Kennedy's War

Based on True Events

D0729229

DAVID LEE CORLEY

Sign-up for my newsletter and you will receive a free book – Prophecies of Chaos in addition to new release updates, special offers, and my thoughts on history. Here's the link:

https://dl.bookfunnel.com/5tl2favuec

DAVID LEE CORLEY

DEDICATION

To all of those men and women that fought and died
for their country. History will not forget your
sacrifices.

PROLOGUE

On January 20, 1961, John Fitzgerald Kennedy became the youngest United States President ever to be sworn into office. He was forty-three years old. During his inaugural address he said, "To those people in the huts and villages of half the globe struggling to break the bonds of mass misery, we pledge our best efforts to help them help themselves, for whatever period is required—not because the communists may be doing it, not because we seek their votes, but because it is right. In the long history of the world, only a few generations have been granted the role of defending freedom in its hour of maximum danger. I do not shrink from this responsibility—I welcome it. I do not believe that any of us would exchange places with any other people or any other generation. The energy, the faith, the devotion which we bring to this endeavor will light our country and all who serve it—and the glow from that fire can truly light the world."

When his presidency began, Americans were full of hope that a new age of liberty and justice was dawning across the planet. Few fully understood the sacrifices that would be required, including Kennedy. He would find out soon enough.

Kennedy governed in a time of unprecedented danger and global upheaval. Especially in the early days of his presidency, JFK was naïve and indecisive. Like all great leaders, his mistakes cost human lives and those sacrifices weighed heavy on his conscience. But with each mistake, Kennedy learned. The man that flinched during the Bay of Pigs Invasion was not the same during the Cuban Missile Crisis. He had grown in his understanding of the foes and threats his nation faced. Failure had educated him, and he knew then the importance of standing firm against the communist tempest.

Kennedy did not recoil from his pledge to promote liberty wherever it blossomed. He was steadfast in his commitment to Vietnam and holding back communist expansion into Southeast Asia. But he was also cautious and unwilling to commit American forces required to stop the communists. Like Eisenhower, he believed that the Vietnamese people should fight their own battles, and in so doing, value the price of freedom. Kennedy committed vast sums of money, equipment, and supplies to support the South Vietnamese. He sent tens of thousands of military advisors to train their troops and aid workers to build their roads, schools, and hospitals. At times, he felt he was fighting an uphill battle with his allies as South Vietnamese leaders continually thwarted his efforts.

He was a leader of great vision and inspiration, nonetheless, he was far from perfect and made many mistakes that had disastrous consequences. Though he projected self-sacrifice, there were times when he acted in his self-interest. Even as his myth continued to grow after his untimely death, many of his faults were revealed. But most Americans loved him and forgave him for his sins. Few would question that he has become a legend.

He was president for less than two years, and yet, during that pivotal moment, Kennedy had a profound effect on the future of America, Vietnam, and the world. Much has been said about what Kennedy might have done in Vietnam if his presidency had not been cut short. He often commiserated with his advisors and cabinet members, many of whom wanted to pull out the underappreciated American advisors risking their lives and even cut off aid to South Vietnam. But no matter what was said in the privacy of the oval office, history has shown us that JFK kept faith with the people of South Vietnam and his pledge to support them until the very end. This is the story of John F. Kennedy's Vietnam War...

"Victory has a hundred fathers,
but defeat is an orphan."

Original Author - Galeazzo Ciano

Requoted by John F. Kennedy

RICE IS LIFE

April 10, 1961 – Hanoi, North Vietnam

Rice was life in Vietnam. Those that had survived the famine near the end of World War II when the Japanese had taken control of Indochina, remember what life was like without rice. The Japanese had raided the warehouses throughout the country and confiscated all the rice to feed their troops invading China. Over 1,000,000 Vietnamese civilians in the north starved to death. It was a horrible way to die. Wasting away until one's organs shut down. The only thing worse was watching the children fade away and not being able to do anything about it. Any rumor of a rice shortage in the North caused many older Vietnamese to tremble with fear. And that was exactly why Lucien Conein and his paramilitary team had been ordered to destroy the rice exchange in Hanoi.

René Granier, the other CIA team commander, was gone. Two weeks ago, he had left in hurry after a phone call from Washington DC. Conein had no idea why he left or when he might return. Granier's absence was good news no matter the reason. Conein despised Granier. He believed Granier was a traitor and possibly a double agent for the communists. Although he couldn't prove it, Granier had twice prevented Conein from killing the Viet Minh commander, Le Duan, who had become the communist party leader and the First Chair in the politburo. In Conein's mind, killing Le Duan could have prevented the upcoming civil war between north and south. It was Granier's fault, but for some reason, only Conein saw it that way.

Their commander, Colonel Edward Lansdale, saw the unfounded accusations as a squabble between two of his best warriors. Lansdale liked and even promoted competition between his commanders. It kept them sharp. Lansdale had been pissed off when the unexpected call came from Washington for Granier. Why was the White House talking to one of his subordinates and not him? It didn't make sense, Granier jumping the chain of command like that. He would have a few words for him when he returned... if he returned. In the meantime, Lansdale had folded the two paramilitary teams that Conein and Granier commanded into one large team under Conein's command. It wasn't ideal. Granier's team members were irate at being put under Conein's command. They didn't like him and they sure as hell didn't trust him. But Conein was an effective commander and Lansdale was sure he would make good use of the extra men. Conein was sure that Granier's men would come around after a few missions. In Conein's mind, it was his victories that won loyalty, not his behavior.

Vietnam was the world's largest producer of rice because of its exceptional amount of rainfall and fertile fields. Over five million tons of rice passed through the Hanoi rice exchange on its way to China and throughout North Vietnam. The multiple warehouses that made up the exchange were filled to the ceiling with burlap sacks of rice.

By attacking the rice exchange, Lansdale was not trying to purposefully starve the North Vietnamese civilians. He was making a political statement and hoping to embarrass Ho Chi Minh. Lansdale like many

Americans and South Vietnamese believed that Uncle Ho was still in charge in the north. He wasn't.

Although Ho was still revered as the father of the revolution, Le Duan had taken control of the day-to-day operations of the North Vietnamese army and government. He was also secretly in charge of the Viet Cong and their insurgent activities in the south. Ho had become a figurehead. Age and frail health had caught up with him. He couldn't keep up with the load of work required to run the country and prepare for the upcoming war. He spent most of his days visiting farmers and peasants in the countryside, touring public work projects, and visiting with foreign dignitaries. Le Duan often asked Ho, whom he admired, for advice. Ho was only too happy to help but knew that it was important for Le Duan to carve his own way as the leader of North Vietnam. He, therefore, kept his advice to a minimum and only counseled Le Duan in private. The reunification of Vietnam was what Ho wanted to see most before he died. For the revolution to win its final victory and reunite the country, Ho needed Le Duan to succeed.

It didn't matter who was the leader of North Vietnam if the raid on the rice exchange was successful. The loss of such a large amount of rice would strike the fear of famine in the people of the north and they would hold their leaders, whoever they were, accountable. It would also cut off the rice shipments to China to pay for the weapons and ammunition they were supplying to North Vietnam and the Viet Cong.

Lansdale had no illusions that a single raid would bring the North to its knees. It was just a piece of a complex propaganda puzzle he toyed with in his mind. One more straw on the camel's back. Having fought insurgent tribes in the Philippines during World War II and after, Lansdale knew what well-designed propaganda could do to the enemy. While the effect of a single campaign was minimal, it was the consistent chaos that propaganda created that brought about the demoralization and eventual defeat of the enemy. Lansdale, a former advertising executive, was a master at "the big lie" and wielded it like a knight wields a sword.

As the sun set over Hanoi's skyline, Conein and his team prepared for the night raid. Even with the help of his in-country intelligence agents, it had taken him and his team a full week to steal across the border and travel to Hanoi undetected. Just as the North had agents in the South, so the South had agents in the North. The South Vietnamese agents had arranged transportation, food, and a well-hidden staging point near the rice exchange for Conein's team. Upon arriving in Hanoi, his team was tired from all the traveling. But Conein knew the longer they stayed in enemy territory, the higher the risk of being caught. Conein was the most experienced troublemaker in all of Vietnam. He had learned his trade from the Corsican mafia during World War II. They were masters of deception and mayhem - destroying German boats and trains, counterfeiting the Reichsmark, and misleading entire divisions during the German invasion in Southern France. They created massive chaos and still earned a tidy profit from their endeavors. Such was the Corsican way. Conein soaked in their tactics making them a permanent bag of tricks he would use after the war was won. It was part of what made him special. The other part was his narcissistic and unpredictable personality that craved the adulations of his commanders. It was a strange combination, but it worked. Conein had a reputation of being a highly effective paramilitary commander and it caused his commanding officers to overlook much of his unseemly behavior, especially his womanizing and excessive drinking. His brand of anarchy was something his commanders needed from time to time, and he knew it. More than his fellow officers which often derided Conein, Lansdale valued Conein's abilities and used them to achieve his objectives. As the CIA director's hand-chosen leader of all paramilitary operations in Vietnam, Lansdale's mandate was bedlam. Without a doubt, Conein was a loose cannon, but he was Lansdale's loose cannon.

At the moment, Conein's only real problem was that rice was not easily destroyed, especially a huge amount of rice. It was a simple plan. Take out the guards and burn all the warehouses to the ground. The extra men in his team made such a plan possible. Although the men from Granier's team grumbled from time to time, they were veteran soldiers and understood the need to obey orders. The new team was comprised of ten Americans and thirty-six soldiers from the 5th Bureau, South Vietnam's counterintelligence group trained by the CIA and loaned to Lansdale whenever requested. It was a huge team by paramilitary standards and was supposed to be covert. That wasn't easy with so many men.

The team was gathered in an abandoned theatre that was previously used for performances of shadow puppet shows and was only a few blocks from the rice exchange. Torn and dusty paper cutouts of the puppets were scattered across the floor of the stage where they once performed to the delight of children and their parents. The American team members used their Zippo lighters to cast shadows of the broken puppets on the wall making them perform lewd acts one against another. The 5th Bureau found the performance entertaining which encouraged the Americans to get even more obscene in their presentation. Conein let them have their fun and waited until midnight before ordering the team to move out.

Just before midnight, a truck backed up to the theatre's rear loading door. Several 5th Bureau soldiers unloaded the back of the truck and carried the contents into the theatre. They placed well-used weapons on the floor along with ammunition. They also unloaded forty containers of kerosene and a large number of civilian clothes.

Conein ordered his team to exchange their modern weapons for the old weapons and to change from their uniforms into the clothes that had been dropped off. The clothes resembled the suits that Hanoi gangsters wore – black suits and ties with white shirts and fedora-style hats. The weapons were also similar to those used by the gangsters. Conein's soldiers didn't like the idea of using antiquated weapons this far behind enemy lines, especially the Americans. "For the mission to succeed, it's important that the police report that it was gangsters that raided the warehouses. If we show up with modern weapons, nobody will believe the ruse," said Conein.

"Some of these rifles are muskets," said an American. "If we get in a firefight, we're dead meat."

"So, let's not get in a firefight. If we do our jobs right, we are in and out in less than thirty minutes."

"Thirty minutes is gonna be a long time under fire, especially with these old clunkers."

"Just do your job and leave the worrying to me."

After changing into the gangster's clothes and exchanging their weapons, each team member picked up a can of kerosene. Just past midnight, Conein led the team out the back of the theatre and moved off in the direction of the rice exchange. The team made their way through the streets, sticking to shadows, and leapfrogging to cover one another. Conein didn't want a fight. Just the opposite. Any altercation with police or North Vietnamese soldiers put the mission in jeopardy and his men in danger. They had made it this far into the heart of Hanoi without being discovered. All they needed was another thirty minutes of luck. Luck was the one thing he could never plan on and yet that was exactly what Conein had done. It was sloppy and he knew it. But he didn't see another way. The good news was that his team was made up of dedicated American veterans and well-trained Vietnamese. If anyone could pull off a mission like this, they could, especially under his leadership.

Conein always thought highly of his ability, but his former commanding officers did not always agree. His military record was sprinkled with derogatory comments, and many questioned his ability to lead. Despite their criticisms, Conein was the go-to guy when presented with a mission that nobody else wanted. He planned the mission out in detail but relied on his vast experience and quick thinking when things did not go as planned, which was often. Conein knew his reputation and liked it. He didn't want to follow the path of others. He often thought out of the box which surprised the enemy and his commanders. There was a bizarre brilliance in the way he thought combined with his cavalier attitude that made it all work to his advantage.

As the team approached the rice exchange, they broke off into squads of nine or ten men. They approached the warehouses from different alleys. The Americans covered their faces with handkerchiefs to conceal their nationality. The squads were synchronized to all strike at the same moment so as not to allow the night guards to warn each other or call for reinforcements.

When the team attacked, they did so aggressively and with overwhelming force quickly surrounding the guards who surrendered without a fight. They did not kill the night guards. Instead, they blindfolded them and tied their hands and feet with a cord. Part of Conein's plan of deception was to let the captive night guards overhear conversions between his men seeded with the names of gangster bosses. When they were finally freed, the night guards would report what they heard and that would support the evidence that it was the Hanoi gangsters that raided the rice exchange.

With the captured guards sequestered in an office, Conein's team went to work dosing the rice bags with kerosene. They had not understood Conein's instructions during the pre-raid briefing. Orders were often mistranslated or misunderstood. It was part of the problem with using native soldiers commanded by foreigners. "No," shouted Conein. "Don't soak the bags of rice. Put the kerosene on the columns and walls."

The 5th Bureau soldiers looked confused. "I thought we were burning the rice?" said a sergeant.

"We are. But the rice won't burn easily. If we burn the warehouse, the heat from the fire will burn the rice."

They obeyed and splashed the walls and columns with the kerosene from the cans. It dawned on Conein that the other 5th Bureau soldiers were probably soaking the rice with kerosene instead of the walls and columns. He ordered four soldiers to find the other members of the team and instruct them on what he wanted. They moved quickly to the other warehouses.

When they returned to report, they informed Conein that two of the warehouses had already used up all their kerosene by the time they received the new instructions. The team had used all the kerosene in the cans. Conein's plan was already going south, and he needed to innovate to save the mission.

After taking a moment to consider the situation, Conein went to the other two warehouses and ordered that the kerosene-soaked bags of rice be placed against the walls and columns. He knew that it would take time for the two warehouses to catch fire using the bags instead of kerosene directly on the columns and walls. Things were all messed up and the timing of the mission had to be altered to allow for more burn time.

He ordered the men to stack the large rice bags in front of the entrances to each of the warehouses. If they needed the fight, the bags would form a barricade to keep the enemy out and a bulletproof barrier. Bullets would have a hard time penetrating a fifty-pound bag of rice. When the bags were in place, Conein had his men set fire to the kerosene-soaked rice bags in two of the warehouses. Once those fires were burning strong, he would set fire to the columns and walls in the other three warehouses. Conein could see that the kerosene-soaked bags were not catching fire nearly as fast as he had hoped. He ordered his men to tear apart several wooden pallets stacked around the warehouse and use the boards as additional fuel to help the fires. The pallet wood was dry and brittle and caught fire quickly. Things were looking up when Conein heard gunfire coming from one of the warehouses.

He ran to the warehouse to see his men firing their weapons through the main entrance. He watched as several of the soldiers armed with muskets slowly reloaded their weapons. He reconsidered his decision to use the obsolete weapons as part of the ruse. He decided it didn't matter at this point, those weapons were all his men had. He moved toward the entrance and looked out the opening into the street. A bullet whizzed by his head, and he ducked back inside. "What the fuck happened?" said Conein.

One of the American officers reported, "We've spotted about twenty North Vietnamese regular troops with more arriving every minute. They've taken up positions in the buildings down the street."

"All right. Keep 'em pinned down. We need to buy more time to make sure the fires are big enough that the firemen won't be able to put them out before the rice burns."

"How long?"

"Ten to twenty minutes."

"We can hold 'em off that long but not much longer."

"Alright. You need to start your fire now."

"You realize were setting fire to the only cover we have?"

"Yes, but it's the only way. We have to make sure the warehouses are going to burn all the way before we abandon our position."

"I don't much like it, but I understand."

"Good. I'm going to check on the other warehouses," said Conein moving off.

By the time he made his rounds, each of the warehouses was under fire from North Vietnamese forces outside on the street. The enemy seemed to be evenly spread out surrounding the rice exchange.

Conein ordered a fireteam of four to fight their way into an alley to the north of the rice exchange. He wanted to make the enemy commander think that was the direction his team of saboteurs would use to escape. He told the fireteam leader to continue north until he encountered heavy resistance, then pull back to the exchange. Conein emphasized that he was not to risk his fireteam for anything more than a superficial fight. The team commander, a corporal, confirmed that he understood Conein's instructions, and the team moved off.

Once outside the warehouse and exposed with little cover, it didn't take long before the fire team encountered resistance. They moved into an alley and fought their way forward against light resistance. Leapfrogging forward, they were able to move two blocks to the north of the rice exchange before the amount of gunfire increased to an unacceptable point. Before abandoning their position and moving back to the rice exchange, the corporal glanced down a side street. He caught a glimpse of three Panard armored cars advancing toward the exchange. He ordered his men to retreat quickly. They ran backward firing their weapons but not seeking cover.

When they re-entered the rice exchange, the corporal went in search of Conein. When he found him, he blurted out, "Panards. They've got Panards."

Conein was concerned by the report and riddled the corporal with questions, "How many? Why type of armament? Where is their current position? Did you see any —"

Before Conein could finish his barrage of questions, the forward wall of the warehouse exploded with a loud crack followed by an even louder bang like lightning hitting a transformer. Shrapnel from the shattered corrugated metal flew into the warehouse injuring several men. A large piece of metal pierced a bag of rice next to Conein's head missing him by less than a foot. Rice flowed out of the torn bag onto the concrete. "I think one of them had a 75mm cannon," said the corporal.

"No shit," said Conein.

The Revel machine gun on the Panard opened fire punching holes through the sheet metal walls, splintering the wooden columns, and tearing into the rice bags. Conein addressed the team members, "Everyone find good cover and be prepared to pull out at a moment's notice."

"These pop guns ain't gonna do jack shit against armored cars," said an American officer.

"They don't know who we are or what we have in the way of weapons. They'll be cautious. At least for a while. On my signal, we are gonna head out the back of this warehouse, enter the exchange building, then move into the warehouse to your east where we will rendezvous. In the meantime, keep up suppressing fire, but don't anyone be a hero."

"I wasn't planning on it."

"Good. Then you won't be disappointed. If the Panard advances, you fall back deeper into the warehouse. Use the rice bags for cover. They will at least stop the machine gun rounds."

The fire inside the warehouse was growing slowly and filling the space with smoke. Conein left to check on the teams in the other warehouses. As soon as he left, the firing from outside intensified forcing the team members to move deeper into the warehouse. It was only a matter of time before the crew in the armored car realized that the combatants inside the warehouse were no threat and advanced.

Conein ordered his men to ignite the kerosene in all of the remaining warehouses. A cloud of black smoke rose over the rice exchange as the warehouses burned. He wanted to wait as long as possible to ensure that the rice would be destroyed before the flames could be extinguished.

But the North Vietnamese troops outside had other plans and the gunfire increased once again into a cacophony of violence.

Several of the team members were wounded and Conein concluded that their position would soon be overrun if they remained. It was time to go. With fire climbing up the columns and walls of the warehouse, Conein sent word to his men to fire one last barrage of gunfire then to pull back into the warehouse east of the rice exchange. It was an organized retreat, not a rout. His men continued to fire as they leapfrogged backward through the warehouses. Their discipline bought them much-needed time and kept the North Vietnamese troops and armored cars from rushing the warehouses while they escaped.

The warehouse to the east of the rice exchange was burning when the team members entered. They could feel the intense heat from the flames. Conein knew they needed to move quickly through the warehouse and escape through the loading doors before the heat and smoke became too intense.

The moment the first of the team members exited the warehouse, an armored car appeared at the end of the street and opened fire. Several high explosive shells from the Panhard's cannon exploded in front of the loading dock killing one man and driving the rest of the team back inside for cover.

Inside the warehouse, the fire grew into an inferno engulfing the walls and roof. The heat was severe, and the men were pouring sweat as they continued to fight. They were being cooked alive. Conein could see that they would all die within a few minutes if they didn't escape the warehouse. He ordered his men to empty their canteens onto their exposed heads, hands, and feet. It cooled them for a moment but quickly evaporated into rising steam. Conein figured the water gave his men an extra minute of life. An extra minute to find a way out of the furnace. His men were hacking and coughing from the smoke. Their eyes watered and their noses ran as their bodies produced mucus to keep their lungs clear from the noxious fumes. Conein knew he and his men were in deep trouble.

To make matters worse, North Vietnamese troops entered the rice exchange connected to the warehouse and opened fire through the doorway. The team of saboteurs was now flanked between two enemy forces. Conein looked around for another escape route. There was none. He noticed the warehouse's sidewall to the north only had a few bullet holes. "Is there a door on that side of the warehouse?" he shouted above the gunfire, explosions, and flames.

"No," said a sergeant.

"Make one."

The sergeant ordered several of his men to follow him. They moved to the northern warehouse wall and used the butts of their rifles against the sheet metal loosening the nails until one of the sheets gave way. They pushed their way through the makeshift opening bending the sheet metal until it was big enough to fit a man. One of the men collapsed from the heat and strain. The sergeant shouted to Conein that the door was open, then grabbed the soldier that had fainted and dragged him through the opening to the outside.

Outside the warehouse, the sergeant pulled out his canteen and poured his remaining water on the face of the unconscious soldier until he came around. Team members and smoke poured through the opening. The soldiers with blackened faces took up defensive positions on the exterior of the warehouse. There was no enemy fire on the northern side of the warehouse because there was no door that needed to be covered by the North Vietnamese. Men were hacking and coughing from the smoke, but they were alive and grateful to have escaped sure death inside the burning warehouse.

Conein waited for his turn to pass through the opening as the remaining team members pushed their way through. Conein shouted to the two men holding back the enemy at the rice exchange doorway to fall back. As they turned to run, one of the men was hit in the leg and fell to the floor. His comrade went back for him, picked him up, and lifted him over his shoulder in a firemen's carry. The smoke was so thick that the soldier could not see his way through the warehouse. Conein called out to him. Unable to see, the man followed Conein's voice as he made his way through the smoke and flames. Near the center of the warehouse, where the heat was most intense, the two men screamed as they burst into flames. The man carrying his comrade stumbled and fell to the floor unable to continue their escape. Conein moved back into the warehouse to help them, but the heat was too intense. He took one last look at their burning bodies before retreating through the makeshift hole in the wall.

Outside the warehouse, Conein fell to the ground as he hacked and coughed up the black soot from his lungs. One of the men gave him the remains of water from his canteen. It helped. His eyes watered blurring his vision. He knew they didn't have much time before the North Vietnamese figured out where they had escaped and closed in on their position once again. The walls of the warehouse buckled from the heat, popping and creaking. They needed to move. He ordered a sergeant to take a fireteam and find a way back to the theatre while the other men moved into the alley across the street.

Everyone was moving at once. Every foot away from the warehouse was cooler than the last. As if an answer to a prayer, it started to rain. The men laughed as they quickly cooled down. Many had burns on their faces, hands, and feet. Their exposed skin was deep red and covered in blisters and soot. But they were alive.

Conein turned back and looked at the rice exchange engulfed in flames. Their mission was a success, but at a high cost — five dead and everyone wounded, some with bullets or shrapnel, others with third-degree burns and scarred lungs. It was a terrible toll. But Conein knew that the communist leadership would also pay a heavy toll when its people began to starve from the lack of rice and the Chinese cutoff their weapon shipments for lack of payment. Like most wars, it was a question of who could endure the most pain and sacrifice before surrendering. Conein and his men had done their part on that day but would need weeks to recover before they could take on another mission. Conein couldn't help but wonder if it was worth it — the lives of his fallen men for rice.

BLUE BEACH

April 14, 1961 - Washington DC, USA

The White House was abuzz. Something was about to happen, and last-minute preparations were underway. CIA officer René Granier could feel it in the air as he was escorted through the halls and bullpen offices, the tension. Everyone tried to remember what they had forgotten. Nobody wanted to make a mistake. The praise of success meant far less than the blame of failure. Most were just out of college and still unsure of themselves. Their youth was being consumed by responsibility. *They are so young to be running a country,* Granier thought as he looked at President Kennedy's staff. *They should be at the beach playing grab-ass, not stuck in an office.*

His escort, a young man dressed in a suit and tie, stopped at a desk to check in before proceeding. "You can go in. He's waiting," said the woman sitting behind a reception desk.

One of the two marine guards opened the door. Granier walked into the oval office alone, his escort moving off as the door closed. Kennedy was nowhere in sight. Granier assumed he was somewhere else in the White House and would arrive shortly. This was Granier's first time in the president's office. It was smaller than he imagined, yet impressive. The "Resolute Desk," so named because the carved wood was salvaged from the HMS Resolute, sat in front of the tall windows lined with the drapes Jacqueline

Kennedy had picked out for her husband's office. As usual, he was much too busy to care about things like drapes. She, on the other hand, had spent hours searching through fabric samples to find the perfect shade of blue to match the office walls and the changing seasons seen through the windows. Granier walked over to a credenza with a model of a China Clipper sitting on top. 'The Sea Witch was the first ship to navigate Cape Horn in less than one hundred days,' said the plaque below the model. As he studied the ship's rigging, he heard a voice, "Well?"

Granier turned to discover that he was still alone in the office. "What do you think?" said the bodiless voice.

Granier walked behind the desk to find President John F. Kennedy lying on the carpet, his body perfectly straight, his eyes closed, resting. "Your back?" said Granier.

"Yes," said JFK opening his eyes. "Can't sit for more than a couple of hours these days."

"I don't imagine the stress helps."

"No," JFK said reaching up. "Give us a hand, will ya?"

"Will the Secret Service shoot me?"

"Only if I tell 'em to."

Granier reached down and helped the president to his feet. "So, what did you find out?" said JFK.

"You ain't gonna like it," said Granier.

"That bad, huh?"

"Worse."

"All right. You've prepared me, now out with it."

"It's going to fail."

JFK let the news sink in before responding, "How do you know?"

"You don't have enough troops, equipment, or aircraft."

"Eisenhower invaded Guatemala with a third of the men and succeeded."

"You're not Eisenhower and Cuba ain't Guatemala."

"That's a little harsh."

"You want me to soften it?"

"No."

"Look... Eisenhower got lucky. His invasion force was losing to the Guatemalan military until they became demoralized and gave up. The CIA had laid the groundwork with PsyOps for months before the invasion."

"We've done that in Cuba."

"And? Has it worked?"

"No."

"It's because President Árbenz was no Fidel Castro. The people love Castro. And more importantly... they believe him."

"What else?"

"The CIA is not the U.S. Military. They have no business leading an operation this size. Hell, you're three days out and they haven't even picked a landing site."

"Yes, they have. Playa Girón on the southern side of the island in the Bay of Pigs."

"Great. Have they reconned it?"

"They're working on it."

"Right. You get my point?"

"Yeah, I do. I suppose that's why I asked for your assessment. What else?"

"One hand doesn't know what the other hand is doing."

"That's to keep security tight. We can't afford for word of U.S. involvement to leak. The Cuban exiles' commanders are informed of the plan on a need-to-know basis."

"Okay. So, you're gonna keep a secret and lose a war."

"Not everything is going to go wrong, Granier."

"So, your strategy is luck?"

"Don't be a smartass."

"Of course not, Mr. President."

"You don't have to call me that. After all we've been through, we're friends, aren't we?

"We are."

"My friends call me Jack."

"Sorry. Can't do it. You are who you are, Mr. President. Friend or no friend, you are the commander-in-chief."

"Fine. Finish your assessment."

"You don't have enough aircraft, ships, or tanks to overthrow Castro."

"Now you are talking crazy. I've got the aircraft carriers Essex and Boxer, plus eleven destroyers and two submarines on station."

"Yeah, but you can't use them without implicating the United States."

"I don't need to. Just the threat of that kind of firepower will make Castro think twice about attacking."

"Yes. He will think twice. Maybe three times. But in the end, he will attack. He has no choice."

"He could surrender."

"Castro? That's wishful thinking. Che Guevara would shoot him."

"Are you finished?"

"Almost. Lastly, I could be wrong. I am giving you my best guess based on my experience and what I have observed. We both know I'm not a general. And you're right. You could get lucky. After all, you are one of the luckiest guys I know. Winning a war is more about who is the most committed and less about numbers and strategy. If you decide to move forward with the invasion, for God's sake, don't second guess yourself and don't look back. Fight to win, Mr. President. Whatever it takes."

JFK turned and stared out the window as he considered. "Do you know what you are going to do?" said Granier.

"Honestly, no. I campaigned on getting tough with the communists. Kinda hard to back down the first time I get up to bat. Besides, Khrushchev will see it as weakness."

"You think the Soviets know what you are planning?"

"I suspect they suspect. These days that's enough. I never should have let the CIA take control of things. You're right. This is a military operation. They're just going to fuck it up."

"So, don't do it. Don't go forward."

"I wish it was that easy."

"You're the president. It is that easy."

"Now, you're the one being naïve. Things gain their own momentum in Washington kinda like a political freight train. Besides, intelligence reports say that the Russians are almost finished training the Cuban pilots that will fly the shipment of jets that have already arrived in Cuba. If we wait any longer, the Cuban military will be too well-armed. I am told that it is now or never for the invasion. I wish there was more time to think it through. But circumstances demand an answer now," said JFK. "Thank you for your assessment. There are few I trust as much as you, Granier."

"It's an honor to serve you, Mr. President."

"So, are you hungry?"

"Are you?"

"Even presidents gotta eat. What do you say we take Marine One up to Boston and get some lobster stew at the Union Oyster House? You remember the place, don't you?"

"Oh, yes. How could I forget?"

"You know, they dedicated a booth after me. I'll call Patty and Bobby and have them join us. It'll be like old times."

"I'd like that, Mr. President. But I am thinking you have more important things to do than entertain me. Besides, I need to get back to Saigon. I left in such a hurry. My team needs me."

"You don't know what you're missing."

"Oh, but I do, Mr. President. I do."

Granier hated the lobster stew at the Union Oyster House; too salty. The two men shook hands and Granier left JFK to mull things over.

April 14, 1961 – Puerto Cabezas, Nicaragua

There was no lack of gently swaying palm trees, sandy beaches, and semi-active volcanos in Nicaragua. It was a land of huge lakes and straddled two great bodies of water – the Pacific Ocean and the Caribbean Sea. It was also 771 miles from Cuba. This meant a B-26 Invader could fly to and from the island with full armament and without a ferry tank. It was a nation friendly to America and didn't say "no" when asked if the CIA could build a covert airfield to host a squadron of Cuban insurgent fighter bombers.

Tom Coyle, a veteran pilot working undercover for the CIA, stood at the edge of the new airfield watching the last of eight Douglas B-26B aircraft take off into the predawn darkness. They were on their way to Cuba. He, along with 120 Alabama National Guardsmen, had trained the forty pilots and aircrewmen that made up the anti-communist FAL Air Force. They and another 1,400 Cuban exiles were committed to the overthrow of Fidel Castro and his government. They were patriots of democracy and hated communists. They were willing to give their lives to free the country that had been taken from them by Castro and his mob of farmers turned soldiers.

Coyle was concerned. Working with them over the last couple of months, he had seen firsthand that they were good aircrews and dedicated to their mission, but less than half had seen any real combat. He knew only too well that experience played a big part in warfare, especially air warfare. These men had too little experience and the time allotted to train them was too short. He had done what he could, and he hoped that it was enough to bring them back alive.

Coyle had been recruited and put on temporary assignment by his commander at Civil Air Transport (soon to be Air America) in Saigon, Vietnam. Allen Dulles, the Director of the Central Intelligence Agency, had personally requested him. Coyle wondered how someone that high up in the chain of command even knew his name. But Coyle was more of a legend than he cared to admit. He had fought in the Pacific during World War II as a fighter pilot. His aircraft was a twin-engine P-38 Lightning nicknamed "The Fork-tailed Devil" because of its twin booms and fierce reputation. It was powerful, fast, and had a nasty bite when it fired its nose-mounted 20mm cannon and four M2 machine guns, not to mention its twelve M8 rockets. Having shot down his share of enemy aircraft, Coyle was an Ace. He also had held the record of crashing his aircraft more times than any other U.S. Military pilot and surviving. He had fought in China, Korea, and the French Indochina wars. Until being recruited for his current training mission, he was flying for the CIA in Vietnam. Even though he was getting a bit long-in-the-tooth for war, he was one of the most experienced twin-engine fighter pilots in the world. If anyone could keep those men heading toward Cuba alive, it was Coyle whether he admitted it or not.

Most of the training had been performed in Guatemala as the American-made B-26s arrived in spurts and fits. The little air force had ended up with twenty of the medium bombers, most of which were retrofitted with eight M2 machine guns in the nose in addition to three in each wing. Four additional defensive machines guns in the tails of the planes had been removed to make room for additional fuel cells. It was a long way to Cuba and time on station would be short. The aircraft needed as much fuel as possible.

In addition to the armament changes, each of the aircraft was stripped of its insignia and all identification markings. Next, came a new coat of paint and "False Flag" insignia making the planes resemble FAR (Cuban Air Force) aircraft. The CIA had prepared a cover story to be released after the raids that it was FAR warplanes that attacked their own airfields then defected to other democratic countries including the United States.

The battle plan was to destroy the Cuban Air Force on the ground with three preemptive airfield strikes, so there would be little need for defensive weapons during the invasion. The crews Coyle had trained were on their way to do just that... he hoped. "Are you okay, Boss?" said a lieutenant moving up behind him.

"Me? Sure. I ain't flying into that mess," said Coyle.

"Yeah, but you want to, don't ya?"

"We all do. But that ain't gonna happen. It's their country anyway. They should be the ones to fight for it."

"I suppose you're right."

JFK had ordered that no American citizen should fight during the invasion of Cuba. At least not yet. Like Eisenhower during the overthrow of Guatemala, Kennedy wanted to wait and see how things unfolded before committing American forces to help the Cuban exiles.

"Well, they sure are passionate little brown buggers. That's gotta count for something. I just hope it's enough," said the lieutenant.

Coyle didn't respond. He just watched as the last taillight on the horizon flickered out.

San Antonio de los Baños, Cuba

The sun had cracked the dawn giving the countryside a golden hue. The homes were made mostly of wood with terracotta tiles as roofs if you were rich or thatched palm leaves if you were poor. Most in the countryside were poor. Horses, donkeys, and mules still performed much of the backbreaking work required to grow the sugar cane, coffee, and tobacco that were Cuba's main exports and sustained the island's economy. The occasional tractor was Russian and spent more time being repaired than in the field.

Life was simple in Cuba before politics made it complex... and dangerous.

Captain Miguel Santiago sat at the controls of the lead aircraft with his navigator/bombardier in the seat to his right. The third member of the aircrew was the tail gunner. He sat behind the navigator in a jump seat. His normal position near the rear of the plane had been rendered moot when the two-machine gun pods he operated had been removed. He was basically along for the ride but could help if the navigator or pilot were wounded during the mission. He had been cross-trained in the aircraft's controls like all the members of the aircrews.

They were flying low hugging the terrain. Santiago took a moment to glance down at the sugar cane fields sweeping below the aircraft at three hundred and fifty miles per hour. It was Cuba. He tried not to tear up, but it had been many years since he had seen his motherland. The other crewmen looked away hiding their own tears. They all understood what was at stake and were willing to make whatever sacrifices were necessary to rid their country of the tyrant named Castro. Santiago snapped out it when he saw the airfield in the distance. It was time to focus as Officer Coyle had taught him and his crew. "This is it," he said. "We will make one recon pass to identify our targets."

"Roger that," said the navigator.

Santiago broke radio silence and told the two B-26 pilots following his aircraft to hold back while he made his recon pass. They peeled off and circled... waiting for their turn like hungry hyenas.

The twin 18-cylinder, air-cooled Pratt & Whitney engines hummed in baritone. They were powerful beasts that generated 2,000 horsepower each. At maximum speed, they hardly noticed the load like a pair of oxen pulling a plow. "Call it," said Santiago as they passed over the airfield.

"I got two T-33s, a Dakota, and two B-26s," said the navigator.

"Two T-33s and two B-26's on this side," said Santiago.

"I got jack shit. I can't see a thing," said the gunner.

Santiago and his navigator laughed as he banked the aircraft. "Bombay doors open," said the navigator switching the controls.

"We should go for the T-33s on the first pass," said Santiago.

"Roger that," said the navigator.

"You, guys need any help?" said the gunner.

"Shut up," said Santiago and his navigator in unison.

The gunner sat back fuming.

Santiago realigned the aircraft for the bomb run. "Little to your left," said the navigator.

Santiago adjusted the bomber's flight path. "That's good. Stay on that line," said the navigator.

Santiago held the aircraft steady as it approached the airfield on the second pass. He could see men running across the field. Tracer rounds from the anti-aircraft gunner whizzed past the cockpit in a bid to down the aircraft before it could drop its payload. "Bombs away," said the navigator as he pickled the bomb switch.

Santiago banked the aircraft hard hoping to see the explosions. He saw nothing but thought he could feel the concussions as the bombs exploded below. "Coming around for a second pass," said Santiago.

"Roger that," said the navigator.

As they passed over the airfield, Santiago could see that the bombs had landed wide and missed the T-33 jets. "Fuck," he said.

"Bombs away," said the navigator once again pickling the bomb switch.

Santiago couldn't see anything, but he felt the concussion of the bombs exploding, then a second deep explosion that he hoped was the fuel tanks or bombs on the jets. Once again, he circled back and glanced out the window. "Holy shit. I think you may have hit one," said Santiago.

"Yeah?" said the navigator grinning.

"I think so."

"Good. I need a story for my grandchildren."

"You're not even married."

"I will be after this."

The crew laughed, elated.

Santiago moved off to let the other aircraft take their turns at the turkey shoot. Each aircraft made two bomb runs just as the lead aircraft had done. The airfield was ablaze. They had hit multiple aircraft as well as fuel tanks, vehicles, and buildings. Now, it was the pilots' turn. Strafing was what the B-26 did best, and it was the pilot that controlled the aircraft's forward machine guns… all fourteen of them.

As the lead aircraft, Santiago was first. He lined up his sights on any aircraft that were not burning. He found himself a T-33 and unleashed hell. The fourteen .50-cal machine guns fired in unison. The recoil of the volley was so strong it pushed the crew against their harnesses as the aircraft slowed. Tracer rounds filled the windshield. Santiago grinned as he gently guided the stream of red tracers into the T-33, and it exploded. "Hell yeah!" he screamed.

The crew was giddy. Castro only had six Lockheed T-33 jets that were operational. He and his crew had just destroyed two. The jet fighters were the only aircraft capable of overtaking the B-26s. It felt like they were personally flipping Castro the bird.

Santiago took one more strafing run using his machine guns and wing rockets. He took out a Sea Fury fighter and destroyed several buildings and an anti-aircraft gun emplacement. It wasn't what he and his crew had hoped for, but it was enough to feel proud. He banked hard and radioed the other pilots to make their strafing runs.

In all, the pilots reported that they had destroyed all four T-33s, three Sea Furys, a C-47, and three B-26s. The airfield was useless with bomb craters covering the airstrip and multiple buildings ablaze. It was a huge success and a heavy blow to Castro's Air Force capabilities - at least that's what they believed...

Washington DC, USA

After a particularly cold winter, spring had finally arrived in the nation's capital. The cherry trees had blossomed into a pink wave along the shores of the Potomac River and around the national monuments. Lincoln never seemed happier. The gardens surrounding the White House were a carpet of color with thousands of flower buds.

Hearing the results of the air assaults, JFK was delighted. His legendary grin let those in the room know his mood. "That's more like it. It's about time something went our way," said Kennedy. "Is my guy Granier still in DC?"

"No, Mr. President. He took the first flight out back to Saigon," said Allen Dulles.

"That sounds about right. Make sure he gets a coded message of the mission success once he lands."

"Of course, Mr. President."

Kennedy knew he was rubbing Granier's nose in it, but he didn't care. It was his ass on the line if things went south, not Granier's. Granier would appreciate the good news because it helped America was Kennedy's thinking. JFK knew that Granier would caution him not to celebrate too soon and that battles won are not wars won. He still didn't care. He opened his humidor and removed one of his favorite Cuban cigars – a Petite H. Upmann. He snipped the end and lit up. "Fuck Castro," said Kennedy to himself and anyone else in earshot as he blew a grey cloud into the oval office.

April 15, 1961 - New York, United States

To say the Cubans were pissed off would have been a great understatement. They knew the Americans had supplied and trained the Cuban insurgent aircrews and had given them precise maps of the Cuban airfields that they attacked. Castro's Air Force was in ruin, and he was furious.

At the United Nations, Cuban Foreign Minister Raul Roa appeared before the General Assembly and accused the U.S. of attacking Cuba with aggressive airstrikes. Only a few days earlier, the CIA had secretly attempted to entice Roa into defecting. Roa had refused. Now, he understood why. He gave an impassioned plea to the assembly to condemn the Americans for their destructive actions against his nation's military.

U.S. Ambassador to the UN Adlai Stevenson refuted Roa's accusations and stated that the U.S. Armed Forces would not "under any circumstances" intervene in Cuba. He spoke the truth according to what he knew at the time. President Kennedy had not informed him of the secret invasion of Cuba in hopes that Stevenson would be passionate and show the conviction of his denials. Kennedy had been right. Stevenson went on to state that no U.S. citizens would participate in actions against Cuba and that it was defectors from the Cuban Air Force that had carried out the air attacks on the Cuban airfields. He presented a photograph of a Cuban B-26 whose crew had flown to the Miami airport and asked for political asylum after the raid. What the Ambassador did not know was that the aircrew was made up of exiles and the bomber had been disguised to look like one of Castro's planes. It was all CIA propaganda.

President Kennedy appeared before White House reporters and made an announcement supporting Stevenson's statement, "I have emphasized before that this was a struggle of Cuban patriots against a Cuban dictator. While we could not be expected to hide our sympathies, we made it repeatedly clear that the armed forces of this country would not intervene in any way."

Eventually, Stevenson would be embarrassed and angry when he found out he had been purposefully left out of the loop and the CIA had lied to him about the airfield raids.

Havana, Cuba

Castro responded by having the Cuban national police arrest tens of thousands of suspected anti-revolutionary civilians. There were so many people detained, the national police chief was forced to commandeer the Karl Marx Theatre, the Fortaleza de la Cabaña, and the Principe Castle to hold the prisoners. In total 60,000 people were arrested and interrogated.

While the police and military were aware of the pending invasion, there was not much they could do about it. They didn't have enough resources to defend all of Cuba's coastline. They would have to wait and see where the rebel forces landed before forming a plan and assembling forces to repel them.

April 16, 1961 - Washington DC, USA

JFK sat in the oval office going over his schedule with his Chief of Staff Kenneth O'Donnell. It would be business as usual, so as not to tip off the Cuban military of the impending invasion. The receptionist entered and said, "Mr. President, Allen Dulles would like a few minutes in the war room before the afternoon meeting."

"All right. Did he say what it was about?" said JFK.

"Only that he wanted to show you some photos."

JFK's interest was piqued. He had requested copies of the bomb assessment photos that were taken by a U2 spy plane after the Cuban airfield attacks.

Thirty minutes later, JFK met with Allen Dulles, the director of the CIA in the war room. Reconnaissance photos were spread across the table. Kennedy used a magnifying glass to carefully study the photos as Dulles stood nearby. "When were these taken?" said JFK, distraught.

"Yesterday morning, a few hours after the raid," said Dulles.

"These are jets," said Kennedy pointing to the blurry objects on a photo. "The Cubans still have jets. You told me the raid was sure to destroy their T-33s."

"And it did, just as we projected. But it seems the Cubans had rearmed their training jets with machine guns and wing racks for rockets."

"Why didn't we know about these?"

"We believe they were rearmed fairly recently. Probably as a result of the invasion rumors."

"So, you think Castro knew?"

"He's not an idiot, Mr. President. He has an extensive intelligence presence in Miami where we have been recruiting exiles for Brigade 2506."

"Why wasn't I warned about this possibility?"

"Mr. President, this doesn't change anything. Yes, Castro has some jets, but our air force will shoot them down in a matter of minutes once the invasion starts."

"And what if he shoots down one of our planes? He will have the evidence he needs to show the world that America was behind the invasion."

"Perhaps, but what does it matter? By then Castro's military will be destroyed and the new president will be installed as the head of the Cuban government. It will be a fait accompli. There will be little anyone can do."

"Allen, you treat this invasion like it's the only thing on our plate. What about the Soviet Union, China, and Vietnam?"

"A victory in Cuba will show the world our resolve to stop communist expansion."

"...or it could start World War III. Khrushchev is unpredictable."

"I think that is being a little dramatic."

"Perhaps, but I am not sure that is a risk I am willing to take."

"What are you proposing, Mr. President?"

"I am not purposing anything, Allen. I am ordering that no American forces will participate in the invasion of Cuba and that includes our aircraft."

"Mr. President, this operation has been in planning for over a year. It is well thought out and it will succeed if we just push forward."

"And we will, but without US military forces."

"I cannot guarantee the outcome if our Cuban exiles are denied air support that we promised."

"Then maybe we should just call the whole thing off?"

Dulles took a moment to control his temper before responding, "No. No. That would not be wise. I am sure we can make some adjustments and still achieve our goals."

"Then do so, Allen. Now, if you will excuse me, I have a meeting."

"Of course, Mr. President."

JFK left the room in a huff. Dulles, seemingly unsure, collected his photos and slipped them into his briefcase. This wasn't the first time Dulles had convinced a president to move forward with the invasion of Cuba. Eisenhower, who had originally planned the operation, was unsure at times and needed a nudge from Dulles to move forward. Dulles was on the hook for the invasion, and he knew it. If it failed, his Washington career would be over. He was a hardcore patriot and believed the invasion was the correct strategy for America. Communism needed to be stopped no matter the cost.

Puerta Cabeza, Nicaragua

A few miles away from the airfield, Operation Bumpy Road began. A flotilla of ships set sail toward Cuba.

Aboard the five American-made freighters flying Liberian flags was the CIA-trained Brigade 2506 - 1,400 Cuban exiles committed to overthrowing Castro and his government. Two LCIs and landing craft for infantry accompanied the freighters.

Waiting offshore and out of sight from observers on land, an American Taskforce group rendezvoused with and escorted the Cuban Expeditionary Force across the Caribbean. The American naval forces were made up of eleven US destroyers, two submarines, a landing ship dock, the helicopter carrier US Boxer, and the aircraft carrier US Essex. The Essex with its nuclear weapons and 103 warplanes was capable of annihilating Castro's entire military without breaking a sweat. The convoy was overkill meant to deter Castro and any of his allies that might come to his aid.

As planned, the bulk of the American warships stopped and remained at Point Zulu, forty miles south of Cuba, while the USS San Marcos accompanied the Cuban Expeditionary force to three miles off the Cuban shoreline. The American landing ship dock unloaded three unmarked LCUs carrying the M41 Bulldog tanks of Brigade 2506 and four LCVPs to help ferry the soldiers to the shore. The soldiers and their commanders in the brigade knew nothing of the changed plans and that no air support would be provided by the Americans. They sat on the freighters saying their prayers and waiting to meet their fate... whatever it would be.

As the freighters rendezvoused with their landing craft, Grayston Lynch, the CIA officer overseeing the landing, received a coded message from Washington. He was informed that Castro still had operational aircraft and that he should expect aerial assaults from Cuban aircraft at sunrise. His new orders were to offload Brigade 2506 and its equipment immediately. Grayston was stunned by the last-minute update. With sunrise fast approaching, there was no time to send a message back asking for clarification or more information. Troops were already climbing into the landing craft. Grayston realized that given the new circumstances, his orders seemed correct – offload the troops and their equipment as fast as possible. The soldiers stood a far better chance on shore than in the ships should an aerial attack occur. The crews on the ships would be safer once the soldiers disembarked and the ships were free to maneuver as they headed back out to sea. He wondered how serious the threat was. It didn't take long for him to find out…

Informed of the pending attack by Grayston, Brigade commander José Pérez San Román, went ashore to supervise the unloading of men and equipment from the landing craft.

In the darkness, the battle began when a local militia spotted the landing craft on Playa Girón code-named, "Blue Beach." The militia commander immediately sent word to the local battalion commander stationed nearby at the Australia Sugar Mill and word quickly traveled around the island that the invasion had begun.

A skirmish broke out when the Cuban militiamen opened fire on the disembarking soldiers. It didn't last long. The militiamen were swiftly overwhelmed by the aggressive, well-armed exiles. Most of the militiamen fled the battlefield. Some were taken captive and interrogated for information on the location of Castro's forces.

Washington DC, USA

Although Cuba was utmost on Kennedy's mind, other matters needed to be dealt with. One week earlier, the Russians had used their new booster rocket to put the first man in orbit around the earth. "The Russians are winning the space race," said Kennedy to his cabinet. "Soon, Khrushchev will be capable of burying us with missiles."

"It's true that the new Russian rocket is an impressive leap forward in technology. But we should be able to match putting a man in orbit shortly," said Robert McNamara, Kennedy's Secretary of Defense.

"How long is shortly?"

"Six months to a year."

"And how much further will the Russians improve their technology by then?"

"We don't know, Mr. President. But it could be substantial."

"With all that we have accomplished and with great wealth at our disposal, how is it that the Russians are kicking our ass when it comes to space?"

"They grabbed more German scientists than we did when World War II ended," said Dulles.

A messenger entered the oval office and handed Dulles a telegram. "News for Cuba?" said Kennedy.

"Yes, Mr. President," said Dulles. "The Cuban exiles have landed and are pushing inland."

The room erupted with cheers with pats on the back. "No resistance?" said Kennedy.

"Some. But it's light. Mostly militia," said Dulles.

"I'm sure the Cuban forces will need time to get organized and bring up their troops. We should take advantage of their disorder and advance as fast as possible," said McNamara.

"Yes, but with caution," said Kennedy.

"Mr. President, the exile forces could advance quicker and safely if you reinstated American air cover."

"No, Allen. No American aircraft. The exiles must stand on their own. After all, it's their fight."

Havana, Cuba

Fidel Castro was born into wealth. His family owned a 25,000-acre plantation with over 400 employees called "Las Manacas" and located in the village of Birán on the eastern end of the island. He attended a boarding school and was given a quality education. Uninterested in academics, Castro spent much of his time playing sports. It was later when he attended a Jesuit college that he became interested in politics and debate. He went on to study law at the University of Havana. Becoming a student activist, he was anti-imperialism and opposed American intervention in the Caribbean. From the very beginning of his activism, Castro was not opposed to committing violence to achieve his political goals. He carried a gun and joined gangster-type student organizations. He spent years gathering followers and earning their loyalty.

When General Fulgencio Batista seized power through a military coup, Castro started a violent covert group called "The Movement" to overthrow him. As the leader of the revolution against Batista's illegitimate government, Castro became the president of Cuba when the former president fled the country. Having seen several political leaders assassinated over the years, Castro became paranoid and secretive when he took power. He rarely slept in the same location for more than a few nights and owned multiple residences that were well guarded. His paranoia was well-founded. From the moment the Americans determined that he was a communist, the CIA attempted to assassinate him. But he was too clever and continually uncovered the plots against him.

April 17, 1961

Castro was awoken by his secretary and Vice President Fernández Alvarez. Having had too many highballs of aged rum, lime, and soda the night before, it took him a moment to clear his head. But upon hearing the word "invasion," he snapped upright in bed and started asking questions. He was told by Alvarez that enemy forces of an unknown number were landing at Playa Larga and Playa Girón. Castro ordered a message be sent to the local battalion commander at the Australia Sugar Mill, located two kilometers south of the town Jagüey Grande, to resist the enemy forces at all costs and that help was on the way. A few minutes later, Castro slipped on his uniform and left his quarters.

Making his way to the radio room, Castro broadcast a message throughout the country, "All units are to make their way to their respective battalions... Let us face the enemy...with the conviction that to die for the country is to live, and to live in chains is to live in shame and disgrace."

Finally knowing where the invasion was taking place, Castro put into action premade defense plans to fend off the enemy forces. The original leaders of the revolution and the only men Castro truly trusted - Raul Castro, Ernesto "Che" Guevarra, and Juan Almeida were all given command of different areas of the country to defend, while Ramiro Valdez was made responsible for Intelligence and Counterintelligence, and Guillermo Garcia was left with the defense of Havana. No time was wasted. Everyone knew their role in the defense of their beloved country and the revolution they had fought so hard to win. Now, if they could just hang on to it against one of the most powerful nations in the world.

A veteran commander of dozens of battles, Castro processed the mountains of information coming at him from all directions and spit out new orders with uncanny precision and clarity. He had done the impossible in winning the revolution that overthrew President Batista. He trusted his instincts. War was what he knew. War was home.

In addition to the battalion at Australia Sugar Mill, Castro ordered a battalion of militia to push back the enemy at a second landing site Playa Larga, code-named "Red Beach." The Bay of Pigs was four miles wide and eighteen miles deep. The bay was surrounded by a thick swamp with only three gravel roads offering access to the area.

Havana was less than three hours by car. Although he would never admit it publicly, Castro knew that if Havana fell, there was a good chance his government and his army would be forced to surrender. Three more battalions from Las Villas Province were ordered to take up blocking positions along the two highways between the landing site and Havana. His strategy was simple, if his forces could contain the enemy on the beaches for one or two days, he could marshal forces from throughout the island and drive them back into the sea.

With his land forces on their way, Castro ordered his air force to attack the enemy ships and soldiers at first light. The airfield raids on April 15th had whittled down Castro's airpower, from thirty-six to eighteen operational aircraft - six B-26 intruders, six T-33 jets, and six propeller-driven Sea Fury fighters. Although small compared to aircraft on the US Essex, the fledgling air force was a significant threat to the freighters unloading troops and equipment. Since there was no allied air support over the invasion site, Castro's aircraft could attack unimpeded and even take their time choosing their targets.

Playa Girón, Cuba

Castro's warplanes came at dawn with the freighters in the bay still unloading equipment and troops. The Cuban T-33s strafed the landing force already on the beaches with machine guns and rockets killing a dozen and striking fear into the invaders.

Using their bombs, underwing rockets, and machine guns, the B-26's focused on the freighters. The freighters could not maneuver while the landing craft were loading. The captains and crew had no choice but to take a brutal beating as the B-26's unleashed their weapons dropping their bomb loads and firing their under-the-wing rockets. Once the rockets and bombs were released, the Intruders became fighters strafing the ships with their machine guns. The sound of all the plane's machine guns firing was enough to deafen the aircrews.

Within minutes, three of the freighters were sinking. Troops ran to the landing craft abandoning the sinking ships. The landing craft, targets themselves, pushed away with whatever troops and equipment they already had onboard. Several troops fell from the loading nets and dropped into the sea with full packs on their backs and immediately sank to the bottom of the bay.

The landing craft headed for the beaches at full speed while their machine gunners fought off the aircraft above as best, they could. They were too few machine guns, and the landing craft quickly ran out of ammunition. The closer the landing craft moved toward the shore, the less room they had to maneuver. The boats became sitting ducks bobbing in the waves as the Cuban Sea Furies swooped in like angry seagulls unleashing their bombs, rockets, and Hispano 20mm autocannons. The landing craft were blown apart, and several sank. Others tried to escape back out to sea but hit the underwater reefs ripping out their bottoms and sitting helplessly on the coral as the Sea Furies continued their attacks. The surviving soldiers were forced to wade ashore loaded down by their ammunition belts and gear. Many didn't make it, drowning in the surf.

One of the freighters taking on water headed toward the shore at full speed. The captain beached his ship seventy-five yards from the shore. His heroic effort gave his crew and the troops still on board a fighting chance at surviving. With their prey motionless, the Sea Furies blew the stranded freighter apart killing dozens as they climbed down the loading nets still hanging on the side of the ship's hull. Two hundred and seventy waded ashore but most abandoned their equipment and weapons to the sea for fear of drowning. Weaponless and exhausted, they would be of little use in the imminent land battle.

It was only after all the warplanes had emptied their bomb and rocket racks and their machine guns ran out of ammunition, that they finally broke off their attack. Victorious, they headed back to their airbases to reload, confident they could finish off the invaders.

Most of the Brigade's ammunition and supplies had sunk with the three freighters. Badly damaged, the other freighters had turned tail and headed for deeper waters away from the shore. None of the troops still onboard were anxious to join their comrades on the beaches. They had watched the T-33 jets rip them to pieces and they wanted none of it.

Onshore, the officers gathered their men and did a headcount as they prepared defensive position along the beach's shallow dunes. It was fortunate that many of the Brigade's troops and equipment had already landed onshore before Castro's aircraft had attacked. Even with their losses, Brigade 2506 was a substantial fighting force. But without air cover, the Cuban exiles would continue to be harassed by Castro's air force. Because so many of the troops were forced to climb over the sides of the landing craft and wade to shore, all of the portable radios they were carrying were waterlogged and proved useless throughout the entire battle. The invasion commanders had no way of communicating with the freighters, the Essex, their air force in Nicaragua, or Washington D.C. They couldn't even get reconnaissance updates on the position of Castro's troops. They were on their own.

Washington DC, USA

Allen Dulles stepped onto the White House veranda where Kennedy was eating his lunch. "There has been a setback, Mr. President," said Dulles.

"What kind of setback?" said Kennedy.

"The invasion force was attacked by the Cuban Air Force. The losses were heavy. Three freighters and several landing craft were sunk. Much of the equipment and ammunition was lost. Enemy aircraft strafed the troops attempting to make it to shore."

"My God. How many made it?"

"We don't know, Mr. President. The biggest loss was the communication equipment. The saltwater damaged all of it when the troops were forced to wade to the beach. The brigade has no way of communicating with their American advisors at sea or the Exile Air Force in Nicaragua. With the break in communications, they have also lost all intelligence. They have no idea where Castro's forces are located or when they should expect an attack."

"We must have spare radios that we can send them?"

"We did but the freighter carrying that equipment was sunk during the air assault."

"This is a disaster."

"Yes, Mr. President, it is."

"Don't be so smug about it, Allen. You don't know that air cover would have made the difference."

"Of course. Nobody knows. We all have to live with the outcome from the decisions we make."

"Allen, at times, I'm not sure who's side you are on."

"America's, Mr. President. Everything I do is designed to keep our country and its people safe."

"Well, that didn't work out so well this time, did it?"

"Mr. President, the American people will not accept having a communist nation ninety miles off Florida's coast."

"Then those poor bastards fighting on the beach had better win, wouldn't you say?"

"I would, Mr. President."

"See to it, Allen. This was your party from the get-go. Make sure it's a success."

Havana, Cuba

When the reports of the air assault came back, Castro was elated. He ordered the air force to attack again as soon as possible and to keep attacking until the invaders were driven from the country. Castro also knew that the American fleet forty miles offshore of Cuba was capable of obliterating his entire military. But there was nothing he could do about it. In his mind, he would move forward boldly and hope the American president would be unsettled by his resolve. With a little luck and a lot of bravado, Castro hoped to fend off the Americans in one of the biggest gambles of the 20th century up to that point. Little did he know that an even bigger gamble would take place off his shores shortly.

A warrior himself, Castro was feeling his blood run hot. Sitting in Havana waiting for news did little to satisfy his bloodlust. He ordered a jeep escorted by a convoy of crack troops to take him to the Australia Sugar Mill, the command center for the Cuban army and militias. He wanted to see firsthand what was happening. They sped out of the capital heading south along the highway.

Australia Sugar Mill, Cuba

When he arrived three hours later, Castro was unimpressed with the progress that had been made and took command of the forces around the invasion site. Castro knew how to attack the enemy. His experience was apparent to all as he barked out orders and repositioned forces. He did not wait until conditions were perfect for his men to advance. When additional units entered the fray, they took the pressure off the units already engaged with the enemy. He knew when to pull units out of the battle and give them a rest, so they could catch their breath, eat a little something, reorganize, and reenter the battle once again. He knew the enemy lacked that ability. They were already outnumbered by his forces and needed every man to continue fighting to the point of exhaustion. Castro would take his time and pick apart the invaders one unit at a time. When they broke, he would send some of the units to pursue them and shift the rest of his units to other battles. The more small victories his soldiers won, the stronger his overall force became.

Castro knew that war was not about physically destroying the enemy, but more about destroying the enemy's will to fight. He would keep the pressure up as more and more of his companies and battalions from around the country arrived at the battlefield. As his force grew in size, the invaders were being worn down and using up the ammunition they had brought with them. The Cuban army could continually resupply and reinforce its units with ease and abundance.

With three freighters sunk and the other ships maneuvering to avoid another aerial assault, the Brigade onshore only had a limited supply of ammunition and supplies. Several hours after Castro had arrived on the battlefield and had taken command, another wave of Cuban aircraft swept in attacking the beachhead and once again went after the ships just outside the bay. One more freighter being used as a command and communication center is hit by a Sea Fury's rockets just below the waterline. It was a lucky shot. The freighter immediately took on water and began to sink. The crew abandoned the ship and was picked up by another freighter, also under attack. With the command freighter gone, most of the Brigade's only remaining communication equipment was gone too. Orders and reconnaissance reports had to be relayed through short-distance radio handsets. The commander of the beachhead had no direct communication with the CIA, the US Navy, or the Exile air force.

Washington DC, USA

JFK and his cabinet were given hourly reports on the invasion's progress. At first, the reports were positive. It wasn't until later that the reports turned from glowing to dim. Shortages of ammunition, medical supplies, and communication equipment were not welcomed news. JFK had made sure there was enough on hand to sustain the fighting force as they advanced. He and the CIA officers that had planned the invasion had not envisioned losing so many freighters before they could be fully unloaded.

The number of Castro's forces in the area had also been vastly underreported, especially the artillery and armor shelling the invasion forces on the beaches. Cuba's regular battalions had twenty Soviet-built T-34 tanks with 76mm main guns used on the frontline and a number of SU-100 tank destroyers with massive 100mm main guns used as mobile artillery.

The invading anti-communist forces had five M-41 Walker Bulldog tanks with 76mm rifle cannons as their main weapon. Even though they were vastly outnumbered, the M-41 crews gave as good as they got by destroying an equal number of Cuban tanks. But as with many things during the invasion, the exiles didn't have enough to hold back the waves of Cuban forces that continued to arrive as the battle wore on. The Cuban aircraft were also a constant danger and took their toll on the exiles' armor. The Cuban Sea Fury's with their ability to maneuver at lower speeds and wing-mounted Hispano 20mm autocannons were especially effective against the American-built tanks. While the aircrafts' autocannons could not pierce the tanks' armor, they could disable the tanks' treads and drive gears making them immobile. Once motionless, the American tanks were easily destroyed from a direct hit of one of the aircrafts' 500lb bombs.

Being a Navy officer, JFK had never fought on land, but it didn't take much to see that the anti-communist forces were in real trouble. Kennedy did not want American involvement in the invasion exposed to the world. He held onto a strange belief that simply denying accusations would be enough to keep the truth hidden. He held another press conference and publicly declared that American military forces were not involved in the invasion. And that was true for the most part. The soldiers fighting on land were Cuban exiles. But if those soldiers were not helped soon, they would be wiped out and the invasion would be a failure. Realizing that he may have made a mistake by denying air support, Kennedy authorized limited air cover with the remaining exile aircraft in Nicaragua and overwatch from Essex aircraft to protect the freighters and ships off the coast.

During one of the briefings, the president was handed a telegram from Nikita Khrushchev in Moscow, stating the Russians would not allow the U.S. to enter

Cuba and implied swift nuclear retribution to the United States heartland if their warnings were not heeded. Khrushchev and the Soviets were not buying Kennedy's denials of US involvement.

Without question, Khrushchev's cable made things more complicated. There was some question about how many of the Soviets' missiles were truly operational and how effective their targeting systems were over long distances. But there was little doubt the Soviets had enough weaponry to destroy most major U.S. cities and that the Americans could do the same to the Soviet cities. The invasion of Cuba had become a threat to the United States of America. While Kennedy wanted to see a thriving democracy return to Cuba, his primary responsibility was for the safety of the American people. Kennedy immediately questioned his new order to resume air support and ordered that the Essex aircraft only engage Cuban planes if they threatened any of the ships in international waters. After some discussion, Kennedy expanded his rules of engagement to include aggressive Cuban aerial maneuvers toward the anti-communist forces on the beach. The new president was micromanaging U.S. involvement, and his orders were not always clear when initially issued.

Caribbean Sea

Kennedy's revised orders were issued to the commander of the Essex. Unfortunately, the invasion communication vessel had been destroyed and there was no way to coordinate the Navy's aircraft with the invasion forces on the ground. The Essex could not coordinate with the Exile Air Force in Nicaragua either because of a lack of long-range radio equipment.

Puerto Cabezas, Nicaragua

When Coyle had first been given the order to stand down, he knew it was a mistake. The invasion force could be slaughtered without air cover. He had already been through several wars, and he knew what an important role aircraft could play in a ground strategy, not to mention an air strategy. He had aircraft ready to go, but his hands were tied. Coyle obeyed orders even if he knew they were stupid. That's just who he was. That's why so many commanders trusted him. They could rely on him.

Richard M. Bissell Jr. the deputy director of the CIA and chief planner of the invasion was able to send a coded message to Coyle ordering him to attack the Cuban forces immediately with every aircraft at his disposal.

When he received the coded message from Bissell, Coyle knew every minute counted. He had little time to brief his pilots and aircrews on what they were about to face. They would need to rely on the training he and the Alabama National Guard had given them. It worried him. Like a father watching his son step up to bat the first time, he wasn't sure they were ready. They had performed well on the preinvasion raid against the airfields, but this was different. This was combat and anything could happen.

He gathered the aircrews on the tarmac and shouted out his last-minute instructions. Their mission was to protect the Brigade by destroying as many Cuban units and their equipment as possible. Resistance from the remaining aircraft in Castro's air force was expected. The good news was that the CIA had discovered Castro's best pilots were in

Czechoslovakia training to fly the new MiG-21s that would soon arrive in Cuba. The enemy pilots they would face were lacking in experience but still deadly. The Lockheed T-33 jets were to be avoided if possible since their speed gave them a distinct advantage against the twin-engine B-26s the exile pilots were flying. He wished them God's speed and sent them to their aircraft for immediate takeoff.

Playa Girón, Cuba

The squadron of aircraft approached from the south and flew over the beleaguered freighters, several with black smoke rising above them. Nearing the beach, the aircrews saw several American-made tanks and other vehicles burning from the recent air raids. It was not an encouraging picture. The invasion forces were in trouble. The B-26s did a quick flyover to reconnaissance the position of enemy forces. The squadron commander instructed the pilots to form up in small groups so the aircraft could attack multiple positions at the same time.

For the first few minutes, the B-26s pounded the communist forces unchecked. They unleashed their bombs blowing up several artillery emplacements and tanks. Machine guns and rockets were used to strafe the enemy soldiers many of whom were militia that had never been attacked from the air until that moment and broke ranks running for their lives.

Things were looking up for the invasion forces and several of the invading ground units advanced inland. Then came Castro's aircraft. The Cuban B-26s laid into the advancing soldiers and drove them back to their original positions on the beach killing many as they retreated. The Sea Furies and the T-33s went after the anti-communist B-26s.

Since the CIA had painted their aircraft to match the Cuban Air Force, it was confusing who was who. The biggest recognizable difference was the machine gun placements. The anti-communist aircraft had their machine guns in both the nose and wings, while Castro's aircraft only had machine guns under the wings. Castro's B-26 aircraft also had clear noses that were used for more accurate bombing.

Over half of the anti-communist B-26s were shot down by Castro's jets and propeller-driven fighters. Some crashed in the surrounding jungle and swamps while others crashed in the bay and sunk. Few crew members survived. Those aircraft that did survive were damaged with 50-Cal bullet holes stitched across their wings and fuselage. The Exile Air Force broke off their attack and headed back out to sea leaving Castro's air force to continue its assault on the invasion forces.

Puerto Cabezas, Nicaragua

Coyle stood at the end of the airfield counting the returning aircraft. He could see that most of the aircraft were heavily damaged and had barely made it back. At first, he thought the squadron must have split up into two formations. But he soon realized that only nine aircraft had survived the raid. It was a heavy blow that so many of the men he had trained had failed to return.

Ambulances and ground crews raced out to the aircraft and unloaded the wounded aircrews. Blood dripped out of the hatchways and onto the tarmac. They did what they could, but the damage to the squadron was massive. With few aircrewmen remaining, the CIA's anti-communist air force was finished for all practical purposes.

Coyle sent a message to Washington DC informing Bissell of the losses and asking for instructions. Before long, a message came back authorizing volunteer American aircrews to pilot the remaining aircraft and continue the assault on Castro's military. Coyle was stunned. He was no coward as he had proven many times before but returning to continue the fight with highly damaged aircraft against a superior air force was a very risky proposition. The cable from Bissell also stated, "Cannot stress sufficient importance to fact American crews must not fall into enemy hands."

Coyle wondered if Bissell had just ordered that the American volunteers were to fight to the death or commit suicide rather than be captured by the Cubans if they were shot down. *Was the reputation of America and the credibility of its president so prized that the CIA was willing to sacrifice the Alabama National Guardsmen to keep it intact?* The thought chilled him.

Coyle gathered the Alabama National Guardsmen and the surviving exile crew members in a hangar and briefed them on the impending mission now code-named "Mad Dog Flight." He explained the situation on the ground – the invasion force was being wiped out and without air, the cover would not last long. He asked for an update from the ground crew chief on how many aircraft were still operational and was told six. He told the group of the new authorization and asked for volunteers. Four Alabama aircrews volunteered along with two Exile aircrews to fly the six planes. At the last minute, Coyle replaced one of the younger and less experienced Alabama Guardsman pilots deciding to pilot the plane himself as a squadron leader. He would do his best to get these men back alive even if it meant sacrificing his own life.

An hour later, the six serviceable B-26s were refueled and rearmed. They took off and headed for Cuba. Some of the ground crew that had cleaned the carnage from the planes after the last raid, questioned if it was a suicide mission that pilots and crews had volunteered to fly. They would soon find out...

Australia Sugar Mill, Cuba

As the battle continued, Castro ordered more and more troops, artillery, and armor to the area. A large convoy of private buses, supply trucks pulling artillery, and tanks on carriers was nearing the beachhead when the Mad Dog squadron arrived and opened fire. Bombs, napalm canisters, and rockets destroyed a large number of vehicles killing and wounding the occupants. It was a heavy blow against Castro's forces. During the middle of the aerial attack, Castro's air force reappeared and engaged the six B-26s.

A T-33 jet swooped in behind Coyle's plane and opened fire with its machine guns. Bullets pierced the B-26's fuselage and set one of the plane's engines afire. With little hope of outmaneuvering the enemy jet, Coyle reduced power in both engines slowing the aircraft to stall speed. Traveling at a much faster rate of speed, the jet overshot its prey. As it passed overhead, Coyle gunned both his engines. He tipped the nose of his aircraft upward and fired all fourteen of the machine guns in a desperate fusillade of gunfire.

The T-33 flew right into the stream of bullets and blew up.

Coyle's crew of guardsmen cheered. Coyle knew their elation would be short-lived if he couldn't extinguish the flames in the damaged engine. He cut off the fuel hoping the wind would put out the flames. After a few minutes of flying on one engine, the flames trailing the burning engine turned to smoke. With only one engine operational, he knew they would not survive another dog fight should the enemy spot his wounded aircraft. Even though his instincts wanted altitude, he kept the plane low hugging the waves as he limped back to Nicaragua.

Major Riley Shamburger and his observer, Wade Gray were hit by a T-33 as they approached the target area. Badly wounded, Shamburger steered his aircraft back toward the sea. The T-33 finished both men off and downed the B-26 into the ocean where it exploded into pieces on impact and then disappeared below the waves carrying the two guardsmen to the bottom of the bay.

Captain Thomas W. Ray, flying with Leo Baker as his observer, was hit by a T-33 followed by ground fire near a Cuban command center northwest of the beach. The B-26 crashed into the nearby jungle. Both men survived and dragged themselves from the wreckage. A militia platoon was sent to examine the aircraft and ensure the crew was dead. Ray and Baker opened fire with their revolvers as they attempted to escape through the trees. The militiamen gave chase and fired their rifles at close range killing both Americans. Their uniforms had all insignia removed making identification of country origin impossible.

The Essex had been ordered to provide limited air cover for the B-26s, but lack of communication and last-minute changes in the plan had prevented the aircraft aboard the carrier from taking off. The planes were still on the flight deck forty miles away by the time the B-26s were downed and the four Americans were killed.

Puerto Cabezas, Nicaragua

Coyle and his crew made it back to Nicaragua and landed safely along with three other B-26s. Mad Dog Flight was too little too late. It was the last ground support mission to fly during the invasion.

Blue Beach, Cuba

The troops on the beach were now on their own and the situation was quickly deteriorating as Castro's forces tightened their perimeter and closed in on the anti-communists.

Washington DC, USA

It was late in the evening. Kennedy was in his study reading the first volume of *The Emergence of Lincoln* by Allan Nevins. It was one of his favorites. He could relate to Lincoln and the onslaught of problems he faced from the very beginning of his presidency. The account made Kennedy's own problems seem less overwhelming. JFK's assistant knocked lightly and entered. "Secretary Dulles has requested a few minutes of your time, Mr. President," said the assistant.

"Of course. Show him in," said Kennedy marking his spot and closing the book.

Dulles entered. "Working kind of late, aren't you, Allen?" said the president.

"Yes, Mr. President. I have an update that I thought you should hear," said Dulles.

"I suppose good news could have waited until morning."

"Yes, Mr. President. When the Cuban exile aircrews returned from their last mission, many were seriously wounded, and most of the planes were heavily damaged. The ground crews were able to repair and arm six aircraft. The problem was that there were not enough aircrews to fly the planes. The Alabama National Guardsmen and a CIA officer that had been training the exiles took it upon themselves to fly four of the aircraft in another air assault against Castro's forces."

"…took it upon themselves?"

"There is no record of any orders being issued from Washington DC or the Essex."

"And you had nothing to do with it?"

"No, Mr. President. I obeyed your directive. I believe there may have been some confusion when the communications were cut off with the beachhead."

"Did the Americans in Nicaragua attempt to communicate with the officers in charge of the operation?"

"Not that I know of, Mr. President. I believe the American aircrews saw the need for action and acted on their own to assist the invasion forces."

"Even though I gave strict instructions that they were to do no such thing?"

"Yes, Mr. President. But in their defense, there has been a lot of mixed signals."

"Allen, it's not a mixed signal when the president of the United States gives a command."

"No, Mr. President… it's not and I will get to the bottom of it."

"As soon as possible, Allen. And make sure there are no more mixed signals from the CIA."

"Yes, Mr. President."

"So, what were the results of the air assault?"

"The aircrews were able to assault the government forces attacking the beachhead and inflict significant damage. If anything, the air assault bought our ground forces some time."

"Well, I guess there was some good that came from their insubordination."

"Yes, Mr. President… but at a cost. Two of the planes were shot down and crashed – one in the jungle and another in the ocean. We believe all four of the crew were killed in the crashes or shortly thereafter."

"My God. Where they…?"

"Americans? Yes, Mr. President."

JFK was stunned and took a long moment to consider the repercussions. "So, the world will know that America was involved."

"Not necessarily. The American crewmen were not wearing their National Guard uniforms. They were dressed as the exile aircrews and carried no identification. Since there were no survivors to interrogate, I think it is safe to assume that Castro will believe the dead aircrews to be Cuban."

"We have to recover the bodies for the families."

"And we will, Mr. President. But later, through negotiation."

"Seems like a chicken shit way of respecting our dead."

"Perhaps, Mr. President. But it's the right way to do it."

"Fine."

"There is one more issue."

"What's that?"

"We can save lives if you rescind your order for no American air cover."

"Allen, we've already been through this. Nothing has changed."

"I respectfully disagree, Mr. President. We're losing."

"They're losing."

"Because we broke our promise to supply air cover."

"You mean, I broke my promise."

"Yes, Mr. President. It was your decision to agree to it in the first place. And your decision to rescind that agreement."

"It's late. Let's cut to the chase. What is it that you would have me do, Allen?"

"Just the mere presence of American fighter aircraft will cause Castro and his air force to break off their attacks on the beachhead. That could buy anti-communist forces the time they need to organize their defenses."

"And if the Cubans attack our aircraft?"

"I don't think they will, Mr. President. Castro's air force has suffered a heavy blow. He's lost over half his planes. I doubt he will risk losing more."

"You might be right."

"It could be seen as a humanitarian move on our part – separating the two sides until a ceasefire could be negotiated. I think the U.N. would accept that explanation."

"Alright. I'll give the order for Essex to fly air cover over the beachhead and the surviving freighters in the bay."

"Thank you, Mr. President."

"Good night, Allen."

Australia Sugar Mill, Cuba

Informed of the two downed B-26s, Castro knew that he had won. Without air cover to protect the exiles, his forces would strangle the anti-communists like an anaconda. His big concern was not the cost of victory, but to ensure that none of the American-trained exiles escaped into the mountains where they could become guerillas and continue to cause problems for his people. As resistance lessened, Castro ordered his commanders to spread their men out to guarantee there were no breaks in the front line as they advanced.

Watching as the troops on the beach took a heavy beating from artillery and mortar fire, the captains of two of the freighters waiting offshore took matters into their own hands and moved their ships as close as possible to the beach.

The troops dropped their weapons and waded out into the surf in hopes of making it to the approaching ships. Many were raked with enemy machine-gun fire while others simply drowned in the waves. A few dozen were picked up by lifeboats lowered from the freighters. But it was a momentary victory.

A team of SU-100 tank destroyers onshore opened fire with their 100mm guns and shelled the two freighters punching large holes in their hulls. The captains had no choice but to abandon their rescue attempt. Having saved what they could, they turned the ships back out to the safety of the sea.

Running low on ammunition and weighed down with heavy casualties, the invasion commander recognized the futility of the situation. In the early afternoon of April 20th, the surviving invasion force surrendered to the Cuban military and local militia. Over one thousand exiles, most of whom were wounded, were taken prisoner. Hostilities ceased. The invasion of The Bay of Pigs was over. Castro and his revolution had won.

Washington DC, USA

It was Allen Dulles that broke the news of the defeat to JFK. "The dead and wounded?"

"Over one hundred dead and three hundred severely wounded," said Dulles.

"How many prisoners were taken by Castro's forces?"

"It's difficult to say exactly. Many that tried to swim out to the freighters were drowned and carried out to sea. But we estimate it is somewhere in the area of twelve hundred prisoners."

"I suppose it is some consolation that they didn't die."

"Yet, Mr. President. They are traitors in Castro's mind. He has said such to the world press. We don't know what their fate might be."

"I would have thought he'd have called them "American pawns.""

"He may in time. We might be able to negotiate their return, but it would be like admitting that we had backed them."

"I don't care about that now. The cat is pretty much out of the bag. We will continue to keep up the appearance of neutrality in the affair, but nobody is going to believe us. We'll leave it to the diplomats to perform damage control."

"I don't imagine this is easy for you, Mr. President. If you wish, you may have my resignation."

"No, Allen. I'm not letting you off the hook. At least not yet. You will do your best to clean up the mess you've helped make. Castro remains in power, and we have a communist nation within spitting distance of our coast. We need foreign intelligence more than ever."

"I will see to it, Mr. President. Is there anything else?"

"I want the names and phone numbers of the American families that lost loved ones when those planes crashed. I'll be calling them as soon as the smoke clears. We need to get their bodies back, Allen."

"I will do everything I can."

"Good. That'll be all. I'm sure we'll talk in the next day or two."

"Good night, Mr. President."

"Good night, Allen."

Over the next few days, President Kennedy made several statements to the press in which he declared, "There is nothing in the neutrality laws that prevent refugees from Cuba returning to that country and engaging in the fight for freedom... There is nothing criminal about an individual leaving the United States to join an insurgent group... or encouraging others to do so. The message of Cuba, of Laos, of the rising din of communist voices in Asia and Latin America – these messages are all the same. The complacent, the self-indulgent, the soft societies are about to be swept away with the debris of history. Only the strong, only the industrious, only the determined, only the courageous, only the visionary who determine the real nature of our struggle can survive."

A week later, President Kennedy, having been consistently hounded by reporters, gave a short speech that began, "There's an old saying that victory has a hundred fathers and defeat is an orphan... Further statements, detailed discussions, are not to conceal responsibility because I'm the responsible officer of the government."

JFK never admitted that the United States military was directly involved in the invasion of Cuba. A few months later during a peace conference, Che Guevara slipped Kennedy a note that said, *"Thanks for Playa Girón. Before the invasion, the revolution was weak. Now, it is stronger than ever."* Kennedy was said to have crumpled the note and deposited it in a nearby trashcan.

The invasion of Cuba only lasted four days, but the repercussions lasted throughout JFK's presidency and affected many of Kennedy's decisions, especially when it came to Vietnam. As a new president, he was naturally nervous about his first military action as commander-in-chief. Having failed that test, Kennedy became overly gun shy and lost much of his confidence. He did not plan the invasion, that belonged to Eisenhower, but Kennedy approved and executed the plan. It was Kennedy that owned the fiasco called "The Bay of Pigs."

The biggest irony from the failed invasion was that the new president, after being elected by the thinnest of margins, became more popular than ever with both Democrats and Republicans. Instead of being seen as a pacifist liberal unwilling to confront communism, JFK was labeled a strong leader that would do what was necessary to protect America and promote democracy. The American people forgave the failure and applauded the effort. Few of his opponents questioned that Kennedy had the luck of the Irish. But then came Vietnam…

A MEMORABLE EXPERIENCE

Hanoi, South Vietnam

In a neighborhood not far from Building D67, the politburo headquarters, there was a rather small two-story house. The French yellow walls and green shutters were faded, a sign of neglect and dark mold had set in as it often does in Vietnam. It was located on a quiet residential street with dozens of homes just like it. Few realized it was the home of the most powerful and secretive man in North Vietnam – Le Duan.

Known as "Spitting Woman" to the American soldiers she had fought alongside during WWII, Suong sat on a stool with a wailing baby on her lap. She could not believe how loud the infant could scream, especially when it was hungry or needed its diaper changed which was often… too often. Gifted with natural immunity, mothers can put up with an amazing amount of shit, piss, drool, mucus, and vomit from their children. But the thing on her lap was not hers. It belonged to Le Duan's other wife, Le Thi, who was grocery shopping with her eldest daughter. Suong wondered why she had been asked to watch the baby and Le Thi's other two children while the daughter, who was old enough to care for children, went with the mother. But Suong said nothing. Things were difficult enough without her making more trouble.

Le Thi was not happy when Le Duan had brought home his new bride. Duan had not asked Le Thi before marrying Suong. Instead, he simply told her to move all the children back into one bedroom so that Suong could have her own room. When Duan's second wife arrived, Le Thi had cried for days causing Duan to work even more late nights at the politburo. Suong was left alone to deal with Le Thi's abusive tongue and the bulk of the housework and laundry.

As the second wife, it was a tradition that Suong obey Le Thi, the first wife. Suong did not care much for tradition, especially that particular tradition. When she felt she was being treated unfairly, she simply left the house and wandered the neighborhood streets thinking about her life in the mountains before she met Duan. It was a good life full of adventure and danger. She was a scout for the Viet Minh in their war against the Japanese and later the French. Ho Chi Minh was their leader and she respected him more than any other man. Suong was like the Viking warrior maidens she had read about when Ho had taught her to read and speak Vietnamese and French.

She had killed many enemy soldiers without remorse, knowing it was her duty to do so and she was good at it. When Ho had commanded her to betray the American soldier Granier, she obeyed, although not without a heavy heart. She loved Granier, but she loved her country and Ho more. She longed for the nights when Granier and her slept together in a mountain cave or the jungle. She missed Granier.

She missed her children that were now grown and living on their own. She missed her mother and father, still living in her mountain home. She thought about returning but found the thought of leaving Duan unbearable. She was stuck. Damn all love.

When darkness descended and she finally came home, Duan would lecture her about how she needed to try harder to get along with Le Thi and respect her. Because she loved Duan, Suong would pretend to listen, but she thought Duan was full of water buffalo manure and had told him so on many occasions. She imagined that was one of the reasons he loved her… she was honest and not afraid to anger him with the truth if required. But lately, it seemed Duan just wanted to shut the world out while he was home.

As Chairmen of the Politburo and Secretary-General of the Communist Party, he was constantly dealing with problems and trying to satisfy his fellow board members. Life was far from easy for Duan and now having two wives made it even more complicated. He just wanted a good night's sleep before going back to the office in the morning.

Sex with either of his wives died off to one or two times a month and never together. Each had made her feelings clear when he had brought up the idea. It was bad enough sharing a house, they refused to share a bed with one another. So, the wives came up with a schedule and stuck to it no matter what happened during the day. Any deviation was met with anger. For Duan, polygamy had enslaved him. He loved both his wives but often preferred to be alone. It was just easier that way. He had asked Suong to marry him because several older members of the politburo were complaining that as chairman it wasn't proper for him to keep a mistress. A man in power should have high moral standards and set a good example for the people.

Finances were not easy either. Suong was another mouth to feed. His politburo position, even though lofty, didn't pay much in keeping with the communist principles. He had originally considered two households for each of his wives but abandoned the idea once he had calculated a monthly budget. They would just have to share the same house. That was all he could afford.

As time moved on, Suong had become quieter, keeping her thoughts to herself. Day after day, scrubbing the laundry, wiping the baby's ass, then peeling and cutting the vegetables for the evening meal and sweeping the floor with a worn-out broom. The joy of life leaving her. The drudgery set in and overtook her like a dark shroud or an evil spell. She was not living the life she had imagined when she agreed to marry Le Duan, and she was worried she was getting fat.

Binh Duong Province, South Vietnam

It was a day like many, the was sky covered with a thin layer of clouds making the terrain look flat and without form. The promise of rain to some, but not for First Lieutenant Pham Phu Quoc and his wingman Second Lieutenant Nguyen Van Cu. Each officer was flying a Douglas A-1 Skyraider over Binh Duong Province, part of the iron triangle and a Viet Cong stronghold. They were hunting the VC and wanted a clear view of the ground below.

There had been a brief but vicious attack against a government platoon patrolling the villages. As usual, the platoon leader had quickly broken off the attack and called in for air support. Most ARVN commanders believed it was smarter to use artillery and aircraft to fight the Viet Cong rather than South Vietnamese soldiers. Although bravery was encouraged, loyalty to President Diem and keeping those safe under one's command earned promotion. Diem did not like when his army suffered heavy casualties. His troops were needed to protect Saigon, and even more important… him.

Quoc and Cu would do their best to find the Viet Cong before they slipped back into the cover of the woods. They both knew it was a long shot, but they had to try. They were in luck and spotted a group of men and women running through a cluster of rice paddies less than a kilometer from the edge of a forest. They made a quick pass to ensure that the group below was indeed Viet Cong and not a bunch of scared villagers. They could see the men and women below wearing black pajamas, conical hats, and carrying a mix of rifles. That was enough to identify them as Viet Cong and allow the attack to go forward.

Quoc gave a quick set of instructions to Cu over the radio. Quoc would attack first then Cu. They would perform a bomb run then strafe the Viet Cong with rockets and machine guns. Quoc had recently been personally commended by Diem for his achievements in combat, having been honored as one of the best pilots in the Republic of Vietnam Air Force. Quoc made his turn and arced around in a broad circle. Cu followed giving his commander room for his attack.

The two Skyraiders were propeller-driven attack aircraft developed after World War II. They had unusually long fuselages and a long-range flight capability. They carried 8,000 lbs. of bombs and rockets on their fifteen hardpoints and the four 20mm auto-cannons onboard gave them an extra punch after their bombs and rockets were expended. In many ways, it was an ideal aircraft for Vietnam where dogfights were few and air-to-ground attacks were commonplace.

Quoc launched his rockets from a distance then dropped his bombs. The barrage of high explosives was devastating to the enemy below and killed four on the first pass. Cu followed up with the same mix of rockets and bombs. Three more Viet Cong would fight no more. The surviving Viet Cong watched as the two warplanes turned for another pass. They ran for the tree line splashing up the muddy water in the rice paddies making them more noticeable to the two pilots. The aircrafts' autocannons killed three more before the Viet Cong reached the safety of the tree canopy and began firing back at the aircraft. The gunfire was of little use. The planes were moving far too fast and climbing into the grey sky to be bothered by small arms fire. The occasional lucky shot was not to be had.

Quoc and Cu headed for home. It was a good day for the South Vietnamese Air Force.

Bien Hoa Air Base, South Vietnam

When Quoc and Cu landed at Bien Hoa Air Base sixteen miles outside of Saigon across the Dong Nai River, a private working in the communications building delivered a message to Cu as he stepped down from his aircraft. As the private moved off, Cu read the message. His expression revealed his distress. "Bad news?" said Quoc.

"My father has been arrested," said Cu.

"I'm sorry," said Quoc. "Diem doesn't like opposition."

"It was Brother Nhu's doing."

"It comes from the same roots."

"I need to go and find out what happened."

"Yes. Go. I will see to your aircraft and make the after-action report."

"Thank you, Commander," said Cu moving off quickly.

The government interrogation center on the outskirts of Saigon was new; built with American aid money. It looked like most of the modern buildings of the time, except for the windows which were more narrow than usual. There was a perimeter wall with one gate that served as entrance and exit to the compound and was guarded 24/7 year-round. There were also guards in the reception area inside the front doors of the building. The movement of suspects to interrogation rooms and back to their cells was well secured by two transport guards and a set of manacles with sharp edges that cut into the skin if worn too long. Few struggled. It was hopeless anyway. Escape meant you were guilty.

If someone succeeded in escaping from the facility, they would be hunted down and most likely executed on the spot. And if they couldn't be found, their family would suffer the consequences of their treason. It was unjust and barbaric but effective.

Cu was the second son of Nguyen Van Luc, a leader of the Vietnamese Nationalist Party (VNQDD), which opposed the Diem regime. He was arrested by Nhu's secret police force and taken to be interrogated. There was nothing unusual about this. Almost all prisoners began their internment with interrogation. Luc was no different. During interrogation, no visitors were allowed, not even lawyers.

After the day's interrogation was finished, Cu was able to bribe a guard with what little money he had saved from his officer's salary for three minutes with his father. When Cu entered his father's cell, he was surprised and grateful to see he had not been beaten… not yet. Knowing their time was short, they talked quickly. "Father, tell me what to do?" said Cu.

"There is nothing to be done, my son," said his father. "They will do with me as they wish. You cannot stop them."

"I refuse to accept this."

"But you must. My life is of little consequence. It is the movement to remove Diem and his family from power that must survive. If not, our country and its people are doomed."

"But Father, can't you see? The movement still needs you."

"No, my son. It needs you and young men like you. You are the future. True democracy will be your legacy, not mine."

"I am not here to discuss politics with you. There is no time."

"There is always time to discuss what is right."

Cu considered for a moment, then said, "Alright. If you feel this is my calling, then what would you have me do, Father?"

"You know the leaders of the Vietnamese National Party. Contact them. Become their vessel and heed their counsel. Do their bidding whatever it might be."

The guard unlocked the door. Time was up. "If you are the man that I think you are, carry our message and show the world the truth."

"Yes, Father. I will do as you ask," said Cu, his eyes welled up with tears.

They hugged. The guard entered and pried them apart. The father watched as his son and the guard exited the cell and the door slammed shut. Both son and father wondered if they would ever see one another again.

Cu knew the leaders of the party. They had late-night meetings at his family's house many times. Most were former politicians and retired military officers; well respected and revered by their followers. Because his father had been arrested, the leaders were fearful of meeting with Cu knowing that he was probably being watched. Instead, they sent a woman, Thi Pham, to make contact.

Pham met with Cu at a brothel where she was disguised as one of the working girls. Few would suspect the young lieutenant visiting a brothel and even fewer would suspect one of the working girls of being an opposition party operative. They met in the privacy of a bedroom. "You are Nguyen Van Luc's son?" Pham said.

"Yes," said Cu.

"When you turned eight years old where did your father take you for your birthday?"

"He took me to the Golden Dragon theatre to watch the water puppet show."

"A memorable experience."

"Yes. Can you help my father?"

"I am afraid there is little we can do. Nhu's grip is strong. He will not let your father go until he is sure he has revealed all that he knows."

"My father would never give up his friends."

"I know. That is why we fear for him. Nhu's interrogators can be very persistent."

"So, you are going to let him rot in prison?"

"No. We will use whatever influence we can to free him, but I fear it is a worthless cause and we do not want to endanger other members of the party if the chance of success is limited."

"You are cowards."

"We are practical. Revolutions are not won by the impatient."

"Patience does not help my father."

"I know it is difficult. We have had many of our members arrested in the past. The waiting seems unbearable."

"Torture is unbearable."

"Cu, your father is a very smart man. He will allow them to torture him for a time then give the secret police the name of one of our enemies as a member of our party. That may be enough to win his freedom."

"Or death."

"Like all of us, your father knew the risks when he joined our cause. What about you?"

"What about me?"

"You have seen firsthand what Diem and his family are capable of. Their desire to stay in power outweighs the war against the communists. If the people do not act, I fear our country will be lost. How far would you go to remove them from power?"

Cu thought for a long moment before responding, "I don't know."

"Consider the question. When you have an answer, contact us again. We have work for you if you want it."

"Work?"

She smiled and exited the room without explaining further and left Cu to ponder.

Saigon, South Vietnam

When Granier returned to Saigon, he immediately reported to Lansdale and found that his team was still on a joint operation up North with Conein. Even though their mission had been completed, it would take another week for them to work their way back out of North Vietnam. "There is nothing you can do until your team returns and even then, from what I have been told, they will need time to recoup from their wounds," said Lansdale.

"Wounds? What the hell did Conein do to my team?" said Granier.

"They ran into some trouble in Hanoi. Something about a fire. We'll know more when they get back. In the meantime, take some time off and relax," said Lansdale. "The beaches at Vung Tau are great this time of year."

"I don't need a vacation. I need a mission," said Granier.

"Unfortunately, I don't have anyone that needs whacking at the moment," said Lansdale.

"It doesn't have to be wet work. I could blow a bridge or something."

"Sorry. No bridges either. However, I do have a bit of intelligence work that needs doing."

"Yeah. What's that?"

"It's really below your skillset."

"I don't care. What is it?"

"I need some surveillance photos taken."

"Surveillance photos?"

"Like I said… below your skillset."

"Yeah, but… you need it done, right?"

"Yes, I do. It is a request from Nhu, President Diem's brother and head of internal security."

"I know who Nhu is. Wait a minute... Nhu must have a dozen photographers at his disposal. Why is he asking you to do it?"

"The surveillance target is politically and financially connected. He wants to avoid any link between the surveillance and the government."

"He means Diem?"

"Yes... he means President Diem."

"So, who is the target?"

Lansdale shuffled through a stack of manila folders on his desk and pulled one out. He opened it and read the name, "Zhou Youyong. He's a trader in investment-grade gems here in Saigon. We have his address. He mostly deals with government and military officials."

Granier had heard the name before but couldn't place it. He knew that in the espionage business it was always best to keep one's mouth shut until you had all the information. "So, what did he do?" said Granier.

"Nothing that we know of, but a Viet Cong sympathizer under interrogation suggested that he might be an intelligence officer for the North."

"So, confirm it and shoot him. Why the photos?"

"We want to see whom he is talking to before we take more permanent measures."

"Sounds simple enough."

"Good. You want an operation... It's yours."

A few hours later, Granier took a trishaw to the neighborhood where Youyong's office was located. It was upscale for Saigon with clean streets and no food carts insight. The restaurants, tea rooms, and stores were well kept with patrons that wore suits and dresses. He had decided to scout the location first and locate a good position to take up surveillance before he brought his camera gear.

Dropped off on a corner, the driver pointed at an alley as the address he was given. Granier paid him. The driver motioned with his hands that he would wait for the American so he could take him back when he was finished with his business. Granier motioned for him not to wait, but it didn't seem to have much of an effect as the driver climbed onto the passenger bench on the front of the trishaw to take a nap while waiting – a common practice.

Granier rounded the corner and headed down the alley which was covered in cobblestones and was surprisingly clean. He imagined the businesses connected to the alley to be offices and high-end boutiques rather than restaurants that would stack empty crates in the ally and have several overflowing trash bins with the remains of rotting vegetables, eggshells, and fish bones. The alley had none of that and there was no smell of urine or feces. It was well-kept for wealthy patrons to pass. There were even lanterns that hung between the buildings to illuminate the alley at night. He stopped for a moment and studied the building addresses. He saw that he was heading in the right direction.

As he resumed his search, he noticed a young Vietnamese woman walking toward him from the opposite end of the alley. She was wearing a white ao dai and carried a bamboo umbrella to shield herself from the hot sun and surprise cloud bursts that were common at that time of year. The woman averted her face and did not make eye contact with him. It was a common practice among attractive married women not wanting to attract a male's attention, especially a foreigner. Granier only had a brief glimpse of her face as they passed each other. She was pretty with clear skin and silky black hair. As Granier moved farther down the alley, he looked back and saw that the woman was already gone. He was disappointed. She was intriguing.

The end of the alley opened into a mini-square with five doors. Above each door was a plaque with an inscription and symbols explaining the business inside. He found the door for Zhou Youyong – a gem trading company. It looked less fancy than the other doors and plaques. Granier imagined that a gem dealer might not want to advertise too heavily that there were valuable jewels inside the building. He considered entering the building to get a better look, but he knew he would probably run into Youyong, and he didn't want to raise his curiosity.

He surveyed the end of the alley and saw a fire escape attached to the building above one of the doors. He was sure he could get a good angle on Youyong's doorway. The only problem was that anyone below would be able to see him. He decided to bring a bucket of paint, a paintbrush, and a tarp and disguise himself as a painter repainting the fire escape. Even though he was a big Caucasian, he surmised that from the ground nobody would be able to determine his height. A conical hat and some ragged coveralls would complete the disguise. It wasn't perfect but it didn't need to be. Just enough to satisfy nosy eyes.

He went back to headquarters and gathered the camera gear and the other things he needed. It was almost the end of the day before he made it back to the alley and climbed up the fire escape. He watched while pretending to paint as several people exited the various doors in the alley. But nobody exited Youyong's door. He wondered if Youyong was even in there today. As the sun set, the business owners exited their respective doors and locked up… all but Youyong. Still no sign of him. Granier continued to wait.

As day turned to night, the alley became dark, and the lanterns turned on. They were electric which was a luxury. More signs of wealth. Just as he was about to give up, Granier saw the door open and Youyong appear. It was hard to see and even harder to see through the camera lens. Youyong locked up his business and turned. Granier snapped a photo and was surprised by the loudness of the shutter. Youyong hearing the shutter stopped and glanced upward. Granier quickly set down the camera and picked up his paintbrush. He realized how stupid he looked painting in the dark.

Youyong studied the painter for a moment then called up to him in Vietnamese.

Granier, unable to understand what Youyong said or reply, grunted and turned away as if ignoring the man below.

Youyong called out again and received no response. He considered for a moment then shrugged and walked up the alley.

Granier wondered if he had blown his cover just as the operation had started. It was a rookie mistake. He hadn't thought it through correctly. He packed up his things and left.

When Granier returned to headquarters, he told Lansdale what had happened. Lansdale was peeved but didn't make too big of a deal about it. He asked for the film and said he would have it developed. Granier said he doubted that the photo he took would even come out because it was so dark. Lansdale said he wanted it anyway. Something was better than nothing.

Granier thought nothing of it until the next morning when he was getting ready to go back to his surveillance spot. A messenger dropped off a manila envelope from a local photo lab and Granier signed for it. Curious, Granier went into the toilet, closed the door for some privacy, and opened the envelope. There was one photo inside. It was very grainy. But Granier recognized the face and suddenly remembered where he had heard Zhou Youyong's name.

It was during the Indochina War. Granier was a bodyguard for Congressman John Kennedy and his brother and sister as they toured Vietnam. Having seen his former lover – Spitting Woman in a park, he followed her. Granier was ambushed by a group of communists and knocked unconscious. When he came to, he found himself in a room with Zhou Youyong, who introduced himself and apologized for the rough treatment. Youyong was a Chinese intelligence operative in Saigon. Youyong warned Granier that the French might attempt to assassinate the Congressman to keep him from discovering and revealing the truth about the war – the French were losing – which meant that the Americans might cut off financial and military aid that the French desperately needed. Once the message was delivered to Granier, he was freed and left the building unhindered.

Making his way back to the Hotel Continental where they were staying, Granier decided not to tell anyone about Youyong and his message, so he did not endanger Spitting Woman. He realized that was a mistake. Youyong had continued to operate in Saigon for over ten years spying for the Chinese and most probably for the North Vietnamese. The problem that Granier faced was that he still could not tell anyone without getting into a lot of trouble and having his commanders question his loyalty. He concluded that the information of Youyong's identity didn't matter since Lansdale and Nhu already suspected Youyong to be a spy. No harm, no foul. He would remain silent. He placed the photo back in the manila envelope and delivered it to Lansdale.

Over the next few days, Granier snapped photos of anyone going in or out of Youyong's office and delivered the film to Lansdale just as he had been ordered. He had no idea who the people were, but he was sure that Nhu would have them picked up for questioning. Granier was confident that the identity of Youyong and his co-conspirators would be discovered by Lansdale and Nhu and no harm to South Vietnam or the US would occur. What was done, was done and nobody could change the past. Even so, Granier had trouble sleeping as he replayed what had happened and how he would have changed things if given the chance.

A HORSE NAMED "TABASCO"

Washington DC, USA

Once the Bay of Pigs invasion had failed, the CIA wanted to cover its tracks as much as possible to prevent blowback. The surviving Alabama National Guardsmen were ordered back to their base in Birmingham. The CIA contractors and officers that participated in the invasion were scattered to the wind with many, including Coyle, returning to their assignments overseas. The CIA made sure that anyone who was there was well briefed on how to respond to questions from journalists. The most popular response was, "Fuck off" which could not be quoted and therefore was useless.

Coyle was happy to be done with Cuba. It was one of the biggest failures of his career. He was unable to protect the men he had trained and commanded just as he had been able to protect his friend Earthquake McGoon during the fall of Dien Bien Phu. Once again, the memories came flooding back of that terrible night when McGoon died in a fiery crash after having been hit with Viet Minh anti-aircraft shells. Coyle was with McGoon when he died and pledged to find his friend's two live-in whores and help them. He had failed at that too, unable to find either of the girls as the French surrendered and Hanoi fell to the communists.

Before going back to Vietnam, Coyle flew to Washington D.C. and was debriefed by the CIA at their Foggy Bottom headquarters. The CIA didn't want Coyle or anyone that had participated in the Bay of Pigs invasion anywhere near the White House where Kenney was besieged by journalists and photographers. The fewer questions the better.

The old office buildings at Foggy Bottom would soon be abandoned by the CIA in exchange for its new headquarters in Langley, Virginia. Officers and office workers were packing up everything to get ready for the move. Each box was carefully labeled and stamped with Top Secret, Secret, Confidential, USAP, or ACCM depending on the security level required to view the items inside. There were already thousands of boxes stacked in rooms and overflowing into the hallways making it difficult to maneuver one's way through the maze. Upon checking in, Coyle was escorted to a room with a table, three chairs, and a tape recorder. He sat and waited for his inquisitors. He didn't wait long…

His debriefing took five hours and was conducted by two CIA officers. The windows and door were kept closed for privacy, making the room hot and stuffy. The questions were probing and uncomfortable at times. The officers were sticklers for accuracy and asked most questions several times to compare the answers and determine their truthfulness. Coyle felt he was being treated like the enemy, but he didn't complain. He wanted to get the whole thing behind him as soon as possible and move on with his life. Besides, he knew that the officers were just doing their job and that a record of what happened was needed. In between questions, he wondered how many people would read the historical record the two CIA officers would help create. Reports of a victory were rarely overlooked. But the Bay of Pigs operation was far from a success and Coyle was fairly sure his answers to their questions would be locked away for years to come. *It was a shame really*, he thought. *One can learn just as much from failure as success. Even more perhaps. But such was not the CIA's way of doing things.* Not yet anyway…

When he was finally done, the officers thanked him for his cooperation and his service to his country. It was a small acknowledgment when compared to grilling he had been given, but he accepted it and left the building.

He went back to his hotel downtown. It wasn't a fancy tourist hotel, more business than pleasure, but the bed was comfortable and there was a restaurant attached to the lobby. He opened the menu on the nightstand next to the bed and ordered room service for dinner – a chicken-fried steak smothered in white gravy with mashed potatoes, peas, a dinner roll (to sop up the gravy), a small salad with thousand island dressing, and two domestic beers. He had no desire to interact with other humans at the moment and was only too happy to spend the rest of his per diem for the day to avoid eating out. He just wanted to take a cold shower and eat something decent before retiring for the night.

After finishing his meal, he stripped down to his underwear, brushed his teeth, climbed into bed, and turned out the light. After a few minutes of staring at the ceiling, he turned the light back on, slipped out of bed, and pulled an envelope from his duffle bag. He climbed back into bed and read the name on the return address on the envelope – Janet Scarborough. He knew the name well and remembered how they first met…

August 21, 1941 - Northern California, USA

Rumors of war were spreading quickly when Coyle, a young lieutenant, was stationed at an airbase outside of San Francisco for flight training. He had been assigned to fly the new Lockheed P-38 Lightning with its distinctive twin booms and a central nacelle containing the cockpit and armament. He had completed his initial training on the aircraft and was preparing for his final check flight.

It was a warm summer morning as Coyle approached his assigned aircraft. There was no training officer to accompany him. He was beyond that and clocking solo flight hours. If he got into trouble, he was on his own. It was a scary yet liberating feeling. He climbed up on the wing careful to step where instructed so as not to damage the aircraft's butt-jointed aluminum panels. Unlike most military aircraft, the Lighting's skin was flush-riveted giving it a smooth appearance and cutting down on wind resistance. With two 1,000 hp turbosupercharged 12-cylinder Allison engines, she was fast. The first American-built military aircraft to fly over 400 mph. She was a beauty and Coyle knew he was lucky to fly her. He climbed into the cockpit, strapped himself in, lowered the bubble canopy, and rolled up the side windows. In the event of an emergency during flight, he had been instructed to turn the aircraft upside-down, open the canopy, release his harness, and fall out of the aircraft. The parachute would do the rest assuming it deployed properly which was by no means guaranteed. In the event that it and his backup parachute failed, he would shortly become a pink pancake. Believing it would be a comforting thought, his instructor assured him that he would not feel anything. It wasn't.

He went through his checklist and fired up the engines. The Lightning was one of the few military aircraft that had mufflers on the engine exhaust making it unusually quiet during flight. The propellers rotated in an opposite direction offsetting the twin engines' torque. This made the plane amazingly stable and easier to maneuver. It was a remarkable machine.

Coyle taxied to the beginning of the runway, stood on the brakes, and advanced the throttles to achieve 3,000 RPMs and forty inches of manifold pressure. The engines roared. He released the brakes. The aircraft accelerated down the runway. At seventy mph he eased back on the stick and the Lightning lifted into the air. He retracted the tricycle landing gear and the aircraft increased speed to 150 mph. As the plane gained altitude, he eased back on the throttle to reduce the manifold pressure and decreased the propellers' RPMs to 2,700. No need to burn up the engines.

He had enough hours behind the stick to know what the P-38 could do. He increased altitude to 20,000 feet and practiced a series of emergency drills such as engine stalls and inverted flight for bailing out. The twin-engine could only endure flying upside down for ten seconds or less because of the loss in oil pressure. That wasn't much time to bail out of an airplane, so he practiced until he was confident, he could do it within the allotted amount of time.

Engine stalls were always a gut-wrenching exercise. Fortunately, the Lightning had two engines and could safely fly level on just one. It could even take off and land on one engine. It was a remarkable aircraft. There was a lot to learn in the short time he had to practice each day. But Coyle was a natural flyer and things seemed to come more easily for him than most of the trainees.

With time running short, Coyle decided to push his aircraft to top speed and fly as low as he dared. He figured he might need to fly a low-level assault one day and wanted to be ready. At 100 feet off the deck, the green hills below raced beneath him. He flew his plane at its top speed of 400 mph hugging the contours of the landscape. He was at the edge of control pushing his limits. One wrong move and his short life would be over. He imagined it was the same feeling he would get his first time in combat. It was exhilarating.

He dipped the plane down into a valley and up over a gentle hill. He saw a small house in the middle of a pasture with a horse grazing. A woman was hanging her laundry on several clotheslines. Everything appeared so fast there was no time to alter course. He flew directly over the little farmhouse. The horse bolted. The woman's laundry was caught in his tailwind, torn from the clotheslines, and whipped into the air as if snatched by a twister. He turned around to see the woman's dress flying upward revealing her undergarments and her slim figure. Her hair twisted in a tangle. "Oh, shit," he said to himself as the plane climbed over another hill and disappeared.

When landed back at his airbase, Coyle could see the base commander and his flight instructor waiting for him on the apron. He taxied over to his aircraft's assigned parking spot, cut the engines, and climbed out. Even though he knew better, he behaved as if everything were normal. "How was your flight, Lieutenant?" asked the base commander as Coyle saluted.

"Fine, sir," said Coyle.

"Uneventful?"

"Ah, well… I've never known flying to be uneventful."

"Yeah, I guess that's true. So, you think you're ready for your final check flight?"

"I've got a little more work to do, but I think I'll be ready."

"That's a shame."

"A shame?"

"Yeah. To be so close…"

"I don't understand."

"Well, Lieutenant, let me see if I can explain it to you. Do you know General Scarborough?"

"No, sir. I don't believe I do."

"He's the base commander over at the Presidio. Most of us commanders see that as a plum job. The Presidio being next to the Golden Gate Bridge. Helluva view. Anyway, he called me this afternoon and asked what kind of chickenshit outfit I was running here. Naturally, I took umbrage at his choice of adjectives until he told me that one of the pilots flying a P-38 buzzed his daughter's ranch, scaring the shit out of her horse and sending her laundry to hell and back. I told him that was impossible. None of my pilots were that stupid and would never disobey a standing order of always flying 800 feet above the deck unless landing. I was correct in representing the intelligence of my pilots, was I not, Lieutenant?"

Coyle knew he was caught and that if he tried to wiggle out of it, it would just make things worse. And so, he said, "I may have been flying a bit low this morning."

"A bit low?"

"Yes, sir."

"I see. I guess I owe General Scarborough an apology. That's gonna be uncomfortable. At least until

I assure him that the pilot involved has been grounded until his daughter decides that pilot has matured an appropriate amount and is ready to fly again."

"What?! But my final check flight is next Tuesday."

"Was next Tuesday, Lieutenant. Was."

Coyle was crestfallen and feeling like the asphalt had disappeared from beneath his feet. "Now, if I could give you a bit of friendly advice, Lieutenant," said the base commander. "If I were you, I'd requisition a vehicle from the motor pool and haul ass over to Janet Scarborough's property, where I would fix whatever needs to be fixed, then beg her forgiveness for your juvenile stunt. And I sure as hell wouldn't set foot on this airbase again until Miss Scarborough has written a note saying all is forgiven and she thinks you're ready to fly again. Is that clear enough, Lieutenant?"

"Yes, commander."

"Better get to it then. Daylight's burning."

Coyle saluted and moved off to secure his aircraft.

Coyle drove one of the new Willys jeeps that had been issued to the airbase. It easily handled the three-mile dirt road leading to the Scarborough ranch. Clouds rolled in over the green hills typical of Northern California and threatened rain. It hadn't dawned on him that he might get drenched if the clouds let loose. He had bigger concerns on his mind as he pulled up in front of the farmhouse. The laundry was once again hung on the clotheslines. He could see the silhouette of someone standing behind the front door screen. On the drive over, he had decided that a contrite attitude was probably his best chance at saving his flying career. He climbed out of the jeep and walked toward the house. "Are you the asshole that scared my horse and ruined my laundry?" said a woman's voice.

"Yes, ma'am. That would be me," said Coyle shifting his eyes downward hoping to demonstrate a guilty conscience.

"My father said you'd probably be coming out here."

"I'm really sorry for any inconvenience I caused you."

"You should be. My horse was so damned scared he broke through a fence. You're lucky he didn't hurt himself or I would be pointing a shotgun filled with rock salt at you."

"It was a bonehead move on my part. I never meant to harm anyone or anything, especially a horse. I like horses. Look I am happy to pay for any damages I caused."

"You any good with tools?"

"Excuse me?"

"I don't need money. I need my fence fixed."

"I could do that. And rewash your laundry too."

"Laundry's already been rewashed and hung. Besides, I don't want you poking around my undergarments."

"Of course not. I completely understand. Do you have any tools?"

"In the barn. You can find wood in there too. Stacked in the back. This isn't the first time Tabasco has broken a fence."

"Tabasco?"

"The horse you scared with your P-38."

"Tabasco, cuz he's a chestnut?"

"You know horses?"

"I know the color of their coats. Not too much more. You know planes?"

"I know that plane. You're not the first Lightning pilot to buzz my property."

"Again, I am really sorry about that."

"Don't be sorry. Fix my fence."

"Right away, ma'am."

"And stop calling me 'ma'am.'"

"What should I call you?"

"Janet."

"I'm Coyle."

"That's your first name?"

"No. It's Tom. But everyone calls me Coyle."

"Well, Tom, you better get to work before it starts raining. The broken fence is just beyond that crest to the south."

"And Tabasco?"

"Don't worry about him. He'll find his way back when it's time for his evening grain. He's got a sweet tooth for molasses."

"I'll get right on it," said Coyle moving off toward the barn. Janet continued to watch him from behind the screen door.

It was getting late when Coyle was nailing in the last replacement board. It was already raining, and the sky was getting dark. He saw something moving in the tree line and wondered if there were bears in Northern California. The hammer he was using had a claw on the opposite side of the head. He flipped the hammer around to use the claw as a weapon and realized how stupid that would be. Much better to outrun the bear than fight it. But first, he needed to finish the fence. He flipped the hammer back around and pounded the last nail into the board.

Coyle heard someone banging on the side of a bucket. He turned to investigate and saw nothing.

When turned back to the fence, he saw a brown mass break from the trees and charge straight at him. He froze until he realized it was Tabasco heading for his evening oats and closing fast. It occurred to Coyle that he had repaired the only way Tabasco knew how to get back into the pasture. As Tabasco leaped into the air, Coyle hit the deck. The horse cleared the top rail with a good foot to spare, landed on the other side, and galloped toward the house on the other side of the knoll. Coyle rose, his uniform muddied, and cursed the beast, "Well shit, if you could jump the damned thing why did you have to break it, ya dumb mule!"

Coyle finished up and carried the toolbox and broken boards back to the barn. As he walked through the barn door, he caught a glimpse of Janet for the first time. She was feeding Tabasco, now in his stall, his evening oats. Coyle was taken aback. She was beautiful. Tall and full-figured but with a face like Vivien Leigh. She wore tight jeans and a loose blouse that hid her large breasts. "Done?" she said without looking at Coyle.

"Good as new," said Coyle.

"Bullshit, but I'm sure it's fine."

Coyle pulled out the bent nails from the broken boards and set them in what he thought was a scrap pile of wood to be used as kindling for a fire. He used some hay to scrape off as much mud as possible from his uniform. "I should probably get going," he said

"Don't you need a hall pass?" she said looking over at him as she started brushing the dried mud and sweat off Tabasco with a six-circle curry comb.

"What?"

"My dad said I needed to write you a note permitting for you to fly again."

"Yeah, well… if you wouldn't mind."

"You've done your penance. Let me finish up with Tabasco and I'll write you a note."

"Thanks. Can I give you a hand?"

"Sure. Pulldown a couple of alfalfa bales from the loft and cut one open. There's a pair of wire cutters hanging on a post by the ladder."

"Will do."

He climbed up the ladder and tossed down two bales from the loft. He climbed back down and cut the 14-gauge wire on one of the bales. "How many flaks?" said Coyle.

"Just one. Otherwise, he'll get fat," she said grabbing Tabasco's long mane as if teasing.

Enjoying his oats and molasses, Tabasco ignored her. "How long have you owned him?" said Coyle breaking apart a flak of alfalfa and pushing it into Tabasco's feeder.

"About five years. My dad bought him for me after my mom passed away."

"My condolences."

"Yeah. Those were a tough couple of years but, like all things, the colonel and I soldiered through it. He was a full colonel."

"So, this is his place… your father's?"

"Yeah, still is, but he rarely comes out here anymore. Too many memories, I suppose."

"So, how often do you see each other?"

"First Sunday of each month… for golf."

"You golf?"

"Yeah. I shoot too. Skeet."

"Your father taught you?"

"Nope. My mom. She was a helluva shot."

Coyle laughed. "Ah, you're one of those," she said.

"One of what?"

"A man that thinks a woman should stay in their place, get married when they're young, and pop out as many babies as they can."

"Me? No. I figure a woman, or a man can do whatever they want as long as they don't hurt nobody. Although, nothing wrong with kids… if ya want 'em."

Coyle finished stacking the wood and Janet finished with Tabasco. "Coffee before you head back?" said Janet.

"Sure. Much obliged."

They left Tabasco munching on his alfalfa and headed out the barn door toward the house. The rain was steady.

When Coyle woke up the next morning, the rain had stopped, and the sun was shining through the curtains. *Curtains?* He thought. *This isn't my bed.* It wasn't. It was Janet's. He had stayed the night. He looked over at the pillow next to his. It was crumpled but empty. He was alone and naked. He searched for his uniform. It was nowhere in sight. He rose and walked into the bathroom. He relieved himself in the toilet, washed his hands and face, then grabbed a towel and wrapped it around his waist. It suddenly dawned on him that he had not reported to his commander. But considering that he had bedded a general's daughter, he thought that being AWOL from the airbase was the least of his concerns. He could smell bacon cooking on the stove and hear its faint crackle. He also smelled coffee which in this crazy mixed-up world seemed a higher priority than bacon. He walked out of the bathroom and into the hallway.

Through the screen door, he could see Janet walking toward the house with his uniform and undergarments neatly folded in her arms. She was wearing a red flannel shirt and her rubber mud boots. She was not wearing any pants. Coyle realized he was starring as she walked up the stairs and slipped off her boots. He moved into the kitchen. There were two plates on the table with a coffee pot and a vase of fresh-cut wildflowers between them. He poured himself a cup of coffee and sat. Janet walked in. Neither spoke. Coyle watched out of the corner of his eye as she used a fork to collect the bacon from the pan and placed it in a pie tin with a dishcloth on the bottom to collect the grease. Coyle noticed that the bacon was not rigid from being overcooked, just the way he liked it. She dumped out most of the bacon grease into an empty coffee can sitting by the stove. She placed the bacon tin on the table next to the coffee pot. With a little grease left in the hot skillet, she cracked five eggs which she scrambled in the pan mixing them with the grease, and sprinkled them with salt and pepper. It took less than two minutes to cook the eggs. Still, no words had been spoken between them.

When the eggs finished cooking, she scooped the majority on Coyle's plate and the rest onto hers. She sat across from him without a word. They began eating. "No toast?" said Coyle.

"This ain't the Biltmore," she said.

Sassy, thought Coyle. He liked her. Curiosity got the best of Coyle as he chewed on his bacon. He dropped a spoon off the edge of the table and went down to pick it up. Janet did not move to hide anything. After a long moment, Coyle rose with his spoon in hand. "Find everything you were looking for?" said Janet.

"I did," said Coyle.

There is definitely going to be a round two, thought Coyle with a slight smile.

As punishment for being AWOL, Coyle was not allowed to take his final flight check. Instead, he was forced to wait a week and repeat the last part of his flight instruction. He didn't mind. It gave him a chance to see Janet again on the weekend. Somehow, he was able to wrangle a pass. He suspected Janet's father might have had something to do with it.

They spent most of the weekend in her bed and ended up so sore, neither could walk well. Coyle took her for an ice cream sundae in the nearby town and they picked up worm medicine for Tabasco at the feed store.

When they got back to her house, they climbed back into bed and held each other until they fell asleep. It was wonderful.

When he finally took his flight check, Coyle passed with flying colors and graduated. He saw Janet one more time before he shipped out to his first assignment – patrolling the Aleutian Islands in Alaska. Although it sounded like a terrible first posting, it was actually very important. Tensions were rising between Japan and America. Army Air Command was concerned that the Japanese might try an end-run assault by way of the Aleutians. The P-38 was perfect for patrolling the area because of its long-range ability.

Their last night together was filled with passion. The next morning, they said their goodbyes. There were no tears. They hadn't known each other long enough for tears, but there was sadness. They promised to write to each other and then Coyle was off. As Janet watched his jeep disappear over a knoll, the tears began to flow. Coyle never saw them and wondered what he meant to her... and what she meant to him.

They wrote to each other for six weeks, then Janet stopped responding to Coyle's letters. It was like a light switch, once on, now off. No explanation. Just nothing.

Washington DC, USA

Coyle snapped out of his daydream. He considered for a moment, then retrieved the letter inside. It was a cordial, straightforward letter lacking the passion they once shared. Coyle found it cold. Janet asked if Coyle could come to visit her in Virginia, next time he was in Washington DC. There was an important matter she needed to discuss with him. She signed the letter with regards Janet Anderson, not Janet Scarborough like the return address. As far as Coyle could figure, she had taken another man's last name. The letter made Coyle angry. After all these years of no explanation about why she had cut off communication with him and now she finally wanted to talk. Coyle threw the letter into the trash and turned out the light. As much as he tried, he could not fall asleep until he had retrieved the letter from the wastebasket and placed it on the nightstand. He would decide what to do in the morning.

Virginia, USA

With the letter in hand and wearing a cleanly pressed shirt and trousers, Coyle walked down a hallway lined with book lockers. He stopped at a classroom door and peered through the window. Janet, twenty years older, stood at the front of a classroom filled with high schoolers. Coyle was mesmerized as he watched her explain their weekend homework assignment. She was beautiful just as he remembered her. He became conscious of his looks. He no longer had the lean body of the young lieutenant she once knew. Gray hair invaded his short sideburns and he wondered about his wrinkled face from too much sun.

Janet felt someone staring at her and looked over at the window. She was surprised to see Coyle's face and could not help but smile. Coyle held up the letter like it was a hall pass. The recess bell rang, and the high schoolers poured out into the hallway. Coyle waited until the flow of teenagers ceased then entered. "Your gardener told me where you worked," said Coyle.

"Good," Janet said. "I mean… you look good. Healthy."

"You too."

"I have two more classes to teach. Why don't you let me make dinner tonight? We can talk then… that is if you have the time?"

"I'll make the time."

"Good. Six, okay?"

"Sure. You want me to bring anything?"

"Just you and an appetite."

"I'll be there," said Coyle with a sheepish smile as he left.

Coyle arrived with a bottle of wine at Janet's house. When she opened the front door, she was wearing an apron and Coyle got a heavy whiff of the roast she was cooking. They moved into the kitchen where Coyle opened the wine and Janet finished cooking mashed potatoes on the stove. Their conversation was light, neither wanting to discuss delicate subjects… not yet.

They made it through dinner without discussing the elephant in the room. Having waited patiently, Coyle finally asked the question he had longed to ask for so many years, "Why did you stop writing?"

Janet didn't answer straight away. Instead, she removed her apron and sat down across from Coyle. "I was pregnant," said Janet studying Coyle's reaction.

"What?!" said Coyle. "Mine?"

"Yours. Twins in fact. A boy and a girl."

"Why didn't you tell me?!"

"I wanted to. More than anything. But I knew you'd try to do the noble thing and that was not what I needed at that point."

"The noble thing?"

"Marry me."

"Well, yeah. Of course. What was wrong with that?"

Janet waited a long time before answering. Coyle could see that it was difficult for her. "I knew the war was coming and that you'd be in the middle of it. I knew the odds of a fighter pilot surviving."

"You thought I was going to die?"

"If I am being honest... yes," she said looking away, afraid to make eye contact. "I needed stability. And you couldn't give me that. Not while becoming a hero."

"I wasn't trying to be a hero. I was doing my duty."

"Yes. You were. Country above all else."

"What's wrong with that?"

"Nothing. I was proud of you. But that was not what I needed to raise a family."

"You needed stability?"

"Yes."

"You should have told me and let me make a choice."

"Really? Would you have chosen differently?"

"Would you have wanted me too?"

"No. That's the point. I loved you for who you were. I didn't want to change you."

"You loved me."

"Of course, you idiot."

"That was a strange way of showing it."

"I know. But it was the right thing to do... for my children... and for me."

"This is bullshit."

"Listen... it's not. Before I met you, I was dating an officer under my father's command. He was a good man. He didn't know about you... or us."

"And you didn't tell him?"

"No. As far as he knew, the children were his. That's all he ever knew. That's all my children knew."

"You mean our children?" Coyle said sharply.

"Yes. Our children. He was a good father."

"And I wasn't?"

"You weren't available."

"You don't know what I would have done."

"You loved flying. You weren't going to give that up, and if you did, you would have resented me. Of that much, I was sure."

"We could have worked something out."

"Maybe. But I couldn't take that chance."

"So, you lied to me?"

"I didn't lie. I just didn't tell you."

"It's the same damned thing."

"Maybe, but I didn't do it to hurt you."

"Well, you failed at that."

"I can see that. I'm sorry that I hurt you, but not for doing what I thought was right for my—our children."

"So, why tell me now... after all these years?"

"Your son needs you."

"My son. How does he need me?"

"He's in flight school in Alabama. Fort Rucker for advanced training. He'll graduate soon."

Coyle hid his pleasure at hearing his son was being a pilot. "What's wrong with that?" he said.

"Nothing. I think it's great. He's a natural pilot like you."

"And you thought that would make me happy?"

"Doesn't it?"

"Sure. But it doesn't make up for the years I lost seeing them grow up. Being there for them."

"I know. But there is something else…"

"What's that?"

"He wants to go to Vietnam. They desperately need helicopter pilots, so it's almost guaranteed he'll go if he were to request it."

"Why isn't he flying fixed-wing… or jets?"

"I don't know. He chose helicopters."

"Well, that was his first mistake."

"So, don't let him make another. Convince him to request a different assignment."

"Why isn't his *father* talking to him?"

"He passed away a few years back."

"And that's why you need me… to talk him out of it?"

"Yes."

Coyle rose from the table and said, "No."

"Tom, please."

"It's not right… contacting me after all these years and springing this on me. Find some another schmuck to do your dirty work," said Coyle and walked out of her house leaving her in tears.

Washington DC, USA

Although things were far from calm, Kennedy knew that there was no time to wallow in self-pity. In the world's eyes, he failed his first test as commander-in-chief. There was little he could do about that now. It was the past and he had little control over it. His diplomats in State were picking up the pieces and putting America's reputation back together as much as humanly possible. In the meantime, there were more problems on the horizon. Big problems. He, his cabinet, and his advisors needed to move forward and deal with the things they could control or at least influence.

He had gathered his National Security Council figuring that the safety of the American people was his highest priority. The international community doubted America's intent. The Soviets and Chinese were seeking to take advantage of the situation. Trouble was brewing and JFK needed to make sure it didn't accelerate into a crisis.

Meeting in the Cabinet Room of the White House, the National Security Council was an eclectic mix – Vice President Lyndon B. Johnson, US Attorney General Robert Kennedy, Under Secretary of State George Ball, Secretary of State Dean Rusk, Secretary of Defense Robert McNamara, Chairman of the Joint Chiefs of Staff General Maxwell D. Taylor, Special Counsel to the President Ted Sorensen, Special Assistant to the President for National Security McGeorge Bundy, Secretary of the Treasury Douglas Dillon, Director of the Arms Control and Disarmament Agency William C. Foster, and Director of the Central Intelligence Allen Dulles. All of them were highly educated and very intelligent. Not one was a political appointee. They were Kennedy's "Whiz Kids" – the best and the brightest.

The president listened to the reports of each of the cabinet members and advisors. As suspected, the news was not good. The Soviets were angry and making more threats than usual. Even America's allies were critical of the invasion of Cuba. Nobody seemed to understand why America should feel threatened by such a small nation off their coast. Most of it was posturing and Kennedy commented that he was sure they would feel differently had the invasion been successful. He told the group that he would take full responsibility for what had transpired while not admitting to any wrongdoing on behalf of the United States. It was everyone's job to repair the damage where possible but to keep their guard up.

After the meeting, Kennedy walked out on the South Lawn and spent several moments in reflection. He blamed himself for the lives lost and the damage to his country's reputation. He knew he could not show a penitent face but needed to show confidence and strength instead. America was in danger. He had helped put her there and it was his duty to guide her out of harm's way. Ted Sorenson, Kennedy's policy advisor, and long-time friend walked out to join the president. "Are you okay, Mr. President? It's been a rough couple of weeks."

"I think that's the understatement of the day, Ted," said Kennedy.

"I knew you'd appreciate it," Sorenson said with a smile.

"Did we inherit these problems or are these our own doing?"

"Oh, probably a little bit of both. Does it really matter?"

"I suppose not. You know, the only thing that surprised me when I got into office was that things were just as bad as we had been saying they were."

"Yeah, surprised me too," said Sorenson with a laugh. "Ya know, Mr. President, we're gonna make it out of this. I've never seen so many smart men, so determined to win as your cabinet."

"Yeah, they are an impressive bunch. All except for Allen. He's got to go. I imagine he knows it too."

"He had a good run. We'll find a replacement."

"Best get Shriver on it."

"I'll let him know."

"I can't believe Allen gave me such bad advice. The Joint Chiefs too. They all approved the plan. Every one of them. Now they're all hemming and hawing. Pointing figures at each other."

"Generals do that, Mr. President. It's how they stay generals."

"It doesn't matter. In the end, I was the man in charge. It was my poor judgment that got us into this mess. I can't believe I was that stupid."

"There were a lot of factors, Mr. President."

"Don't start sugar coating things, Ted. I need honesty more than ever right now."

"I'm not sugar coating. I believe you had tough choices that needed to be made and inaccurate information from people you trusted."

"You know, my friend Granier said it was going to fail. I wish I had listened to him more."

"He's not the president. He doesn't bear that weight on his shoulders."

"You're right, he doesn't. Oh, well, just think of what we'll pass on to the poor fellow who comes after me."

Two friends walked back to the White House. "So, Ted… have you ever had the lobster stew at the Union Oyster House in Boston?" said the president putting his arm around Sorenson.

MR. THANK YOU, THANK YOU

Bien Hoa Air Base, South Vietnam

After landing in Bien Hoa Air Base near Saigon, Coyle headed to the closest Go-Go bar. Feeling like a complete jerk for the way he has treated Janet, he started with beer then switched to whiskey as his self-loathing grew. Finally, he purchased a bottle of snake wine with a cobra coiled up inside the bottle ready to strike the consumer. Having finished half a bottle, the snake struck, and Coyle ended up in the bar's toilet emptying his stomach to the porcelain god.

After an hour of more dry heaves than he cared to count, his stomach felt better, but his conscience was still ridden with guilt. Not wanting to bring about another bout of dry heaves, he rose and exited the bar in search of something to eat. Food, especially when drunk, was one of the great things he loved about Saigon. Day or night, he could always find something good to eat at the vendors that lined most big streets in the city.

The street by the airbase was filled with carts holding propane tanks and a fire ring on which sat a steel wok. The wok was the most useful pan ever invented. The vendors could cook just about anything in their woks. Most specialized in three or four dishes that used similar ingredients. Bunches of local vegetables hung from the iron supports on which stretched the canvas roof that protected their cart from the rain and sun. Vietnamese food carts were efficient workstations that provided a decent living for those that could afford the initial investment.

Coyle wanted Vietnamese pancakes stuffed with shrimp but knew the oil used to fry them would probably upset his stomach even more. He settled for a Bahn Mi, a small loaf of fresh French bread split open and stuffed with vegetables, meat, and just enough chilis to give it a kick. It was a good choice. The bread soaked up the remaining snake whiskey still in his stomach. He felt much better after eating.

It was late and Coyle considered staying in the officer's quarters on the airbase. But he had enough of the military for the moment. He needed a break until he had to report to Lansdale on the following day. Although he didn't use it much, he kept a bungalow in Saigon between Lansdale's headquarters and the American embassy. It was small, but he didn't need big. It was just him and that suited him fine. Normally he took the bus leaving the airbase every fifteen minutes. But his queasy stomach suggested a taxi was a better idea. It was rude to puke out a bus window. Too high up. The overspray was sure to hit something or someone. A taxi was much lower to the street and more controllable. He could pay the driver a vomit fee if necessary.

Once he had flagged down a taxi and negotiated the price, he hopped in the backseat and rolled down the window... just in case. He usually ran a slight fever after drinking heavily and the night air felt good against his skin.

Saigon, South Vietnam

As the driver passed over a bridge, Coyle could see a South Vietnamese patrol boat shining its light on a sampan traveling upriver. It was a common occurrence to check boats in the river. The South Vietnamese Navy was tasked with finding contraband and weapons from smugglers that preferred the shadows of night. Coyle wondered if the sampan's pilot had enough money to bribe his way out of being arrested for the infraction rather real or not. Such was the way of Saigon.

After twenty minutes, he arrived. There wasn't much traffic this time of night. He paid the driver and walked up to the dark house. When he had first seen the little house, it reminded him of McGoon's bungalow where he had stayed for several months after he had arrived in Hanoi. As a true friend, McGoon shared everything including his two live-in whores. There were only two bedrooms in his bungalow and McGoon didn't feel right about kicking the girls out to sleep on grass mats in the living room or on the back patio overlooking a stream. Much better to divide them up and share the available beds. Coyle remembered being shocked at the suggestion, but soon grew accustomed to the arrangement.

He used his key to open the door and flipped the light switch. Nothing happened. He had forgotten to leave money with the neighbors to pay the electric bill. No matter. He was exhausted. He felt his way through the darkness and managed only to smash into furniture twice. Navigating his way into the bedroom, he fell facedown in the bed with his boots still on and fell fast asleep.

The next morning when he awoke, Coyle paid for his indulgence in snake whiskey with a mean hangover. It wasn't the worst he had ever had, but it was close. His head was throbbing. He made his way into the toilet, opened a small cabinet, and retrieved a bottle of aspirin. He tried to gauge how many of the tablets he should take based on his headache. He decided on a small handful. He was going to take them without water but concluded that was a bad idea. He slipped them into his pocket. He relieved himself in the toilet, then made his way into the kitchen. He grabbed a half-clean glass, turned on the sink tap and nothing came out. He had forgotten to pay his water bill too. He didn't panic. Panicking was for shavetail lieutenants. Instead, he headed out the front door like a man on a mission.

Coyle landed at his favorite coffee shop around the corner. It was a nice little place with a tree-covered patio and wooden tables covered with tablecloths. The owner was a Vietnamese woman that had married a French soldier who had been killed during the Indochina War. She spoke Vietnamese, French, and just enough English to attract the Americans in the neighborhood in search of their morning coffee and perhaps one of the fresh croissants she baked herself every morning. Coyle sat and waved the woman over as she finished ringing up a couple on their way out. He ordered a black coffee and let her talk him into a croissant with jam even though he wasn't really hungry.

As she moved off to the kitchen to prepare his order, Coyle reached into his pocket, pulled out the aspirin, and placed them in a small pile on the table.

His head was still throbbing when the woman used her imported expresso machine to make his coffee. The high-pitched hissing didn't help. His mouth was dry. He decided he could muster enough spit to down two of the aspirin. It wouldn't be enough to make a real difference, but it was a start. He popped two tablets in his mouth. One stuck to the roof of his mouth and the other to the side of his tongue. They weren't going down. They began to dissolve leaving a horrid taste in his mouth. Now, was the time to panic. He looked around for something to drink. There was nothing in sight, except a glass of water on a table in the corner where a Vietnamese woman wearing a white ao dai was sitting with her nose in a book. Coyle was not a rude person, but this was an emergency. He rose and trotted over to the table. The woman, engaged in her book, noticed someone was standing over her and looked up. Unsure if she spoke English, he pointed to her glass of water, then to his mouth. She looked confused. He stuck out his tongue with dissolving aspirin on the side. She recognized the problem and nodded her consent. Coyle picked up the glass, gulped down the water, then made a disgusting hacking noise like a cat trying to puke up a hairball. A moment later, he set the glass down and said, "Thank you," in a raspy voice.

"You're welcome," said the woman without even the faintest accent.

"You speak English," said Coyle looking at the book in her hand – Crime and Punishment in Russian, "…and read Russian."

"Yes."

Coyle noticed her ao dai was neatly pressed and lacked the embroidered dragons, birds, and flowers of most silk dresses worn by Vietnamese women. It seemed... more formal. Her coal-black hair was long and neatly combed. She wore no makeup that he could detect beyond a light coating of red lipstick and yet her face was eye-catching; not unusually beautiful but unique... memorable. "Thank you again. I'll get you a fresh glass of water," said Coyle realizing he was starring.

"That won't be necessary. I was just leaving."

"Oh well, thank you."

"That's the third time you've said thank you. Once was sufficient. Twice was overly polite. But the third time makes me question your confidence."

"Sounds about right," said Coyle noticing her eyes for the first time. They were arresting and full of mystery.

"Good day," she said rising and walking to the register. Coyle felt strange and it wasn't the hangover. He didn't want her to go. "Will you at least let me pay for your coffee?" he blurted out.

"It was tea and no, thank you anyway."

"I insist. It's my way of saying... uh... of showing gratitude."

"Okay. But only because you didn't say 'Thank you again."

"Yeah well... I'm a fast learner."

"Ah, civil society is saved," she said turning and exiting.

The owner appeared in the kitchen doorway and walked to Coyle's table with the coffee and croissant. "Please put the woman's tea on my bill," said Coyle pointing to the empty corner table.

The owner nodded. "Does she come here often? ... the woman in the corner?" said Coyle.

"Never see before," said the owner setting his order down and leaving.

Slightly disappointed, Coyle sat down and sipped his coffee. He used a small knife to smear cherry jam on his croissant and took a bite. It was fresh and delicious. Another sip of coffee and he downed the rest of the croissant in one very big bite. Surprisingly, his headache was gone.

Coyle stopped by the coffee shop several times over the following week. He sat near where the woman had sat hoping to strike up a conversation when she arrived. While sipping his coffee, he thought about what he might say and how she would respond. He played the conversation over and over in his mind until he had perfected it. Just the right amount of wit. But she never appeared. The one chance he had was wasted by a hangover and bad-tasting aspirins.

He considered his situation and decided not to give up hope. He expanded his search to other coffee shops and foreign bookstores in the area. Seeing Coyle repeatedly cruising the aisles of their shops and never buying anything, the owners wondered if the foreigner was stealing. When confronted, instead of getting angry, Coyle asked about the Russian and English-speaking women in the neighborhood. The owners were no help. He spent much of his free time looking for the woman and drinking too much coffee which upset his stomach. There was no sign of her, and nobody recognized her description – Vietnamese, slender, sophisticated, a flawless English accent, and beautiful eyes filled with mystery. He became more obsessed and began to wonder if he had imagined her. Not a good affliction for a pilot. He had been under a lot of stress since the Cuba invasion. He hoped it would go away… the thought of her. It was becoming painful and overwhelming. He suspected that if he ever did see her again, he would have built her up in his mind so much that she would appear quite plain, and he would wonder what all the fuss was about. The spell would be broken, and he could get on with his life.

Bangkok, Thailand

Communist expansion was a growing concern in Southeast Asia. Neighboring countries could see what was happening in Vietnam, Laos, and Cambodia. It seemed no country was immune as insurgencies sprang up and attacked government facilities and troops. Thailand was especially concerned since it shared a border with China, Laos, and Cambodia.

The Kennedy administration considered Thailand as a potential bastion against communism. Unlike the other countries in Southeast Asia Thailand had never been a colony of a Western power and therefore did not carry the stigma of colonial rule. The Thai did not loathe Western countries like the Vietnamese, Laotians, and Cambodians. Instead, the Thai sought protection from the West against the growing communist threat. JFK embraced Thailand and promised to help build up Thai military capabilities.

As part of the buildup program code-named Operation Bell Tone, an advanced unit of the USAF 6010th Tactical Group arrived at Don Muang Royal Thai Air Force Base just outside of Bangkok. Six F-100 Super Sabres were designated an early warning system to patrol and protect Thailand's borders. In addition, RT-33 jets flown by USAF pilots were used on covert reconnaissance missions over Laos. The surveillance missions were code-named Operation Field Goal and gave Thailand and the United States, which shared the intelligence, a clearer picture of communist troop movements.

While they welcomed American help in bolstering their air defense and intelligence capabilities, the independently-minded Thai were cautious. They did not want to be drawn into the wars just across their borders and therefore limited USAF activities. However, like the proverb of a camel with his nose in a tent, once allowed onto the Thailand air bases, the Americans gently pushed the Thais to allow more and more aircraft into the country and the operations expanded.

Washington DC, USA

May 12, 1961 – Saigon, South Vietnam

After a long transpacific trip, a Boeing 707 touched down at Tan Son Nhat International Airport five miles northwest of the Presidential Palace. As the jet rolled to a stop next to the terminal, American Vice President Lyndon B. Johnson could hear a band striking up patriotic American tunes all meant to please the distinguished visitor... him. "Now that's how you greet a dignitary," said Johnson to his aides and advisors.

Once he was sure President Diem was outside to greet him, Johnson ordered the aircraft door opened and stepped out into the humidity that was South Vietnam. It was hard to think of anything else when the heat hit his face and he immediately dabbed at the sweat with the handkerchief he always carried in his pocket. He waved to the crowd and stepped down the stairway. As planned, Diem and his family were there to greet him. Hands were shaken and photos were taken. Everyone smiled. The drama would come later in private. Nobody wanted the world to think anything other than America and South Vietnam – the best of friends and allies forever pledged to each other. It was a façade that few believed but even fewer questioned. At six foot four inches, Johnson towered over the Vietnamese. His broad shoulders made him look substantial, almost intimidating except for the smile he brandished whenever possible. His smile made folks feel more comfortable like he was an oversized teddy bear. Nothing to be feared unless that was what he wanted to portray. His glare could dissolve the will of the most determined government official. It's how he got his way – sugar or Castor oil, depending on the situation.

Diem would have preferred a visit from President Kennedy and his beautiful wife, Jacqueline because they were both Catholic and he trusted Catholics. But he would settle for Johnson, who was a Protestant and play the role of a gracious host. He needed a United States presidential visit to bolster his sagging popularity, even if it was a vice president. Diem was facing increasing criticism from Buddhist factions for his bias toward Catholic institutions. He could not understand why the Western press which was mostly from Christian nations was siding with the Buddhists. While his brother Nhu was able to silence some of the critics, the overall number of those against Diem and his family was rising at an alarming rate. In addition, the war with the Viet Cong was not going well as the rebels occupied more and more of South Vietnam. A visit from a high-level executive from South Vietnam's most powerful ally was easily manipulated into a show of support and strength. During Johnson's visit, Diem made sure there were no public protests and that everything appeared to be under control.

One week before the visit, Brother Nhu had rounded up anyone he thought might be a troublemaker or protestor. He threw them all in detention centers without so much as a hearing. He would release most of them once Johnson had left. But some of the more egregious offenders would get lost in the shuffle and never be heard from again. Nhu took opportunities such as a foreign dignitary's visit to chip away at his brother's enemies and his own. He was also not above arresting one of his business competitors and disappearing him. It was all for the good of the family. Family was everything to Nhu.

Johnson's visit to South Vietnam was at the request of JFK in hopes that his vice president could get to the bottom of what was going on and help figure out a path forward. Since becoming vice president, Johnson had been jockeying for more power and visibility. This was a convenient way for Kennedy to keep Johnson happy and hopefully gain some traction with a key anti-communist ally. Johnson was a strong believer in the Domino Theory and said so on many occasions when the press was listening. On this occasion, Johnson spoke briefly to the press and made sure to coin the phrase "The Winston Churchill of Asia" to describe his host, President Diem. The press ate it up as Johnson knew they would.

Johnson knew that most of Kennedy's cabinet, especially the president's brother Attorney General Robert Kennedy, either undervalued or completely despised him. He didn't care. He wasn't in politics for them, and he sure as hell wasn't about to let this opportunity pass him by because of their ivy-league snobbery. This was a chance for him to shine and get something valuable accomplished at the same time. All the world's eyes were on him during his short visit. Whenever a picture was snapped, Johnson was sure to flash the Texan grin that had made him liked by all.

May 13, 1961 - Tan Son Nhut Air Base, South Vietnam

Operating under the cover of the 3rd Radio Research Unit, a company of 92 Rangers arrived at Tan Son Nhut Air Base outside of Saigon and established a communications intelligence facility in several unused warehouses on the airbase. Their mission was to monitor enemy radio transmissions and train South Vietnamese units in radio reconnaissance. Unlike the American advisors already in-country, this was the first full deployment of a US Army unit to South Vietnam.

Saigon, South Vietnam

Johnson was careful not to visit the new American military arrivals. He didn't want their arrival in-country to alter the news cycle which was currently focused on him and his trip to South Vietnam. This was his time to make hay, not theirs. Besides, it was better to downplay anything that might have been considered a treaty violation which deploying US Army personnel in South Vietnam definitely was. It was a stretch claiming they were just advisors when they arrived as an intact military unit with all their electronic gear.

Johnson and Diem had one formal meeting during which the press was invited in to snap photos and ask questions. The guests were served steak which Johnson ate but did not particularly enjoy. In his mind, the only good beef was American beef which had more fat than the lean Vietnamese beef. He said nothing but grinned while chewing when asked by Madame Nhu how he liked his meal. She claimed the steaks were cut from their finest bulls and aged for two months before his arrival. Johnson nodded politely and thought she was full of bullshit. The meat was tough and chewy with no real flavor and full of gristle. As a Texan, Johnson knew good steak and that wasn't it. He washed it down with a glass of Fresca which Diem had flown in special knowing it was the vice president's favorite. Johnson was pacified after the bad steak and appreciated Diem's effort.

There were also several dinners hosted by Diem during which the conversations between them continued. None of the press wanted to rock the boat. Johnson's visit to South Vietnam was enough to capture the headlines. The questions were softballed and the answers were vague with strong expressions for the photographers.

Johnson's press agents created plenty of opportunities for the films of the vice president riding rickshaws, shaking hands in crowds of smiling Vietnamese, and eating dumplings at a famous restaurant. He also toured several South Vietnamese military bases and talked with the help of a translator to some of the troops. He inspected the US military equipment and weapons provided through American aid. He visited a hospital built with American dollars and chatted with Vietnamese doctors trained at American universities. He even grabbed a shovel and helped road workers build a highway under the supervision of American engineers. Through his entire visit, Johnson appeared on the nightly news of all three American networks.

The US Embassy was a five-story art deco-style building located on 39 Ham Nghi Boulevard in downtown Saigon. By the time of Johnson's visit, the Ham Nghi embassy had already endured a car bomb attack, and the need for a defensive perimeter was apparent. Designs had already begun on a new embassy compound to be built nearby. During Johnson's visit to the embassy South Vietnamese security units blocked off all the streets around the building and kept civilians at a safe distance. The South Vietnamese would ensure the Americans were safe while the world's eyes were on Saigon.

Newly appointed US Ambassador to South Vietnam Frederick Nolting was a career diplomat. He had few ambitions beyond just getting the job done right and serving his country with honor. Kennedy had wanted to stabilize what he felt was a deteriorating situation in South Vietnam and Nolting was the epidemy of stability.

Johnson met with Nolting and his staff deep within the embassy where an enemy rocket could not penetrate. Lieutenant General Lionel C. McGarr was the MAAG commander in charge of US Advisors assigned to South Vietnam and briefed Johnson on the current disposition of South Vietnamese and Viet Cong forces. Johnson was stunned. "Are you telling me that a third of South Vietnam is under the control of the Viet Cong?" said Johnson incredulously.

"Yes, Mr. Vice President. That is exactly what I am saying," said McGarr. "But to correctly surmise the situation it is important to recognize that VC forces do not occupy any major city in South Vietnam. They are still a guerilla force, and with more advisors, we hope to keep them that way."

"More advisors? I thought Diem was against putting American advisors in ARVN command positions."

"He was, but with more Viet Cong victories he is changing his tune. We would like to see the current limit increased to 685 advisors in-country."

"It's starting to look more and more like boots on the ground, General."

"I know it appears that way, Mr. Vice President, but US advisors do not directly participate in any combat operations. They are strictly there to advise and provide leadership when necessary."

"And the increase in helicopters you requested?"

"Helicopters have proven to be an effective force multiplier. With more, we can deploy and reinforce South Vietnamese units faster than the enemy. This gives the ARVN a substantial strategic and tactical advantage."

"So, are these additional advisors and equipment going to be enough to keep the cork in the bottle?"

"I'd be lying if I didn't say that with the increased Viet Cong assaults on ARVN forces the situation in South Vietnam is fluid."

"Fluid? That's not very reassuring, General."

"No, Mr. Vice President. It's not."

Johnson pulled off his glasses, rubbed his hand through his hair, and let out a sigh. "All right. It is what it is. I'll talk to the president as soon as I return. So, what is going on with President Diem and his family? We're hearing horror stories, but I ain't seeing nothing out of the normal."

Nolting jumped in, "Yeah, they're behaving themselves while you're here. But I assure you, things are far from normal."

"All right. We are on the same team. What is it?"

"The main problem is his brother Nhu and his wife. They lack any moral boundaries when it comes to achieving their goals. I believe they have President Diem's well-being as their main goal. But they are willing to do unthinkable things to keep him and themselves in power."

"I'm not sure that's our concern. Diem was a democratically elected leader. If the people don't like him, let them throw him out at the polls."

"To say he is a democratically elected leader is a bit ingenuine. He was elected over ten years ago and there have been no elections since then, nor do I think there will be while he remains in power."

"President Kennedy says he was elected fair and square. So, America is going to support him. You guys need to get behind that. I ain't saying he is so honest you could shoot craps with him over the phone, but he's the only guy we got in this neck of the woods. Unless you know something, I don't?"

"No, Mr. Vice President. There are others that might be able to replace him. But it is doubtful they can hold the country together like he has."

"Well, you see, there is a good reason."

"Mr. Vice President," said McGarr piping in. "...the main problem that concerns us is President Diem's persistent interference in military matters."

"Well, he is commander-in-chief, is he not?"

"He is, but a good commander-in-chief does not involve himself in day-to-day operations or politics within the military."

"Is that what he is doing?"

"He and his family."

"In what way?"

"Officers within the military are promoted based on bribes and their loyalty to Diem and his family.

Such interference demoralizes the entire officer corps. The other problem is that the officers are punished if they lose too many men. They are given orders to attack the enemy, but they execute those orders with little gusto and overuse artillery and air power instead of engaging the enemy directly."

"You do realize that we can't tell the man how to run his country or his military?"

"Yes, Mr. Vice President. But if something doesn't change, I fear he will lose his country before too long."

"Are you serious, General?"

"As serious as a heart attack, Mr. Vice President."

"I don't think it is quite that bad. But I do agree with General McGarr that Diem and his family do tend to stick their noses where they don't belong when it comes to the military. We've already had one coup. We don't need another."

"Is that a possibility… a coup?"

"It's Southeast Asia. There is always a possibility of a coup."

"Bit negative, don't you think?"

"Yes, Mr. Vice President. Look, if we get the additional advisors that we need and scatter them among the ARVN units, we can probably increase morale to the point they can defend the country and stop the communists."

"Now, see… that's something I can chew on. Let's stop worrying about the things we can't change and start worrying about the things was can. My big question is how are you going to cut off the weapon and supply shipments coming into the South? From what I have seen on the intelligence reports the North Vietnamese have a free hand on their supply route through Laos and Cambodia."

"I would agree with that assessment, Mr. Vice President. We've tried to intervene but with little success. The route travels along the mountains in both countries and is heavily forested. It makes it very difficult to pinpoint. In reality, it is not just one route but many routes running in parallel. We plug one hole only to have another pop up overnight."

"Okay. I see the problem. Now, what is the solution?"

"We have been working on a plan to recruit the native hill tribes in the region. So far in the conflict, they are an untapped resource that the South Vietnamese government has refused to train or supply. The government is concerned that if they are armed, they might rebel and start fighting for autonomy."

"And what makes you think that Diem will accept using them now?"

"If we restrict their operations to the Laotian border and only use them to cut off the supply routes, he will see them as less of a threat. But we are going to need more special forces to train them."

"I suppose those indigenous folks would be pretty good at traveling through those mountains."

"They know the terrain very well and from what we can tell they will be good fighters. It's part of their culture."

"How many special forces are we talking about?"

"About four hundred Green Beret ought to do the trick."

"General, I don't know how we can do that. We are already over the American force limit set by the Geneva Accord."

"I understand that. We were thinking that the new forces might be given special status as "Dedicated Advisors to the indigenous tribes along the border.""

"That might work, especially if we threw in some money for building roads and villages."

"Exactly, Mr. Vice President. It could be seen as a humanitarian operation."

"And you think that will be enough to cut off the Viet Cong's supply line?"

"Maybe not completely cut it off but certainly curtail it."

"What does Diem think about the idea?"

Nolting jumped in, "We haven't discussed it with him in detail yet. We wanted to see your reaction first. But I can assure you that President Diem will like anything that increases military or financial aid to South Vietnam and does not involve tying up more of his military forces."

"All right. It's a good idea. I'll advocate it to President Kennedy when I get back," said Johnson.

During a farewell dinner at the presidential palace, Johnson took the opportunity to reassure the South Vietnamese president. Johnson encouraged Diem to view himself as indispensable to the United States and promised additional military aid to assist his government in fighting the communists. In return, Johnson asked Diem to step up his attacks on the Viet Cong and retake the territory they now controlled. Diem gave Johnson his word that it would be so. But Diem would have promised anything to secure more aid from the Americans and ensure that Johnson's visit was seen as an overwhelming success to his people.

When Johnson's airliner lifted off, Diem turned to his brother Nhu and said, "The Americans are a peculiar people, especially those from Texas."

"Yes, but I like their cowboy hats," said Nhu. "Do you believe he will convince Kennedy to give us what we need to fight the communists?"

"I imagine so. Johnson is very big and intimidating. How can Kennedy refuse him?"

Washington DC, USA

On returning to the United States, Johnson briefed Kennedy and his cabinet on what he had learned, and the proposals offered by the in-country team. JFK was receptive and asked General Taylor to prepare plans to deploy US Special Forces. Kennedy was a fan of the Green Beret. He saw the Special Force units as the right type of soldiers to enlist indigenous help and fight guerilla insurgents. He also liked their hats. He personally approved the exclusive wearing of the green berets by US Special Forces. The berets didn't provide much protection from the sun or rain, but women thought they looked exotic and that was good for morale.

Johnson delivered a rousing speech on his return during a planned press conference. He championed the Domino Theory and stated that if Vietnam was lost, the United States would be fighting the communists on the beaches of Waikiki and eventually on the homeland's own shores. The press ate it up and their editors gave Johnson's comments front-page coverage. It was exactly what Johnson had wanted. Fame gave him power. Power he would use to advance his plans and programs for America.

By the end of May, four hundred Green Berets with hundreds of crates of new weapons and ammunition arrived in South Vietnam and headed for the mountains near Laos. They carried with them the promise of financial and military support if the hill tribes agreed to cut off the Viet Cong supply route. It was mostly the Montagnard tribe that took up the challenge. With 40,000 militia troops within their ranks and armed with new American weapons, they alone could stop the North Vietnamese from infiltrating into Southern Vietnam.

The Montagnard were broken into small groups and were given several Green Beret advisors for each. Unlike the American advisors in the lowlands, the Green Beret were less concerned about being seen fighting alongside the tribesman and directly engaged the enemy during battles. They knew the Montagnard culture and that the tribesmen were more likely to follow a fellow warrior than an advisor. The Green Beret lived with the Montagnard in their villages and camps. They ate the same food, drank their homebrewed alcohol, and often consorted with the tribe's single women when asked. They were professional soldiers with a special mission. Trust was key. Communion created bonds.

Before long, the Green Beret financed and helped the Montagnard build fortified "fighting camps" all along the Laotian border and sometimes within Laos itself. Like medieval castles, the outposts were used to threaten, and eventually cut off the enemy's supply lines and infiltration points into South Vietnam.

The special forces fighting camps were different from the firebases and outposts built by the regular army. They were capable of defending against major assaults, prolonged sieges, and could project powerful assault operations against the enemy when required. The tactical area of operation for combat troops based in the camps was up to six miles in any direction and they would still fall under the protection of the camp's artillery umbrella. This meant that the camps could be safely located twelve miles apart.

The camps were built with inner and outer defensive rings. The inner rings which were highly fortified contained all the key operational buildings such as the field hospital, ammunition depot, fuel depot, communications bunker, headquarters, power generators, and the artillery firing pits. All facilities were built three feet below ground and had reinforced roofs cable to withstand a direct heavy mortar hit. The ammunition and fuel depots were protected by high earthen berms. The heavy machine guns were usually given high unobstructed positions that could fire in any direction. Surrounded by three layers of sandbags, the machine gun positions could withstand direct fire from the enemy's heavy machine guns and recoilless rifles.

The Special Force's preferred artillery were 81mm mortars and 105mm howitzers which provided the high arc needed for the mountains and a powerful punch. Even though they required more soldiers to operate, more smaller artillery pieces were more desirable than fewer big artillery pieces.

The outer ring was filled with blockhouses, sandbag-lined trenches, and layers of concertina wire with minefields to keep the enemy at bay. Outer ring weapons were a mixed bag of recoilless rifles, light machine guns, and the individual soldiers' rifles and submachine guns. Napalm canisters were also strategically placed in the wire of the most likely path of attack. Tanglefoot wire was used in-between the layers of concertina wire and at times was even stacked with layers of concertina wire on top. To avoid the extensive wire defenses which took time to remove or disable, the enemy was forced to assault the camp in narrow lanes with cleared fields of fire. Trip flares were used throughout the strike base to warn of enemy incursions. Each corner of the base had two light machines and a recoilless rifle positioned to provide covering fire for the troops on the perimeter defensive line.

Fighting camp commanders knew that waiting for the enemy to attack was folly. They constantly sent out platoons to patrol the forest and jungles surrounding the camps. Even though they were well protected by the camps' fortifications and defenses, the soldiers inside the camps were far better off knowing that the enemy was coming. A surprise attack was never a good thing unless they initiated it. A well-supplied fighting camp could fend off even the most determined enemy for hours, or even days, until reinforcements arrived.

Weapons and reinforcements going to the Viet Cong were greatly reduced until the communists could develop strategies to bypass the Special Forces' fighting camps and Montagnard outposts. And therein lied the main problem - the enemy's ability to innovate was limitless. Short on supplies and often using inferior weapons, the North Vietnamese and their allies excelled at learning from their defeats which allowed them to create new tactics for defeating what should have been a superior enemy.

In the first year of the Kennedy administration, military aid increased from $50 million per year to $144 million. It was a major escalation designed to stop the progress of the Viet Cong. Diem agreed to allow American advisors into ARVN command positions for battalions and below. He was still unwilling to let the Americans take control of his military divisions and South Vietnamese generals could still countermand American advisors' orders if they felt it would overly endanger their troops. The South Vietnamese saw the new policy as being generous while the Americans saw it as a continuing obstruction that prevented the South Vietnamese forces from defeating the Viet Cong.

Although out of office, former Vice President Richard Nixon still wielded a tremendous amount of influence with many in congress. He was the de facto leader of the Republican party, especially since Eisenhower participated less in politics as his health declined. Kennedy knew that he could not afford to ignore Nixon if he was going to move his agenda forward.

Having an obstinate liberal wing in his party, Kennedy often needed bipartisan support on many issues including civil rights and funding for the war in Vietnam. Kennedy also believed that any intelligent, well-informed individual could come up with a good idea no matter their political leanings. Nixon was both intelligent and well-informed. Kennedy did not trust Nixon, but he listened to him even when their discussions often turned into father-to-son type lectures that drove Kennedy crazy. It helped that Kennedy realized that Nixon probably didn't know he was being obnoxious. Nixon was full of ideas on how to win the battle against communism and they usually involved aggression of some sort. He believed that America should use its power to bend other nations to its will.

JFK listened patiently and at times even accepted Nixon's advice. In return, he asked Nixon to support some of the programs Kennedy was trying to push through congress. While well-versed in international politics which is what he cared about, Nixon tended to ignore lesser domestic issues and occasionally gave his support to Kennedy. The two politicians had run contentious campaigns for the presidency and that didn't make things easier between them. But they made their relationship work for the good of their country.

Saigon, South Vietnam

As time went on, the image of the woman in the corner of the coffee shop faded from Coyle's memory. He was released. Once again, he could concentrate on his flying. His relationships with women were temporary. A straightforward transaction. Mostly bar girls that he met by the airbase. For a few moments, he was happy, and they were happy. A perfect relationship that required no more than a few dollars and a couple of hours of free time. He didn't need or want anything else. Then one day…

He was coming back from the airbase on the way to his bungalow. He had flown some supplies to De Nang and picked up two MAAG advisors for his return leg back to Saigon. It wasn't a particularly hard day. Boring in fact. Flying for the CIA was boring most of the time. It was like a taxi service – constantly picking up and dropping off. But when something went wrong, it usually went very wrong. He could go from sipping coffee to full-on, heart-pumping adrenaline in a matter of seconds. Lives were on the line and people were depending on him for their survival. If he were being honest with himself, he lived for those moments.

But nothing like that happened that day. It was uneventful. It was late in the afternoon, and he knew if he headed for Saigon, he was sure to hit traffic. He considered stopping by one of his favorite Go-Go bars, but he decided he was too tired and hailed a taxi. He could doze off in the backseat if the driver hit a traffic snarl.

It was slow going once the taxi hit the outskirts of the city. Mostly thousands of motor scooters mixed with cyclos and an occasional car or truck. Riding a motor scooter in Saigon was not for the faint of heart. The unspoken strategy was not to slow down or brake from anyone. By keeping a constant speed and direction, everyone knew what the other drivers were doing. There was a hierarchy of right-away. A truck or bus always had right-away because of its size and that the driver couldn't always see the vehicles next to him in his side mirrors. Everyone knew it was best to stay out of their way. Next came cars, then cyclos, and finally motor scooters. Because of their ability to maneuver quickly and get out of the way, motor scooters were at the bottom of the pyramid and could go wherever they wanted as long as they didn't crash into anyone. Some of the more daring motor scooter drivers would even go the wrong way to avoid traveling to the next U-turn crossway. The only thing lower than a motorbike was a bicycle or a pedestrian. Both were considered fair game if they steered or stepped in front of a motor vehicle. It didn't matter what the law was, drivers rarely stuck around after an accident, especially if someone was seriously injured or killed. After work traffic was always exciting for someone that had not driven much or was hitching a ride on the back of a friend's scooter.

Coyle was asleep in the back as the driver bluffed his way through the tangle of traffic – moving to cut someone off then braking when they didn't stop or gunning his engine if there was the faintest hesitation by the other drivers. It was all about confidence and the will to kill or maim to get a few feet further toward one's destination. The taxi driver slammed on his brakes to avoid colliding with a cement truck. Coyle tumbled to the floor. "So, sorry," said the taxi driver. "Truck drive crazy."

"You mean taxi drive crazy," said Coyle lifting himself back on the seat.

Now awake, he could see that they were close to his bungalow. He stared out the side window and caught a glimpse of a cyclo heading in the opposite direction. Sitting in the front passenger seat was the woman from the coffee shop. Coyle couldn't believe his eyes. "Turn around," yelled Coyle.

"Why? We almost there," said the confused taxi driver.

Coyle didn't have time to argue. He pulled out a wad of bills and pushed forward offering it to the driver. "Go that way," said Coyle pointing.

The driver turned the taxi around in the middle of the street causing a bigger traffic snarl in both directions. Once righted, he increased speed honking his horn and threatening to run over anyone in his way. It worked. They moved forward quickly. "Where we go?" said the driver excited to be in a chase.

"The girl in the cyclo. Catch up to her," said Coyle.

"Okay. Which one?"

The driver was right to be confused. Five cyclos were heading in the same direction and Coyle couldn't see the faces of the passengers sitting in front. "Just drive," said Coyle.

As they caught up to a cyclo, Coyle looked over at the passenger. Each time, it wasn't the woman from the coffee shop. When they finally caught up to the last one and saw the passenger – an old man cursing at the crazy taxi driver, Coyle realized that he had again lost her. He was crestfallen.

That night, he couldn't sleep. His mind was racing trying to find a solution to a puzzle. When he saw the woman, the taxi was near his bungalow and the coffee shop where they first met, so she most likely lived in the area. It was almost six o'clock which meant that she was probably coming home from work. The solution was simple. It just required a bit of stalking.

The next day, around the same time, Coyle stood on the sidewalk watching the traffic go by. Next to him was a motor scooter with a driver standing ready. Coyle paid particular attention to the cyclos but also looked at the passengers in any taxi or car that went by. He ignored the motor scooters figuring she was too sophisticated to ride on the back of a motorbike. He was again building her up in his mind.

After several hours and near the end of the evening rush, Coyle saw her in a cyclo as she passed. She was wearing her white ao dai and reading a book. The wind had caught her coal-black hair twisting and tossing it behind her.

Coyle jumped on the back of the motor scooter and pointed at the passing cyclo. The driver pulled into traffic and followed. Coyle had given him instructions not to follow too closely. He didn't want her to see him pursuing her like a lunatic. There was no way to explain above the noise of the traffic. He wanted to see where she was going, then figure out his next move.

The driver followed the cyclo as it turned onto a side street then through the twists and turns of a neighborhood of tube houses with storefronts on the bottom floors facing the street. When the cyclo pulled to the curb, Coyle motioned for the motorbike driver to keep going. The motorbike passed the cyclo and turned down the next corner. Out of sight, Coyle hopped off the back of the scooter and peeked around the corner of a hair salon.

He watched as the woman paid the cyclo driver, then walked into a storefront with a two-story residence on top. Coyle didn't know if she was visiting the business or if she lived in the house on top. It was a typical setup for many homes in Saigon where land was valuable – family business on the bottom floor with family living quarters stacked on top. The bigger the family, the taller the building up to five floors which seemed to be the limit for the neighborhood. The storefront looked well-worn while the residence on top seemed well-kept with a fresh coat of paint and no broken tiles on the roof. Each floor had a small patio with tall windows and a double door. Flowers grew in boxes on top of the decorative railing.

It suddenly dawned on Coyle that the woman could be married and even have children. He thought back to the coffee shop and didn't remember her wearing a ring. But not all Vietnamese women wore wedding rings. Wedding rings were a Western tradition brought by the French. He wondered if that was the reason she had been aloof. There was no way to know for sure. And it wasn't just marriage... There were other potential problems too. Although she did not act like a young woman just out of school, it was hard to tell age with Vietnamese women. He suspected he was at least ten years older than her and maybe a lot more. And there were the obvious cultural and religious differences. He was a non-practicing Christian and imagined her a Buddhist or maybe a Taoist. He was miffed at what to do next. He decided to push forward in his pursuit knowing he could make a complete ass of himself. She was worth the risk.

He waited for over an hour, watching. He realized it was her home above the shop when she appeared on the second-floor patio with a small watering can. She carefully watered the flowers in each planter box and picked up any fallen petals or leaves. When she finished, she looked out on the horizon. The sun was setting, and its golden light illuminated her face. Coyle couldn't help but stare. When she turned, her eyes went downward and glanced in his direction. Coyle panicked and jerked his head back around the corner like a scared rabbit. *This is insane. You're a damned stalker,* he thought.

He decided that a quick retreat was called for and hopped on the back of the motorbike. He pointed the driver in the opposite direction, and they sped off.

Coyle sat in the front room of his bungalow and stared at the empty wall. He played out different scenarios in his mind, even coming up with witty sayings to impress her. All of them ended in her laughing at him like he was a fool. He finally settled on a casual bump-into-her meeting as his next move. He considered waiting near her house until she emerged but decided that was way too obvious. It wasn't a neighborhood that a foreigner would frequent, and she would know he was following her. He wondered where she might work and thought that might be a good place. He knew that at some point she would need to hail a cyclo for her return home. Maybe he could be passing by and just say "Hey, aren't the women who saved me from choking on my aspirin?" He could even offer her a ride home. It was simple and smacked of genius. He liked it.

The next morning, Coyle used the same motorbike driver to take him to the woman's house and wait around the corner while he watched. A cyclo stopped in front of her house a little before 8 am and waited until she appeared. It seemed like a regular arrangement. Coyle and the driver followed the cyclo from a distance.

Coyle was surprised when the cyclo stopped in front of the presidential palace and the woman climbed out, paid the driver, then walked through the main gate where the guards recognized her. He didn't know what to think. *Did she work at the palace?* His pursuit of the still nameless woman suddenly became more complicated to his career as a pilot. Lansdale was often in the palace consulting with President Diem and his family. He wondered if he had been set up and that the woman had been sent to spy on him. He thought back at their meeting in the coffee shop. He had approached her, not the other way around. He quickly concluded that she was no spy and that it just was a crazy coincidence that she worked in the palace. He knew so little about her. He was more intrigued and determined than ever.

Late that evening during another sleepless night, Coyle came up with a plan to meet the woman and perhaps impress her at the same time. It was a risky plan, and it could get him in trouble. He felt his pursuit of the woman had turned into more of a quest that required uncommon bravery to achieve. At the same moment, he wondered if he had gone off his rocker and it was time to seek help. *Nope. Forward. Always forward.* Coyle needed a reason for Lansdale to take him into the palace so he could bump into the woman.

The next morning, Lansdale was busy writing a report to his boss in Washington DC, Allen Dulles. When Lansdale first accepted the assignment to head up psyops and paramilitary operations in Vietnam, Dulles had told Lansdale to report to him directly circumventing the CIA station chief at the American embassy. While this created friction between the regular CIA and Lansdale's "special branch," it did make Lansdale's job somewhat easier. It was the same amount of effort sending reports to Dulles as it would have been to the CIA Chief of Station. Dulles, who was too busy running a large organization, rarely had time to advise Lansdale or even approve his missions. As long as Lansdale produced results, he and his paramilitary teams would be left alone. In addition to his paramilitary teams, Lansdale had Coyle and his flight crew assigned to him. He had the pick of whichever aircraft he needed. Few wanted to cause problems for a man that had direct access to the director of the CIA. It was easier to just give him what he wanted and not ask a lot of questions. "Are you busy?" said Coyle standing in the doorway after having knocked lightly.

"Yes," said Lansdale curtly.

"I'll come back later," said Coyle.

"No. You've already broken my train of thought. What is it?"

"It's nothing really. I just had some thoughts about the presidential palace security."

"What in the hell do you know about security?"

"Not much. But I did notice a few things during our aborted parachute drop."

"Like what?"

"Well… there are almost no air defenses and yet a parachute drop is a highly probable method of attack."

"What about the machine gun emplacements?"

"Yeah, about those… they are in the wrong place."

"What do you mean 'the wrong place'?"

"They are in the front and back of the palace, which is north and south, but that is not the likely flight path of a plane dropping paratroopers. It would fly east to west."

"How do you know that?"

"That's the path I chose during our mission."

"Yeah, I got that. But why?"

"There were many factors. I'd be happy to explain to them if you have the time."

Lansdale glanced at his watch. Lunchtime was approaching and he needed to finish his report. "I don't right now. But I'm not the one you need to convince anyway. I'll set up a meeting with the head of security at the palace. You can explain it to him. Is that okay with you?"

"Yeah. Sure. I'll let you get back to your letter."

Lansdale resumed his writing as Coyle, pleased with himself, exited.

Several days passed, with no word from Lansdale about the meeting. Coyle wondered if Lansdale had forgotten. It wasn't like him. Lansdale was sharp and unusually talented at multitasking. Although a bit egocentric at times, he was a good commander and rarely let details slip through the cracks, especially when it came to planning missions. His worries were dismissed when Lansdale's secretary, an air force lieutenant, called the airbase when Coyle returned from another cargo mission and informed him that a car would pick him up tomorrow morning from his bungalow and take him to the palace. The lieutenant asked if Coyle still had his uniform and if so, would he wear it tomorrow for the meeting. Coyle responded that he did, and he would. He was going to ask why but figured Lansdale had probably made the request and he had his reasons.

On his way home from the airbase, Coyle stopped by a barber to have his hair trimmed and a shave. He wanted to make a good impression this time if he found the woman from the coffee house.

As he sat in the chair with a hot towel on his face to soften his whiskers, Coyle thought about the woman. He still didn't know her name. He imagined what it might be. He knew a lot of Vietnamese men's names because he primarily worked with soldiers, but he knew very few women's names. He asked the barber which were the most popular women's names. The barber spoke poor English but understood the question and rattled off a list of names in Vietnamese along with their meanings. Coyle settled on "Mai" which sounded nice and meant "blossom of apricot." He knew the odds were very long that Mai would be her name, but he decided he needed to call her something besides "woman from the coffee shop" until he knew her real name.

The next morning a sedan pulled up in front of Coyle's bungalow. When Coyle, wearing his uniform, stepped into the backseat, he was surprised to see Lansdale already inside. "Good morning, Commander," said Coyle.

"We'll see," said Lansdale scribbling notes on a pad of paper.

The car drove off. Coyle realized that there was little to worry about. Lansdale often went to the palace to meet with the president and there was no reason not to share a ride. The drive was quiet as Lansdale seemed busy and Coyle looked out the window at the passing cyclos and taxis for any sign of the women. It dawned on Coyle that the woman might not actually work at the palace and was only visiting that day. In that case, all his machinations were for not. He decided it was stupid to think that way when he would know for certain in a few minutes. *No sense in creating bad juju,* he thought.

As the sedan pulled up to the main gate of the palace, it was waved on through and the driver pulled up to the stairs leading to the main entrance. The palace had French colonial architecture featuring two two-story wings connected by a large reception hall in the middle topped with a high-pitched copper cupola. Like most French buildings the entire affair was perfectly symmetrical and painted in French yellow with white trim. Lansdale and Coyle stepped out. Lansdale slipped his notepad in his satchel and turned his attention to Coyle, "When we get in there you will speak to the point and nothing else unless asked a question. Are we clear?"

"In where?" said Coyle alarmed.

"With the president."

"We're meeting with the president?"

"Yes… and his family."

"Nhu?"

"…and Madame Nhu. Why so shocked?"

"I thought I was meeting with the head of palace security."

"You are… that's Nhu. He's in charge of all the president's security."

"I didn't know that."

"Relax. It'll be fine. Just layout your ideas and stick to the facts. The president is a very busy man."

"Okay. I think…"

"You look a little green around the gills, Coyle. Are you okay?"

"Yes. I'm fine. A glass of water would be nice."

"They'll serve coffee and tea when we first sit down. There'll be light chit-chat, then I will introduce the subject of the meeting and you're on. Got it?"

"Got it."

Coyle knew he was out of his league. It was one thing to pass his theories about wind patterns and escape routes to a government official. It was another thing to present to the president and his infamous family. He forgot all about finding the woman and tried to focus on what he would say.

After a brief wait in the reception hall, Coyle and Lansdale were ushered into Diem's office where President Diem, Nhu, and Madam Nhu were visiting in a sitting area. Off to one side stood a woman wearing a white ao dai, her eyes straight ahead, motionless like a statue. When Coyle looked up at her face, he saw that it was the woman from the coffee house. Coyle was astonished and wondered what she was doing there. When nobody was looking, she glanced over at him, and their eyes met. She said nothing, but Coyle could see the alarm on her face. He said nothing and tried not to stare at her again.

After the coffee and the chit-chat, Lansdale explained the purpose of the meeting and turned everything over to Coyle. Coyle explained his strategy on protecting the palace from aerial attacks and enemy paratrooper drops. Whenever Diem did not understand a word or phrase, he signaled the woman standing nearby. She leaned over and spoke softly in Vietnamese. Coyle realized that she was the president's personal translator. Coyle used technical terms that he was fairly sure nobody in the room understood but made his presentation sound more credible. Even Lansdale, who was an air force officer, didn't understand much of what Coyle was saying. It was the emperor who had no clothes strategy. When he was finished, nobody wanted to admit they didn't understand, so they used words like "interesting" and "thought-provoking." Nhu asked Coyle to accompany him outside the palace and offer up his suggestions as to where they might locate new gun emplacements. Coyle had little choice but to agree. He didn't trust Nhu. Few did. And he didn't like leaving the woman from the coffee house. He still didn't know her name. Lansdale remained behind to talk with Diem and Madame Nhu.

Outside the palace, Nhu inquired about Coyle's background and why he knew so much about aerial defenses. Coyle admitted that he had firsthand knowledge of what worked and what didn't because he had been shot down so many times. Nhu laughed. Coyle wasn't sure if Nhu laughing was good or not. The man was known to have people tortured and killed on a whim. It was best to keep a low profile around him and not draw his attention. They walked around the side of the palace. "So, where would you put a new gun emplacement?" said Nhu.

"Up there," said Coyle pointing to the palace roof. "It will need a clear line of sight to any approaching aircraft. Down below, the view will be blocked by the walls and trees, not to mention the palace itself. If you put a gun on the roof, it'll have a clear shot at the enemy."

"I see. But I am not sure my brother will like an ugly anti-aircraft gun on the roof of his palace."

"Two would be best. One for each side. I admit. It's a trade-off. Security vs aesthetics. You might consider an M45 Quadmount instead of a traditional anti-aircraft autocannon. It's got a lower profile and you can remove the trailer wheels to make it even lower."

"But isn't an autocannon more effective at destroying aircraft?"

"Well, yeah… if you hit it. But a 'meat chopper' throws up a barrage of bullets in the path of the plane. The chances of hitting something go way up. 'Sides, the tracer rounds alone will put the fear of God in any pilot."

"A meat chopper?"

"Yeah, that's what we call 'em cause they chop up the enemy. It's a nickname."

"I imagine the meat choppers are in short supply and will be difficult to acquire."

"Oh, I don't know. You've got two of 'em protecting the runways at the airbase where I am stationed. I'm pretty sure you could get more if you explained why you need them. I could make a few calls if you want?"

"That would be helpful. Can you also supervise the installation assuming we can acquire them?"

"Well, I ain't no engineer but sure. I can make sure the barrels are pointed in the right direction."

"Excellent."

They started walking back to the palace entrance and Coyle said, "Do you mind if I ask you a question?"

"Please."

"The woman that was translating…"

"Bian?"

"Bian. That's her name?"

"Yes. Do you know her?"

"No."

"But you are interested in her?"

"I was just curious. She seemed very talented."

"She is. My wife stole her away from the Philippines' ambassador when she found out she spoke both Russian and Chinese fluently. Bian is very rare."

"Yes. I can see that."

"Would you like me to introduce you to her?"

"No. Thank you. I was just curious."

It was early afternoon before Lansdale and Coyle left the palace and returned to the teams' headquarters. Lansdale wanted to understand more about the palace defenses and how they could be improved since he saw Diem's interest in the matter. Coyle was far from an expert, but he held his own answering most of Lansdale's questions. When he didn't know, he pleaded ignorance hoping Lansdale would seek advice elsewhere. Instead, Lansdale asked Coyle to keep him apprised of his progress in finding the quadmounts.

When Lansdale finally dismissed him, Coyle left headquarters and headed for Bian's house. It was getting late in the afternoon, and he suspected she would be on her way home soon.

As the taxi approached her neighborhood, Coyle changed his mind and asked the driver to take him to the coffee house where he first met Bian. She would be anxious having seen him at the palace. She would want to find him and ask questions. The only other place she had seen him, besides the palace, was the coffee house. So, naturally, she would go there looking for him.

He was right. When he walked into the coffee house, Bian was already seated in the corner. She looked displeased. Possibly angry. That was not what Coyle wanted. He walked over and sat down across from her without saying a word. Bian studied him like an insect on the end of a pin, then said, "Why have you been following me?"

"Following you?" said Coyle. "I was at the palace on business."

"I'm not talking about the palace."

Coyle took a long moment to consider his answer. He hated the idea of starting their relationship with a lie and said, "Okay. I admit. I was intrigued when we first met, and I wanted to meet you again."

"So, you tracked me down?"

"Yes. But not in a creepy way. I just didn't know how to find you."

"It's called stalking."

"I think that is a little harsh."

"Is it? Perhaps I am not using the correct word. What would you call it when a man secretly follows a woman to her home?"

"Okay. I see your point. But maybe you could see it as a compliment."

"I don't."

"Well, then… I apologize. I didn't mean to make you anxious or feel threatened in any way."

"You work for the Americans?"

"Yes. I'm a pilot."

"You mean you are a spy."

"No."

"Why were you with Lansdale? Lansdale is a spy."

"I don't work for Lansdale. I mean… I do and I don't. I'm on temporary assignment. Technically I am a contractor. But I'm not a spy."

"I don't believe you."

"You don't know me."

"I'm not sure I want to."

"That would be a shame. I'm a pretty nice guy."

"You think a lot of yourself."

"Look, I'm not a spy. I'm a pilot. And I'd like to take you to dinner."

"I'm not going to dinner with you."

"If you go to dinner with me, I will do my best to answer all your questions truthfully. Whatever you want to know."

Bian was intrigued. She wanted to know more. "Alright. But I pick the restaurant and I will meet you there and I will leave alone."

"Okay. That's fine. But I don't eat bugs. So, no place that serves bugs."

"I don't eat bugs."

"Good to know."

"This isn't a date. It's more of a fact-finding mission."

"I understand. You can call it whatever you wish."

"But you are going to call it a date?"

"We'll see how it goes."

"Fine. Tomorrow night. L'orchidée. It's just east of Binh Tay Market. Every taxi driver knows it."

"French food?"

"Yes. No bugs."

"Sounds good."

Like many Western restaurants in Saigon and throughout Vietnam, L'orchidée's décor was based on a theme – orchids. A single orchid floated in a bowl of water as the centerpiece of every table. The lighting was dim with a hint of lavender. Coyle, wearing a white shirt, slacks, and a sports coat that he had purchased that day, was surprised. The restaurant seemed more romantic than he imagined Bian would pick for their non-date. He didn't mind it. It just seemed unusual.

Bian was already waiting in the lounge when Coyle arrived. She was sipping a martini and wearing a Western-style dress that accented her petite figure - a tightly tapered top with a full skirt. Coyle wasn't sure if he liked it. It was attractive on her but seemed slightly out of character for a woman that usually wore a traditional white ao dai. He didn't want her to change because of him. It never dawned on him that she liked the style and wore it to please herself. Such was the thinking of most men. "I hope I am not late," said Coyle.

"You're not. I am early," said Bian.

"I see you started without me," he said referring to the martini in her hand.

"Would you like one?"

"Maybe during dinner. I'm a bit peckish."

"Peckish means hungry?"

"Yes, but not starving… if you want to finish your martini first."

"No. I'll have it brought to our table."

"I made a reservation."

"No need. The maître 'd knows me."

"You eat here often?"

"My uncle owns the restaurant."

"Impressive."

"He's an impressive man."

"With good taste... I hope."

"You shall soon see and judge for yourself."

She motioned to the bartender to bring her drink to the table and rose. Coyle was unsure if he should offer her his arm as they walked. He decided against it. As they exited the lounge, she placed her hand on the crook of his arm and suddenly he didn't know what to think. They walked to the entrance to the dining room and the hostess immediately sat them at a table near a window. A perfect spot to observe the entire room and talk quietly. A Vietnamese musician played a grand piano softly so as not to overpower customers' voices but to provide background for those awkward moments when conversations stalled. When the waitress came over and set Bian's martini in front of her, Coyle ordered a beer. "I would have thought you a whiskey man," said Bian.

"I like whiskey, but I thought it would better to keep my wits tonight," said Coyle.

"And why is that?"

"You have questions."

"And you want to make sure you don't give any state secrets away?"

"Something like that."

"I promise not to probe too deeply."

"Your English is very good. What other languages do you speak?"

"Well, besides Vietnamese and English there's Russian which you already know, um, Mandarin and Cantonese, and French."

"That's amazing."

"I like languages. And you?"

"Oh, ah… a little Spanish in high school, and I picked up some French when I lived in Paris."

"Paris? How lovely."

"Yeah, it was… until it wasn't."

"A woman?"

"Yeah."

"Were you with her long?"

"Like four or five years. I thought we would get married, but she and my friend had other plans."

"I see. Ouch."

"Yeah. Ouch. Have you ever been married?"

"No."

"You're a beautiful and smart woman. Why not?"

"Too busy, I guess. Work gets in the way of life sometimes."

"I guess I could see that. Is it something you want… marriage… a family?"

"Wow, you just jump right into the pool, don't you?"

"I'm sorry. I'm not good at this."

"I can see that. So, what is this?"

"I don't really know what this is. A poor attempt at wooing a girl I suspect."

Bian laughed. It was the first time he had seen her even remotely happy, and he liked it. He relaxed and the conversation flowed more easily.

At the end of the evening, Coyle walked Bian out of the restaurant and hailed a cab. They both said nothing. It was awkward again. Coyle opened the back door and Bian climbed in. "Good night, Mr. Coyle," she said.

"Just Coyle. Can I call on you again?" he said.

Bian took a long moment to study him again, "Will it stop you from stalking me?"

"Probably."

"Then yes."

He wanted to lean over and kiss her lightly on the cheek but closed the taxi door instead. He was learning.

Da Nang Air Base, South Vietnam

A jeep pulled up next to a Cessna O-1 Bird Dog and Coyle hopped out. The Bird Dog was a tandem two-seater scout plane with a maximum speed of 150 mph and had been stripped of decals and identification numbers leaving it non-descript for intelligence missions. Sgt. Rivera a Green Beret dressed in a non-descript camouflage uniform with no insignia rose from sitting on twelve wooden crates. "Are you Coyle?" said Rivera.

"Yeah. You must be my package," said Coyle offering his hand. "You gotta name?"

"I do," said Rivera shaking Coyle's hand but saying nothing more.

"Are you gonna make me guess?"

"Call me whatever you want."

"Alright. How about Smarmy Butt Licker?"

"Seems awfully long."

"I can use Smarmy or Butt Licker for short. Your choice."

"How about 'Blackjack'?"

"Now see, was that so hard?"

"Point taken."

"What do you plan on doing with those crates?"

"We're taking them with us."

"No, we are not… unless they're filled with marshmallows. They ain't filled with marshmallows, are they?"

"Not hardly. They're rifles and submachine guns."

"That's kinda what I thought. Do you understand anything about empty or takeoff weight?"

"Not really, but imagine you are about to enlighten me."

"I am. This is a Cessna O-1 Bird Dog. It's a scout plane. Very lightweight. It has an empty weight of 1,614 lbs. and a maximum takeoff weight of 2,430 lbs. Anything more than that and we don't take off. You follow me?"

"Is there gonna be a test?"

"No."

"Then I follow you."

"Great. How much do you weigh?"

"165 give or take."

"And I am 175… give or take. That's 340 pounds. We have forty-one gallons of fuel which is another 246 pounds and 9 quarts of oil which is eighteen pounds. Two parachutes at thirty-five pounds each. We take all that and add it to the empty weight and that still leaves us with 142 pounds. I'm guessing those crates weigh a bit more than that."

"I've got to take them. I made commitments."

"Well, I guess you're gonna disappoint someone. What kind of rifles and submachine guns?"

"M1 Garands and M3A1 sub machine guns."

"The M1s weigh about ten pounds each and the M3A1s about eight pounds. You can take fourteen rifles or seventeen submachine guns."

"That's not enough of either."

"That's physics and that's all you're gonna get."

"What about the ammunition?"

"I'm not making this up. It's 142 pounds max. That's it. Mix and match however you choose."

"We can take another seventy pounds if we leave the parachutes."

"We ain't leaving the parachutes."

"Don't be a pussy, Coyle."

"Did you just call me a pussy, Blackjack?"

"No, I suggested that you don't become one. Besides, it doesn't mean what you think it means."

"I know what pussy means."

"It comes from the Latin word 'pusillanimous,' which means lacking courage. It has nothing to do with a woman's sex organs or female weakness."

"Oh, great. So, you're calling me a coward. That's better. You can walk as far as I'm concerned," said Coyle turning to walk away.

"No. I can't. Not where I'm going. They said you're the best pilot in Vietnam and that you could get me there."

"Who said that?"

"My commander."

"Well, he's not wrong."

"Look, I need as many guns as we can carry. The ammunition can be dropped by parachute at a later time, but the weapons could get damaged."

"That's not my problem."

"We're flying over jungle and mountains. If we crash, parachutes aren't gonna save us."

"I never liked jumping from a plane anyway."

"So, no parachutes?"

"Alright. But if we crash and I break my legs, you gotta carry me."

"Will do," said the sergeant opening the top crate and pulling out a handful of sub machines, nicknamed "grease guns" for their similar appearance to an auto mechanic's grease gun. Coyle opened the door to the aircraft and loaded the guns on the backseat floor. "So, what happens if I break my legs too?"

"You still gotta carry me."

"You really are merciless."

"Nah. Just lazy. So, where is this landing strip? I didn't see on the map."

"It's not exactly a landing strip."

"What do you mean? Is it a road?"

"No. There are no roads where we are going."

"So, what is it?"

"It's clearing on a mountain ridge."

"Are you serious?"

"Yeah. I checked it myself. My guys cleared out any obstacles and filled in all the ruts from all the rain. Landing's not going to be a problem."

"Great. What about takeoff?"

"It shouldn't be a problem. The clearing is at an angle so that should give you some extra speed. You know… downhill."

Coyle looked unsure and a bit green. Rivera handed him more submachine guns hoping he would continue loading the plane and continue with the mission. He did.

South Vietnamese and Laotian Border

Loaded down with cargo the Bird Dog's 213hp air-cooled, flat-six engine struggled to gain altitude in the mountains. Coyle had to be careful as the aircraft approached stall speed. He climbed as far as he dared then leveled out and flew parallel to the mountain slops gaining speed. "That's the fence," said Rivera pointing. "Just over that mountain ridge."

151

DAVID LEE CORLEY

"I know where the border is," said Coyle frustrated in having to fly an underpowered aircraft. "What I don't know is the location of the clearing?"

"It's about six miles west of the border."

"Can you recognize it from the air?"

"Yeah... I think."

"This is not a good time for guessing."

"I can do it. Everything is starting to look familiar."

"Alright. Let me know when we're getting close."

"Will do," said Rivera staring out the window at the terrain below.

"I don't understand why you didn't just mark it on a map."

"Can't do that. If I'm captured and the map is found, the enemy can use it to locate the others in my group."

"The others?"

"Yeah... the others."

Coyle wasn't trying to pry. Not really. But he felt that he was owed more than a vague explanation. He was risking his life too. He understood that Rivera, in whichever service he served, was like a CIA agent. If caught, the US would disavow him and leave him to the will of the Pathet Lao or North Vietnamese with no Geneva Convention protections. Coyle didn't like him much, but he respected him. He decided to cut him a break and stop busting his chops. They were on the same side, and he needed Coyle's help.

After a few more minutes, Rivera spotted the clearing. Both men were relieved. But the closer the aircraft flew toward the clearing the more Coyle realized that there was a good chance that Blackjack was either crazy or stupid. "You can't be serious," said Coyle. "There is no approach."

152

"Sure there is. You just go along that tree line up the ridge then turn and land in the clearing."

"You really don't know anything about aircraft, do you?"

"No. Not really."

"We're gonna die."

"Nah. They say you're the best."

"I am and I'm telling you we are going to die."

"You can do it. I have faith in you."

"Your faith ain't gonna land this plane."

"You'd be surprised. God and I have a deal – I kill communist atheists and he keeps me alive."

"Did God give you that in writing?"

"Now you're just blaspheming. Bad timing for that, don't you think?"

"Yeah, you're probably right."

Coyle passed over the clearing to survey the area. The soldier was right. The best way to approach the field was to fly along the ridge and then turn at the last minute while diving down toward the clearing. He'd have to pull up at the last minute to avoid crashing. It would be a tricky maneuver, but Coyle was excited by the challenge. "Alright. Here we go."

Coyle started his approach. He had a lot of confidence in his abilities when it came to flying. But he also knew when he was approaching his limits. This was one of those times. The engine sputtered and groaned under the strain. If it stalled, there would be no way to avoid a crash. Unable to continue to climb, the plane would just drop like a rock into the ridge. He took solace that it would probably be over quickly. As he approached the bottom of the clearing, he banked the plane under full throttle and struggled to keep the nose up. The Bird Dog was a taildragger with two wheels on struts below the forward fuselage. If he landed too hard, there was a good chance one of the struts would break whipping the plane around like a toy. If he was too low, the propeller would hit the ground and flip the plane onto its back or side. Either way could be deadly, especially with all the uncrated guns laying on the floor. Coyle realized that there was just too much to worry about and he didn't want to spend the last moments of his life stressing out. He stopped thinking about all the possibilities and let his instincts take over. It was a smart move. Coyle had great instincts when it came to flying.

The nose rose. The wheels hit and rolled up the grassy clearing. The back wheel came down harder than he wanted, but nothing broke and that was a miracle. He throttled down. The plane slowed to a stop after only fifty yards. There was still plenty of field left. He laughed. Blackjack joined him and said, "I knew you could do it."

"Shut the fuck up, Blackjack. You have no idea how close we came to crashing," said Coyle.

"Nah. We weren't gonna crash. God's watching over us. We're the good guys," said Blackjack with a grin.

Coyle taxied the aircraft to the top of the slope and turned it around for eventual takeoff. He could see the problem immediately – there were tall trees at the bottom of the slope that he would have to clear. He decided to worry about that problem later since there was nothing he could do about it, except make the Bird Dog lighter.

Coyle and Blackjack climbed out. Blackjack made a quick survey of the surrounding area, then made a hand signal toward a line of trees to one side of the clearing. Twenty indigenous tribesmen and two Americans emerged from the tree line and approached the aircraft. "How long have they been waiting?" said Coyle.

"Couple days, I would guess. They're very patient," said Blackjack.

The two Americans and several of the tribesmen took up defensive positions around the aircraft while the remaining tribesmen unloaded the weapons and carried them into the trees. "So, I've been thinking… Why don't you come back here tomorrow about the same time, and I'll deliver the rest of your weapons and ammunition?" said Coyle.

"You'd do that?" said Blackjack.

"Sure. Why not? We're on the same side, ain't we? My guess is you and your guys are going to slow the flow of Viet Cong weapons into the South. That's a good thing. I'll do my part to make sure it happens."

"It'll be more dangerous landing the second time at the same sight."

"Yeah, well that'll be your job. You want your guns, you keep the enemy away."

"Will do. And thanks."

"I will expect a free beer next time you're back in civilization."

"You got it."

ANNISTON

May 14, 1961 – Anniston, Alabama

A Trailways bus cruised down a country highway flanked by pine woods, lavender wisteria, and blossoming dogwoods with their brilliant white flowers. There was green grass in every direction sprinkled with firecracker plants, yellow jasmine, and vivid orange Indian paintbrush. It was springtime in Alabama and Mother Nature was showing off.

Sitting by a window, Scott Dickson watched the cascade of color whiz by. He was wearing the green dress uniform that had recently been issued to him by the Army's Advanced Helicopter Training School at Fort Rucker. In a few more weeks, assuming he passed all his exams and his final flight check, he would be a US Army Aviation Warrant Officer.

He was being extra careful not to crease the pants or shirt. There wasn't a lot of time for ironing in between classes and flight instruction. Technically he wasn't supposed to wear the uniform until after graduation, but he thought this might be the only time his twin sister, Karen, was able to see him before he shipped out to his first assignment. He wanted to impress her, although he wasn't sure why. Unlike most twins, they fought like scrapyard dogs growing up. There was pulling of hair, Indian burns, and wedgies in the Dickson household. They were a tough bunch. Military brats.

After their father, Lieutenant Colonel Paul Dickson, lost his arm when the cracked breech on a 155mm howitzer exploded, the twins seemed to calm down somewhat. Maybe they were getting older or maybe what they were fighting about just didn't seem as important anymore. The colonel refused to wear an artificial arm when offered one by the army hospital. He figured an artificial arm was only good as a club and he could still beat the shit of most men without it. He was a man's man — smoked like a chimney, drank like an Irishman, and cursed like a sailor. The men under his command feared him and respected him. He was fine with that. Scott's mother, Janet, naturally wanted to help the colonel when he struggled with the simplest task like opening a can of peaches. But she knew better, and never lifted a finger.

After the accident, the army promoted Scott's father to full colonel and shipped him off to the Pentagon. The army couldn't afford to lose his experience as a veteran artillery commander. His warrior days were over. Conferences, inspections, and reports were his battlefields until he died of cancer a few years later. Some thought it was the cordite he had inhaled during his career with the army. But he knew it was the damned cigarettes. Even when he coughed until he gagged, he just couldn't stop. It was the only mountain he couldn't climb… and it killed him.

The bus made a quick stop in Roanoke. Scott slammed down a bottle of Coke and a Three Musketeers candy bar. The Coke made him wanna pee. He got in line for the white men-only restroom. As he was waiting his turn, the driver called everyone back to the bus. He looked over and saw a man walk out of the colored men's only restroom. The door was slightly ajar, and he could see there was nobody in line and nobody inside. He decided to go for it. He stepped out of line and casually walked past the colored water fountain and slipped through the doorway into the restroom. As he had expected, he was alone. He moved to the urinal and quickly did his business, then moved to the sink and washed his hands. As he moved to exit, the door opened, and a short black man looked up at him. Scott could see that the man was unsure if he had entered the wrong door. He even seemed a bit frightened. Scott averted his eyes, pushed past the man, and headed for the bus.

The last to climb aboard, Scott quickly took his seat as the driver closed the door and drove off. Through the bus window, Scott saw the man leave the restroom and stare at the bus with an accusing eye. It was like Scott had trespassed on what that man called his. Having attended Fort Rucker for just under four months, Scott knew what it was like in the Deep South, but wondered how the man felt living in a society as a colored person that was equal, but separate. Another dozen miles and the bus passed over the bridge across the Little Tallapoosa River heading North.

Scott had been surprised when Karen had asked him to meet her during his upcoming leave. She said she was on a photo assignment and would be in Anniston, Alabama which was only a three-hour bus ride from Fort Rucker. Scott knew better than to ask a lot of questions. Karen would accuse him of being nosey which would lead to a heated argument. Scott wasn't afraid to quarrel with his sister, especially when he felt like he was right, but he didn't feel like this was the right time for one of their knock-down-drag-out arguments. They hadn't seen each other for over a year. Ever since she went off to college, it seemed like Karen was becoming more and more distant from both him and his family. She had stopped coming home for Sunday dinner and even during school breaks. Karen was always a good student and studied hard, unlike Scott, but this was something else. She was changing. Her views of the government and American society were becoming more liberal, and she was more prone to hurl hurtful insults when pressed, even to her mother. She seemed to feel like her eyes had been opened for the first time and she had to tell the world what she now knew to be true. When the family stopped listening, Karen stopped coming for visits.

Scott knew that he wouldn't patch things up with Karen in the few minutes they would share during her stop in Anniston, but maybe it could be a new beginning. Things were heating up in Vietnam and he was pretty sure he would be deployed there before his time was up in the military. There was a big shortage of helicopter pilots and warrant officers would be the first to go when the call-up came. Any deployment was dangerous, but there was something about Vietnam that gave him an uneasy feeling like he might not make it home. He didn't want bad blood between him and his sister. He didn't want Karen to feel guilty if something happened to him. So, he would control his temper and swallow his pride to make peace, even if she goaded him.

Scott had dozed off by the time the Trailways bus entered Anniston. He was awoken when something whacked one of the bus's side panels. Scott looked out to see an angry crowd of white men carrying heavy pipes, headless ax handles, bicycle chains, and baseball bats, many dressed in the Sunday best having just come from church. They were gathered in front of the Greyhound terminal on one end of the town. They were moving toward the Trailway bus that was slowing so as not to run anyone over. Another man used a baseball bat to take out one of the bus's headlights. "Leave 'em alone. That ain't a bus we want," said someone in the crowd. The crowd moved back from the bus and let it pass without further molestation. The driver sped away down main street. "What the hell was that?" said Scott.

"Bunch of no-goods making trouble," said the driver. "Klan, I imagine."

Just the word "Klan" struck fear in the riders at the rear of the bus. In most towns in the Deep South, blacks outnumbered whites, but the law was usually on the side of the whites and many deputies and even sheriffs secretly belonged to the Ku Klux Klan. "But they weren't wearing their masks," said a black woman.

"Don't need to. This is the Deep South. Nobody gonna say nothing about what they do or don't do. 'Less they want a burning cross on their front lawn," said the woman's husband.

It suddenly dawned on Scott why Karen had asked him to meet her in Anniston rather than Birmingham or one of the other bigger cities. "Let me off," said Scott.

"We're all much safer if we stay on the bus until we reach the terminal. We're almost there," said the driver.

"Let me off the damned bus!"

The driver stopped in the middle of the street, opened the door, and let Scott off. Scott headed back toward the Greyhound terminal as the Trailway bus continued towards its own terminal. Scott could hear the crowd in the distance cursing and shouting racial slurs. He heard the thwack and crack of wood smacking against metal. He picked up speed and broke into a run.

When the Greyhound terminal again came into view, Scott saw a Greyhound bus in the bus park behind the building. It was surrounded by a mob of white men smacking the side panels of the bus with bats, bicycle chains, and pipes. One man smashed a side window launching shards of glass into the interior and pelting passengers. The bus driver moved forward threatening to run over anyway that wouldn't get out of his way. A man pulled a knife and slashed the bus's front tire. But the driver didn't stop. He drove the bus forward, slowly at first, then gunned the engine as the mob parted. The bus turned down the main street and headed out of town toward the highway, its flattened tire wobbling from side to side.

Out the back window of the bus, a young woman with a camera appeared, snapping photos of the mob. Someone in the crowd threw an ax handle and smashed one of the back windows. The photographer didn't miss a beat and slid over to the other unsmashed back window so she could shoot clearly. After several clicks, the photographer lowered her camera to reload her film. Scott could see her face clearly. It was Karen.

The mob wasn't giving up. They jumped into their cars and trucks and chased after the bus. "You just gonna stand there, soldier boy," said the driver of a pickup truck. "Jump in the back."

Scott hesitated for a moment, unsure. The truck began to pull away. Scott jumped in the back with seven other men, all whooping and hollering, hell-bent on catching the bus. "We gonna fuck them Freedom Riders up," said one of the men turning to Scott.

"Yeah. Fuck'em up," said Scott. Like a dog chasing a mailman's truck, he had no idea what he was going to do once the mob caught up with the bus.

A black fifteen-year-old, Antwan Lincoln, rode his bicycle along the highway. It was Sunday, Mother's Day. He was heading into town to buy his mother some fresh licorice with the money he had saved working at a neighbor's chicken farm. Each day after school and all summer long, he shoveled chicken shit for twenty-five cents an hour. It didn't add up to much, but it was his to spend however he saw fit. The farmer also gave him a chicken once a week for his family to cook. Antwan, already almost six feet tall and capable of carrying two fifty-pound bags of manure at the same time, was growing quickly as he matured. He needed all the protein his family could afford. The free chickens were always welcomed.

His father was a sharecropper – cotton. He gave his landlord forty percent of his crop in exchange for rent and the use of two mules. That didn't leave much after tools, seeds, and fertilizer which he bought from the neighbor that employed his son. The farm had a large shack in which the Lincoln family lived. The wood was old and greyed, but it kept the rain and mosquitos out. It was the only home Antwan had known.

Antwan's newly freed great-great-grandfather had changed the family name from Washington to Lincoln after the president was assassinated at Ford's Theatre. He figured the sixteenth president had done by far more for his family and people than the first president. Changing the family name and living a good Christian life were the only ways of showing his appreciation for the dead president.

Antwan studied hard during the school year. He knew there was little chance his family would be able to pay for any schooling beyond high school and he wanted to learn as much as he could while he had the opportunity. He saw how hard his father worked every day and decided early on that he didn't want to become a farmer. He didn't know what he wanted to do for a job. He thought he might get a job in a factory in a big city or maybe move furniture because he was big for his age. The one thing he was sure of was that he wanted to leave Anniston as soon as he was able. He hoped his family might follow him once he was stable and could help with the moving expenses. But no matter what, he was leaving. The Klan was strong in Anniston, and he wanted no part of it.

As he was pedaling, he looked down the highway and saw the bus with the flat front tire heading in his direction. He wondered why the driver had not pulled over. Then he saw the reason... cars and trucks filled the men that Antwan knew as the Klan. Antwan steered his bike off the highway, across the grassy strip bordering the road, and into the trees. He hopped off the bicycle and laid it down. He kept low hoping not to be seen and watched...

The driver made it just under two miles out of town when the flat tire dislodged and jammed itself up in the wheel well. Sparks flew as the bus's metal rim met the asphalt. Unable to steer, the driver had no choice but to stop in the middle of the highway. The convoy of Klansmen quickly caught up and emptied out of the vehicles surrounding the bus. They banged on its side panels and doors.

From the tree line, Antwan watched, hidden. He had seen things like this before and they had never ended well. He wanted to turn away, but he couldn't. He would witness it... all of it. But no matter what happened, it was doubtful he would tell anyone beyond his father. Black folk that talked too much rarely lived long in Anniston.

Inside the bus, the passengers and driver were frightened. Leaving the town had been a mistake. There were no witnesses. The Freedom Riders had sworn off violence and held their ground – interracial couples sitting in seats in the middle and front of the bus, ignoring the Jim Crow laws. Not part of the protest, the other passengers were in the wrong place at the wrong time, defenseless. A window in the back was smashed and a Molotov cocktail flew into the bus. It broke on the floor spreading fire throughout the back. A man's trousers caught fire. Another man threw his jacket over the flames on the man's pants and extinguished them. Passengers ran forward avoiding the fire. The bus filled with smoke.

When the pickup Scott was riding skidded to a stop, the bus was already on fire and smoke was pouring out the broken windows. The driver and the passengers attempted to exit through the front door. The Klansmen outside pushed against the door keeping it closed, preventing the passengers' escape. Scott knew it would only be a matter of a minute or two until the passengers were overwhelmed by the smoke and fire. He jumped from the truck and advanced on the mob surrounding the bus. He saw the pickup driver. A revolver was tucked in his trousers behind his back. Scott grabbed the gun. The driver whipped around and began to protest. Scott was in no mood to hear his complaint and decked him with his fist. The man fell to the ground. Scott advanced again, this time raising the pistol in the air and firing two rounds. At the same moment, the gas tank in the back of the bus exploded sending a ball of flame into the air and rocking the bus. The passengers inside lost their footing and fell. The mob, frightened by the explosion and the gunshots, scattered. Scott grabbed the edge of the door and forced it open. The passengers poured out onto the highway, hacking and coughing. A Klansman moved up behind Scott and clubbed him with a baseball bat in the back of the head. Scott crumbled to the asphalt, unconscious.

Antwan had watched the soldier save those in the burning bus. And he saw the Klansman beat him with their clubs after he fell to the ground. Antwan was moved to tears as he watched from the woods, unseen. He wanted to rise up and help the soldier, but he knew what would happen. There were too many of them and he still wasn't big enough to stand against even a few of them. He watched as the Klansman turned from the soldier and unleashed their anger on the passengers from the bus. The mob beat them with bicycle chains, pipes, ax handles, and baseball bats. All fell to the highway, bleeding from the wounds, their bones broken, helpless. Antwan wanted to be brave and stop the Klansmen... he really did... but his courage let him down that day on the highway. All he could do was watch...

When Scott woke, he looked out through blurry eyes. He was lying in tall grass beneath a tree. He saw several ropes with nooses on the ends tossed over a thick tree branch above him. "Soldier boy's first," said the pickup driver, his nose bloodied from Scott's blow.

Two Klansman picked up Scott by the arms and pulled him to a waiting noose. Scott could hear Karen screaming. He turned to see her being held back by a burly Klansman. She kicked and struggled to free herself, but the man was too big and strong. Scott felt his hands being tied behind his back and the noose dropped over his head. It was like a dream. Still dazed from the blow to his head, everything was moving in slow motion. There was nothing he could do. He saw the bus engulfed in flames up on the road. A highway patrol car pulled up in front of the bus and two officers climbed out. One had a shotgun in his hand.

Scott felt the rope tighten around his throat and his body lifted into the air. He couldn't breathe. That was it. He was going to die. *At least Karen saw what I did,* he thought. *She'll tell Mom.* He gagged as he tried to inhale. Nothing. He felt lightheaded. Almost euphoric. *This ain't so bad,* he mused. *It'll be over soon, and I'll be a dead hero.* Just before passing out, Scott heard the boom of a shotgun going off. The mob scattered. He looked over and saw that Karen was free and running toward him. She grabbed his legs and lifted him as everything went black...

Antwan watched as the Klansman got back in their cars and trucks and drove off back toward town. He emerged from the woods and walked across the highway toward the tree. Someone had cut the rope strangling the soldier. The passengers from the bus were helping him down. He wasn't moving. Antwan knelt on the asphalt and wept as the passengers carried the soldier to the highway patrol car and loaded him in the back with a young woman whose face looked similar to the fallen soldier. The patrol car sped away. There was nothing Antwan could do... or was there? At that moment, Antwan made a decision. He would join the military and fight for those that could not fight for themselves. He would take the place of the fallen soldier that stood against the Klan that day.

Scott woke up in a hospital bed. Karen was beside him. "They smashed my camera," she said. "Mom's gonna kill me. It was expensive."

"What happened?" he said, groggy.

"You got yourself lynched. Well… almost lynched. Highway Patrol saved your ass. What in the hell were you thinking?"

"I wasn't thinking. I was reacting. God, my head hurts."

"It should. Nineteen stitches. You got whacked pretty good. You're lucky they didn't crack your skull. Do you want me to call the nurse?"

"No. Not yet."

"Always the martyr."

"Yeah, I guess. Are you okay?"

"Cuts and bruises. I'll live."

"What in the hell were you doing on that bus?"

"Photographing the Freedom Riders."

"Why?"

"What they were doing was important. It's gonna change things. It's gonna be history."

"By the looks of things, I doubt it'll change much."

"Yeah, well… they got a ways to go yet."

"A long ways."

"You're part of it, ya know. What happened. You saved 'em."

"I saved you."

"Alright… me."

"No, thank you?"

"You're my brother. It's your job to protect me."

"You're welcome. Where's my uniform?"

"I threw it away. It was covered in blood and torn pretty badly."

"What?!"

"I'm kidding. It's hanging in the closet over there. But there is a lot of blood on it."

"Shit. My instructor's gonna kick my ass."

"Relax. I'll get it cleaned and patched up. Good as new."

"It's the least you could do."

"Exactly."

"I'm glad you're okay."

"You scared the shit out of me, you know?"

"You scared me."

"I guess that makes us even."

"Not hardly."

They smiled at each other as only twins can do, knowing how the other felt, no words were necessary. "So, you really did it? You're gonna fly helicopters?" she said.

"Yeah, I really did it," he said, proud.

"You gonna give me a ride?"

"It ain't like they give me my own helicopter. But I'll see what I can do," said Scott, then winced from pain, "Maybe you should call that nurse now. Is she cute?"

"You ain't that lucky," said Karen with a wicked smile.

When US Attorney General Robert Kennedy read the reports from Anniston, he was angry, but not surprised. He suspected that something like this would happen when the Freedom Riders first set out from Washington DC. Although he hated the idea of protesters riding through the Deep South to make a point, he hadn't tried to stop them. He understood that they were willing to sacrifice themselves to advance the civil rights movement, and, on some level, he respected them for it. Still, they hadn't made things easier for him and his brother. They were still dealing with the repercussions of the failed Cuban invasion and many congressmen and senators were questioning JFK's ability to lead the country. As one crisis was finishing another was heaped on the fire. And as the chief law enforcement officer in America, this particular fire was right in Robert's lap. Even though JFK was president, and his brother was the head of the Justice Department, the Kennedys still needed the votes of Southern Democrats to pass laws and push their agenda forward.

He called the leaders of the civil rights movement and asked them to remain calm and call off the Freedom Riders. His suggestion was not well received, and some accused him of being a traitor to the cause. Robert attempted to reassure them that he was on their side, and he would do what was necessary to protect the riders for the remainder of their trip. His biggest problem was that almost everyone in power in the South was against the Freedom Riders, even if some supported civil rights. The riders were seen as troublemakers determined to start race riots, not prevent them.

After conferring with his brother, the president, Robert decided on a course of action. He sent his assistant, John Seigenthaler, to Alabama to try to calm the situation. A strong advocate of civil rights, Seigenthaler was trusted by many of the Freedom Riders. However, they would not back down and were determined to continue their journey to New Orleans.

The South exploded with violent protests. Everywhere the buses carrying the Freedom Riders were headed, mobs of Klansmen were waiting. Bus drivers refused to drive their routes for fear of being identified with the Freedom Riders and persecuted for their assistance. After another attack at the bus terminal in Birmingham, Alabama, in which more Freedom Riders were seriously injured by Klansmen, Robert Kennedy had no choice but to protect the Freedom Riders. Although they were breaking many

DAVID LEE CORLEY

local ordinances, the Freedom Riders weren't breaking federal law and were traveling on a federal highway. He ordered the Alabama National Guard to escort and even travel on the buses with the Freedom Riders. The guardsmen rode with their rifles, bayonets attached, at the ready. Robert personally called Greyhound executives and assured them that their drivers and buses would be protected. The executives begrudgingly found drivers that would drive the buses and the journey continued.

Mountain Border, Laos

A North Vietnamese squad approached a V-shaped rope bridge stretching across a mountain gorge. A fast-flowing river wound its way through the steep walls below. The bridge had a thick rope at the bottom of the V on which the travelers could walk while holding the two ropes that acted as guard rails. In high winds, the bridge swayed wildly making the crossing potentially deadly. There was no surviving the fall. Half the squad took up defensive positions along the edge of the gorge while the other half carefully crossed the bridge.

Upon reaching the other side, the NVA troops spread out taking up defensive positions. With both sides of the bridge protected a caravan of civilian porters and youth volunteers loaded down with bundles of weapons and supplies traversed the gorge using the rope rails to steady themselves as they crossed.

An unseen Montagnard tribesman squatted motionless in a tangle of foliage just a few feet from an NVA soldier. His face and body were covered with natural camouflage - wet mud and fresh leaves. He was

170

invisible except for the whites of his eyes which he kept closed. His breathing was controlled and silent. He listened to the bridge as the bearers crossed, some scared and crying. He heard them approaching his side of the bridge. His eyes sprung open, he pivoted and used his long knife to hack off the head of the NVA guard. He wasn't alone. Seven more hidden Montagnard sprang into action killing the NVA. The NVA on the opposite side of the bridge heard the cries of the comrades and watched frozen with fear as the tribesmen tossed the severed heads of the fallen into the gorge. The civilians on the bridge panicked, cast off their heavy loads, and turned to go back. Several slipped and fell to their deaths.

A few moments later, the NVA on the opposite side snapped out of their shock and opened fire with their rifles. It was a long distance, and their aim was inaccurate.

The rest of the hatchet team, made up of two dozen Montagnard, rose from the tall bushes on the ridge and opened fire with their new American rifles. For some, it was the first time they had used the weapons in battle. They were good weapons and brought smiles to their faces as they returned fire at the NVA across the gorge. There was no need to kill the civilians still on the bridge and a waste of ammunition. They were already dead, just didn't know it. Three tribesmen ran to the bridge and used their knives to hack at the rope anchors. One of the rail ropes was the first to snap. With one of their supports gone, more civilians lost their balance and fell into the gorge. When the second rail rope snapped most of the remaining civilians fell to their death. A few of the stronger porters held onto the thick rope on which they had walked. But a few moments later, that too snapped at the anchor and the surviving civilians on the bridge swung downward holding onto the rope until it smashed into the side of the gorge causing all that held on to it to fall and die.

With the bridge down, Blackjack and his two American soldiers under his command stepped from their firing positions behind trees and surveyed the carnage. Blackjack signaled the retreat to the Montagnard tribesmen. There was no need to continue fighting with the few NVA that were left on the opposite side of the gorge. Their work was done, and it was time to celebrate with the pig and whiskey their commander had purchased with his American money. The tribesmen loved to fight and win. The tall American warrior that spoke their language brought them victory and they worshipped him for it.

It was only a small path that was cut off from the Ho Chi Minh Trail. The weapons and supplies would be quickly replaced and rerouted by the North Vietnamese. But word of the loss and the tactic of decapitation spread through the North Vietnamese troops and civilians. The Montagnard had joined the South Vietnamese. Fear spread like wildfire. Nobody in Laos was safe.

THE HIDDEN LIE

August 10, 1961 – Washington DC, USA

August was downright sticky in Washington. The humidity was overwhelming for some. Even the slightest breeze across the Potomac was welcomed.

Bathed in sunshine and cloudless, blue skies the nation's capital was glorious and crowded with tourists visiting its stately monuments. Crowds of visitors snapped obligatory photos in front of the White House, Capitol Hill, and the Lincoln Memorial. The Smithsonian museums were popular with the new addition of air conditioning and restaurants with large awnings or umbrellas on their patios were packed with hungry patrons seeking shade.

Inside the White House, JFK and his cabinet watched a film made by Monsanto on the use of herbicides sprayed from aircraft to clear away heavy vegetation. A plan to deny the Viet Cong the use of cover in and around cities and towns had been proposed by the US military and Monsanto was there to seal the deal. The defoliants could also be used on the sides of highways and roads to create transport lanes void of the snipers that continually plagued South Vietnamese military convoys. They could also be used to deny the enemy the use of forest canopies that prevented reconnaissance aircraft from spotting large troop movements. The British had used herbicides effectively in Operation Trail Dust during the Malaysian Emergency in the 1950s.

When the presentation ended and the lights came back on, Kennedy was full of questions. His main concern was destroying the Vietnamese crops and livestock. He didn't want to make matters worse for the Vietnamese peasants. The Monsanto representative assured the president and his cabinet that their defoliants were harmless when it came to livestock and that it would only destroy vegetation where it was applied. Furthermore, the runoff into the Vietnamese rivers and canals would be minimal. It was a convincing argument that did not risk American or

South Vietnamese lives and yet could greatly improve the military situation.

Kennedy was still hesitant. He agreed to a series of tests to see if the herbicide was effective and if it could be controlled.

Dak To, South Vietnam

The soil around Dak To was rich with nutrients that fed millions of pine trees that grew naturally in the Central Highlands. For centuries, the forests had supplied the farms and villages with all the wood needed for homes and fences. Firewood was easily collected from the fallen trees and broken branches that were common on the forest floor. The shade from the trees cooled the livestock and villagers from the sun.

Four C-123 Providers flew over the forest in a staggered horizontal formation spraying a clear substance over the canopy of pines. The air smelled musty as the liquid descended in the trees. The herbicide landed on the pine needles and branches, while some floated downward until it reached the forest floor. Any wildlife, livestock, or humans living in or passing through the forest were doused with the liquid. The reaction was instant with skin turning red and stinging like little needles. Over the weeks, the planes passed over again and again ensuring strong coverage for the best results.

Twice a day, the C-123s returned to Da Nang Air Base to refill their 1,000-gallon tanks with the herbicide. The defoliant was poured by hand by the maintenance crews at the airbase. Some spillages always occurred and were washed away with high-powered water hoses at the end of the day. The water mixed with the defoliant as it flowed into the storm drains or in some cases into the surrounding grass. Within days all vegetation in and around the airfield was dead.

Throughout 1961, Kennedy's personal approval of each spray test run was required. There was some question as to whether the defoliants were effective against Vietnam's foliage, especially the forests. The solution was to increase the potency of the herbicides using different chemical combinations. The various defoliant used was referred to as Agents Purple, Pink, Blue, and Orange. They were transported and stored in 55-gallon drums marked with color bands matching their description.

For miles around the cities, villages, and surrounding mountains, the forests died. The few trees that resisted the defoliants were bombed with napalm by the South Vietnamese Air Force and torched with flame throwers by the ARVN. Crops died too destroying the farmers' livelihood and driving them into the arms of the enemy. Once Kennedy was convinced that the defoliant worked, the test mission was approved for full deployment. It would be called Operation Ranch Hand and would spray twenty million gallons of chemicals over the South Vietnam landscape and people... including American advisors and soldiers.

August 13, 1961 – Berlin, Germany

Since the division of East and West Germany at the end of World War II, the tensions between the two nations had risen to a fever pitch. Each blamed the other for a multitude of infractions. The East watched as the West lured its best and brightest to the western side of the country. In response, the East German army and police had clamped down, strengthening the border with more patrols and fewer crossing points.

Seeing the opportunity to crossover vanishing before their eyes, thousands of civilians began sneaking across the border to enter the West. Few went the other way. East Germany suffered a brain drain of the most talented of its people leaving their homeland for the greener pastures of capitalism and freedom. The East German authorities were under increasing pressure from Moscow to stop the flow of civilians or suffer the consequences. The East Germans got the message and responded in a dramatic fashion.

Work crews throughout Berlin began the construction of a wall that divided east from west. Doors and windows of buildings on the border were bricked up. The wall was built with amazing speed as the East German government poured more and resources into completing the barrier. Millions of feet of barbed wire were stretched across both ends of a no man's land where escaping individuals would be shot if they tried to cross. Increased East German patrols kept civilians away from the wall and checked papers of anyone that dared approach.

With the nightly news showing desperate attempts to cross the border and the unfortunate outcome usually ending in serious injury or death, the flow of civilians trying to escape East Berlin slowed to a trickle. It had worked. The Soviets had imprisoned their own people.

Kennedy was furious as he watched the human rights of the East German people curtailed. But there was little he could do. NATO was new and its member states were hesitant at best. The United States was not ready to confront the Soviet Union on its own. As much as Kennedy hated to admit, the East Germans were beyond the reach of democracy and freedom. They would have to find their way on their own.

Saigon, South Vietnam

As the chief correspondent for the Associated Press, Malcolm Browne arrived in Vietnam in August. In addition to being a journalist, Browne was an experienced photographer often choosing to take the photos for his stories when his favorite photographer was unavailable. He always carried his Japanese-made Petri 35mm reflex camera with him in a satchel, especially when on an assignment. He had no qualms about snapping off a roll of film even in the most dangerous situations. He often bracketed his exposures between shots to ensure the best exposure and his composition was impeccable. He was willing to put himself in harm's way for a good angle on a subject. Browne wore a gold belt buckle and a money belt, so he always had access to cash in case he needed to bribe his way out of a difficult situation.

Born in New York, Browne's mother was a Quaker with strong anti-war opinions. As a young boy, he attended Friends Seminary, a Quaker school in Manhattan. Later, he attended Swarthmore College in Pennsylvania where he studied chemistry. Browne began his career as a photojournalist when he was drafted during the Korean War. After driving a tank for several months, he was reassigned to Stars and Stripes in the Pacific. He was a hard worker and willing to dig for the truth even when it was frowned upon by his superiors. Not all his stories and photos were printed, and he was seen as a bit of a troublemaker by his commanders. But his editors defended him and praised his work until he was honorably discharged after serving his two years.

Being a journalist was the ideal career for Browne and he kept at it when he returned to the states. He had a natural curiosity. Every day was different, and he was involved in a variety of experiences as he developed his stories.

When he arrived in Vietnam, his mission was simple. He wanted to shake things up. He knew that the Kennedy administration had been increasing the number of advisors which was in direct violation of the Geneva Accords. To be fair, neither the United States nor South Vietnam were signatories of the treaty but had nonetheless complied with its mandates. Browne could feel the underlying tension in Saigon. It was like someone had lit a fuse and everyone was just waiting for the explosion.

Like most journalists, Browne felt himself a patriot of the United States and did not want to do harm to his country. However, he believed that part of being a patriot was to expose the truth to the American people and let the chips fall where they may. The people needed to decide what type of country they wanted and how far they were willing to go to defend their republic. Browne wasn't going to pull any punches no matter who stood in his way.

Browne was a fierce competitor with the other journalists in Saigon, but he was also a reliable friend when serious problems arose. The biggest prize for a foreign journalist was an interview with President Diem or one of his family members. That wasn't easy for foreign journalists since Diem and Madam Nhu saw them as a hindrance. But Browne was determined and immediately went about introducing himself to the staff of the American embassy and offering to write about them if they helped him arrange a meeting between him and Diem. There were no takers. He did find out that there was an American Air Force Colonel named Lansdale that was said to have Diem's ear. Browne decided to track down the colonel in hopes of securing the interview he sought.

The one thing Browne noticed right out of the gate, was that many of military assessments of the war's progress seemed overly rosy. Brown knew that Diem was unliked by a large portion of the South Vietnamese population, especially in the countryside. He found it hard to believe the American military assessment by General Paul Harkins that suggested the war could be won within the year and the American advisors could be sent home. Nothing he was hearing on the streets of Saigon suggested that the people were pacified and compliant with the government. He made a note to himself to dig deeper and find the story behind what he believed was a façade.

Washington DC, USA

When it came to South Vietnam, JFK was at a crossroads. America was supplying more and more advisors to the South Vietnamese military. The advisors' mission was changing from training to leading troops in battle. The American advisors realized that the South Vietnamese officers were not motivated to take risks. In fact, it was just the opposite. They were motivated to keep their men safe and use other means such as air power and artillery to destroy the enemy when they came in contact. When confronted by superior firepower, the Viet Cong disengaged and retreated to the safety of the forest. In the South Vietnamese commanders' minds that was a victory. In the American advisors' minds, it was a defeat. The enemy had been allowed to escape without inflicting heavy damage on them.

The solution for the Americans was simple. They needed to take control of the ARVN troops during the battles. Technically, the Americans could not command the South Vietnamese troops because President Diem did not allow it. He feared foreigners commanding his troops because he could not control them. But the reality on the ground was whatever the Americans advised was to be considered an order and if a South Vietnamese commander chose to discard the advice, he had better have a very good excuse or face demotion by his commanders.

But not all South Vietnamese commanders were reluctant. Some were aggressive and led by example. But they were few and far between. So, the American advisors were forced to lead the ARVN troops in the field through their South Vietnamese commanders. The concept of leading from the front displayed by the American advisors often forced the hesitant ARVN commanders to be more aggressive to save face. Their bravery often put the American advisors in harm's way. Even though there was a standing order for the Americans not to engage the enemy, the advisors ignored the order and armed themselves with their weapon of choice.

Kennedy knew that the American advisors were leading the South Vietnamese troops into battle. Secretly he approved of the advisors' actions. He, like them, wanted to win and American experience and leadership were what was required. The problem was the press. More questions were being asked about the mission of the American advisors in Southeast Asia. Knowing that the press would present the growing number of advisors as a negative, Kennedy called for a meeting of his cabinet and advisors to discuss the matter. "After our debacle in Cuba, I am not anxious to deceive the American public of our use of advisors in South Vietnam. They have a right to know when we place our soldiers in danger even if they are just advisors. But I am concerned that the press will present our actions in an ill light and question our intent," said JFK.

"I wonder if it wouldn't be better just to be upfront with the American people and tell them exactly what we are doing and why," said Robert Kennedy. "If we explain it right, I am sure they will understand and support your decision. After all, when it was all said and done the people supported your actions in Cuba. The vast majority thought it showed courage and determination to attempt to defeat the communist expansion off our shores."

"That may be true, but Vietnam is not Cuba. It's halfway around the world. Most Americans can't even find it on a map," said Pierre Salinger, JFK's press secretary. "It will be difficult convincing the public that a tiny Southeast Asian nation is worth sacrificing the lives of American advisors."

"I don't know. We convinced the public that American lives were worth sacrificing in Korea. Our goal is the same – stop communist expansion. I don't know why the public won't accept that," said McGeorge "Mac" Bundy.

"It's a dangerous gamble. If the press spins this the wrong way, it could endanger our re-election," said the vice president.

"I don't think it is unreasonable to deceive the American public in the name of national security. We do it all the time," said George Ball. "Americans want to be safe. That should be our highest priority, even over the truth. We don't tell them which weapons we are developing or reveal intelligence reports. How is this different? We are simply withholding information for their own good."

"That's true. Stopping communist expansion is for the security of America. I think we could fairly argue that American advisors are part of the strategy and any information we might withhold is for the good of the United States," said Bundy.

"I think it would be difficult to make any more progress in Vietnam without more advisors or Special Forces. Aside from increased military aid, they seem to be the only thing making a real difference in fighting the Viet Cong and the North Vietnamese in Laos. Press or no press, we need to keep the pressure upon the communists in Southeast Asia. That much I know for sure." said McNamara.

"I don't know that I agree with that," said Allen Dulles, the outgoing CIA director. "Covert paramilitary operations are playing a role in keeping the North in check."

"Sure, they play a role, but we can't win the war with paramilitary operations. American advisors leading South Vietnamese troops can take back the territories under the control of the Viet Cong. Plus they are training the ARVN to fight and giving them combat experience. In the end, that's what we want, isn't it? A well-trained South Vietnamese military fighting to protect their own country?"

"And you think that's still possible?" said the president.

"With more advisors and equipment, yes. But it's gonna take some time."

"How much time?"

"It's a moving target, Mr. President. But if I were forced to venture a guess… two, maybe three years before the South can stand on its own."

"I don't see how we can keep a secret from the American press that long."

"I'm not sure we need to," said Bundy. "We just need to ease them into it. If we have positive results, I'm sure the press, as well as the rest of America, will jump on board."

"I'm not sure most Americans want to know all of the dangers our nation is currently facing and how we are dealing with those threats. They elected you, Mr. President. They trust you to keep them safe even if they don't know all the particulars of how you do it," said Theodore Sorenson.

The president considered for a long moment, then said, "Alright. We keep a lid on it for now. We tell the press only what they need to know."

"You realize that deceiving the press could backfire?" said Robert.

"It may. But defeating communist expansion is a higher calling. If it blows up in our faces, we will need to convince the editors that we were doing our patriotic duty."

"By lying to them?"

"Yes. They don't want to see America harmed. Who would they sell their papers to?" said Kennedy.

Saigon, South Vietnam

Lansdale was late. Diem had invited him for lunch at the palace, but he had to finish a report to the incoming CIA director John McCone. Lansdale had mixed emotions about McCone mainly because he knew almost nothing about him. Dulles had been incredibly supportive of his mission in Vietnam giving him and his teams a wide berth. Lansdale was not a fan of change. He liked organization and change tended to mess things up.

There was a lot of talk in Washington about bringing him back to the Pentagon where he could share his knowledge of PsyOps and the North Vietnamese leaders. He was considered by most of the generals and Kennedy's cabinet to be America's leading expert on both. Lansdale didn't want to go. He liked being in the field. A desk job sounded boring compared to running CIA covert paramilitary teams. Unfortunately, he was now a full colonel and for his career to progress, he needed to attend the National War College then get his star making him a brigadier general. He liked the sound of "General Lansdale" but didn't want to leave Vietnam without completing his mission.

When he arrived at the palace, he was escorted to the veranda where Diem, Nhu, and Madam Nhu were talking with Robert Thompson, the new head of BRIAM – the British Advisory Mission. On seeing Thompson, Lansdale was a bit peeved. He had not been told that anyone outside the family would be attending the luncheon.

Madam Nhu tolerated Lansdale, but she didn't like him or anyone else that gave council to Diem. She recognized that was her and her husband's job. She often felt that Lansdale took his position as a special advisor to President Diem for granted and at times seemed to be working against what she knew was good for her country and brother-in-law. Lansdale was cautious. She was not. She especially hated it when Lansdale criticized her or her husband's advice to Diem. She watched with delight as Diem introduced Thompson as another special advisor. She could see Lansdale twisting in the wind.

Lansdale was cordial and hid his loathing well. As usual, the British were horning in where they didn't belong. They had helped create the current mess in Vietnam when they had allowed the French to retake control of the country after World War II. When asked by the United States to contribute resources to Vietnam to fight communism, the British had refused and chose instead to concentrate on the growing communist threat closer to home in Europe. Their advice, which they believed was always welcomed, on how to manage the civil war was freely given. Thompson and BRIAM were the embodiment of that advice.

Diem saw Thompson and BRIAM as a counterpoint to Lansdale and MAAG. He wanted both opinions as he developed his strategy to fight the communists. As of late, Diem had been feeling the Americans were becoming overbearing. He liked the idea of showing the Americans that they were not the only game in town. The irony was American military and financial aid were keeping South Vietnam afloat while the British contributed little in the way of actual support. To Diem and his family, the British served their purpose by just being there and pushing back against the Americans from time to time. "President Diem has been telling me about your counterinsurgency operations," said Thompson. "Some are quite ingenious."

"Interesting. I wasn't aware that we were sharing that information," said Lansdale.

"It is okay, Colonel. Mr. Thompson has our full confidence," said Diem.

"I see. I am sure his advice will be most welcome. The British are known for their advice... especially when others are doing the fighting."

"Colonel, I detect a bit of animosity. Surely, you see the value in alternative opinions?" said Thompson. "After all, we are on the same side."

"I wasn't aware the British had taken a position on Vietnam."

"While it is true that the United Kingdom has its hands full in Europe, we understand the struggle against communism in Southeast Asia. After all, we have been here longer than you Americans."

"Yes. The British Empire once stretched far and wide. How is that working out for you these days?"

Thompson stewed and said nothing in response.

October 11, 1961 – Washington DC, USA

Sitting in the War Room, President Kennedy and the majority of his cabinet listened intently as General Lyman Lemnitzer, Chairman of the Joint Chiefs of Staff finished his presentation. "The recommendation of the Joint Chiefs is to deploy 40,000 combat troops to defeat the Viet Cong and another 120,000 to secure the border as a show of strength should the North Vietnamese or China consider invading the South," said Lemnitzer.

"While I appreciate the time and effort that went into your assessment, that is a pretty big ask, General," said Kennedy.

"It's not an ask, Mr. President. It's the reality of the situation. The Viet Cong are fighting a guerilla war and yet their numbers are increasing daily. If we let this go on much further, the 'ask' as you call it could be well over 200,000."

"Can you guarantee victory with 160,000 men?"

"Mr. President, as you well know, there are no guarantees in war. The situation is fluid. If you allowed us the use of nuclear weapons and bomb Hanoi, I could guarantee you victory. Short of that, we will do our best."

"We are not using nuclear weapons, General. That I can guarantee, you. And as far as 160,000 troops being deployed, I am going to need a little more than 'we will do our best.'"

"You asked for our assessment on what it will take to win. You have our report, Mr. President."

"Thank you, General. I think we are done for now."

The general stood, saluted his commander-in-chief, and left the room. As soon as the door closed, Kennedy said plainly, "This shit has to stop."

"You should fire the belligerent bastard," said Robert Kennedy.

"I would, but I'm not so sure he is wrong. Bob, have run any numbers of proposed troop levels?"

"I have, Mr. President," said McNamara. "While my numbers are slightly lower, I believe the general's projections are in the ballpark of what would be required to defeat the Viet Cong and keep North Vietnam and China at bay."

"160,000 American soldiers. That's insane. Whatever happened to the South Vietnamese fighting their own war against the North?"

"We realized it was impractical, Mr. President. Even with our advisors, they barely hold their own in a battle with the Viet Cong."

"What is it? Are they cowards?"

"No, Mr. President. They just don't believe in their leadership."

"You mean Diem?"

"Yes, but not just Diem. The military leadership seems to reward those field commanders that don't take risks."

"How the hell are they supposed to fight a war if they don't take risks?"

"Exactly, Mr. President."

"So, what's the solution? More advisors?"

"They help the situation, that's for sure. Helicopters may also play a role. Mobility could be a force multiplier for the South Vietnamese forces."

"So, why don't we send them more helicopters?"

"Pilots, Mr. President. They've got no one to fly them. And even if we train them, I'm not sure they would have the needed motivation to use them correctly."

"So, let's send them some damned pilots. That's better than putting American boots on the ground."

"I'll see what is required."

Kennedy did not know Robert McNamara well when he hired him as Secretary of Defense. Robert Kennedy had convinced JFK that McNamara was the right man for the job after the president had attempted to persuade Robert Lovett to accept the position and was turned down. McNamara has served as a statistical control officer in the Army Air Force during World War II and had served under Lovett. During McNamara's interview with the president, McNamara admitted that he knew nothing about being the

Secretary of Defense. To which Kennedy replied, "We can learn our jobs together. I don't know how to be president either." The two immediately liked each other and McNamara soon became the leader of Kennedy's Whiz Kids.

McNamara's former position as the president of Ford Motor Company had proven his theories about using data analysis to control large organizations effectively. He planned to use those same theories to reorganize and run the United States military. That plan extended to the way the military carried out its mission in Vietnam and even how military aid was distributed to the South Vietnamese government. To create policy effectively, he needed data... lots of data... a ridiculous amount of data. He began collecting it through a series of forms that he and his advisors designed, and the military commanders were expected to fill out and submit.

McNamara would also personally interview hundreds of commanders asking them questions and taking notes when they responded. He consumed and processed data like a steel plant devours coal. He used dozens of charts and graphs during his presentations to the president and the cabinet. His conclusions and subsequent solutions were backed by facts and heavy analysis which made them somewhat irrefutable.

Kennedy loved it. It was how he thought the government should be run – facts and analysis rather than anecdotal evidence which would often be biased and lead to incorrect conclusions. JFK knew that when McNamara presented a solution to a problem it was well-thought-out and based on facts. Kennedy enjoyed the complex discussions he had with McNamara about almost anything. The man was brilliant, and his knowledge of an immense variety of subjects seemed endless. Anyone that chose to challenge one of McNamara's proposals, would expect to be buried with a mountain of data analysis, charts, and graphs. It wasn't that McNamara was vengeful toward those that disagreed with him. It was that he believed in his conclusions and, even more importantly, he believed in the importance of his job. Before long, McNamara was transformed from a policy analyst to a policymaker in the president's eyes.

October 26, 1961 – Hanoi, North Vietnam

While the Americans struggled to find solutions, the North Vietnamese leaders had their own challenges. Not everyone approved of the two-track approach that Le Duan and his followers in the Politburo had developed for the eventual victory over the South. The plan had called for limited support of the Viet Cong as they prosecuted the revolution against the Diem government. At the same time, the North would continue to build the communist state to feed the masses and retain the country's independence.

But many saw the efforts of the North as too little too late. Increased American aid in the South was being used to crush the Viet Cong while expanding Diem's power to oppress his own people. The opposition in the politburo cited statistics gathered by the Viet Cong that Diem and his family had killed over 75,000 civilians and imprisoned 270,000 political dissidents. The point was made that if the North did not step up its efforts to assist its brothers and sisters in the South, the war would be doomed and the opportunity to reunite the country would be lost for decades.

The argument did not fall on deaf ears. Le Duan desperately wanted to free the South. Not only would winning the war expand communism, but it would also reduce the requirement for the military which was eating a large hole in the country's yearly budget. The money saved could be used elsewhere to continue the transformation of the country and its people. Victory was the solution, but Le Duan did not know what more could be done with the limited resources of the North. He hated the idea of asking China and the Soviets for more assistance. Like all aid, it came with strings and Le Duan and his people were not puppets.

November 11, 1961 – Saigon, South Vietnam

General McGarr, Chief of MAAG, sat with Lansdale listening to Thompson present his counterinsurgency plan for pacifying the Mekong Delta to Diem and his family. Neither the general nor the colonel looked happy as much of what Thompson was proposing went directly against the American strategy of search and destroy through large military sweeps by ARVN forces. The Americans wanted to wipe out the enemy while the British wanted to pacify the villagers and deny the Viet Cong access to recruits.

Diem seemed to be accepting the British proposal hook, line, and sinker undoing all the work the Americans had done to sell the current strategy. "The concept of 'clear and hold' actions rather than 'search and destroy' may seem at odds. And they are. While search and destroy temporarily secures the area and raises the body count, it does little to pacify the villagers. Once the ARVN forces leave, the Viet Cong return and sow their revenge on the villages, burning them to the ground, raping their women and girls, and killing their men and elders. To the villagers, the ARVN's search and destroy missions have the opposite effect and turn the people even more against the government. Some will even join the Viet Cong out of desperation," said Thompson. "Our plan would be to initially clear the area around the villages using ARVN troops to drive the Viet Cong away. The ARVN would supply the villages with weapons and ammunition to fight off the Viet Cong and provide the villagers the tools and materials necessary to fortify their villages so that when the ARVN finally leave, the Viet Cong cannot just waltz back in and punish the villagers. While these Strategic Hamlets are being built, the ARVN will provide security for the villagers and patrol the surrounding area. The idea is to hold what has already been cleared, so you are not repeatedly fighting for the same territory."

November 22, 1961 – Washington DC, USA

Unlike McNamara, Kennedy knew McGeorge "Mac" Bundy well when he asked him to serve as National Security Advisor. They had met at Harvard where Bundy was a dean and Kennedy was an overseer on Harvard's board. Both were from Boston and had political connections with many of Boston's elites. Known for his peppery personality, Bundy had served as an intelligence officer during World War II. He was one of two Republicans that served in Kennedy's cabinet. He had offered to switch parties to become a registered Democrat when he accepted the position. Kennedy declined that offer, saying he preferred to have a Republican National Security Adviser to rebut charges that he was "soft on communism."

Bundy's knowledge of foreign affairs and history was vast and Kennedy, who also had extensive experience with foreign affairs, relied on him as a sounding board for many of his policies. But Bundy was far more than a sounding board. It was Bundy that was the chief architect of the plan to escalate the war in Vietnam. It began with National Security Action Memorandum, No. 111 which Kennedy signed. The Memorandum authorized the United States to provide additional equipment and support to the South Vietnam military, including helicopters and aircraft to train the South Vietnamese Air Force. While it seemed rather innocuous, the American trainers assigned were in reality USAF pilots that flew the aircraft often with a bewildered South Vietnamese soldier in a backseat. Technically, the US pilots could claim that the soldier was being trained to fly the aircraft. The unknowing soldier was their cover in case the plane or helicopter was shot down.

The military saw the helicopters as a force multiplier and pushed hard to sell Kennedy on the idea. It worked. Kennedy was willing to let American pilots and aircrews fly South Vietnamese troops into battle as long as the training cover was plausible. Kennedy had once again stopped short of what many of his cabinet members had suggested, including McNamara and Bundy: the introduction of U.S. combat soldiers into South Vietnam. Throughout his tenure, Bundy was a strong advocate of the Vietnam War, believing it essential to contain communism.

The Department of Defense which had been preparing for a military buildup was surprised when their advice was again rejected by their commander-in-chief. It was Kennedy alone that vetoed the full escalation to include ground troops. The generals were not happy and questioned Kennedy's ability to command. Many saw him as a political coward unwilling to do what was necessary to stop communist expansion in Southeast Asia.

November 27, 1961 – Washington DC, USA

Kennedy was adamant that he didn't want US troops in Vietnam. He also knew that the generals in the pentagon were dragging their feet on many of his counterinsurgency policies. Kennedy was displeased and frustrated. He called a meeting of the top military officials and brought them to the White House to call them on the carpet, "I know that the US military is not going to get on board with the counterinsurgency program unless the military wants to do it. But dammit, I want you guys to get with it and do the things that need to be done to make this plan work. That's an order from your commander-in-chief. Whether we like it or not, we are fighting a guerilla war in Vietnam and that means we need to reinvent our playbook. You guys need to start thinking about different ways to achieve victory rather than overwhelming force. We need smaller, more effective ways of fighting. We need to use the South Vietnamese troops and leave our American troops out of it. Our role is to train and support, not combat."

"Mr. President, with all due respect, while we appreciate your input, we know how to defeat the enemy. Most of us in this room have been fighting all our lives. The South Vietnamese military is not capable of defeating the enemy," said an army general. "We need American troops under American commanders in Vietnam if your goal is to achieve victory over the Viet Cong and stop communist expansion."

"General, thank you for your insight. But I think you misunderstood. I was not giving you input. I was giving you an order," said Kennedy. "Get with it or I will find someone who will."

"Mr. President, if you have lost faith in my ability to effectively perform my post, I will happily resign my commission."

"Thank you, General, for understanding and honesty. I accept your resignation."

The room fell silent. The general rose, saluted, and left the room. Robert Kennedy leaned over and whispered to his brother, "That may not have been the wisest move."

JFK whispered back, "No. But it sure as hell let them know I mean business."

December 11, 1961 – Saigon, South Vietnam

The USNS Core arrived at the Port of Saigon. Longshoreman and 400 air and ground crewmen immediately began unloading thirty-three H-21C Shawnee helicopters plus spare parts, supplies, and tools to maintain the aircraft.

In addition, the ship offloaded fifteen T-28C Trojans to be conveyed to the South Vietnamese Air Force. Although lacking internal machine guns and autocannons, the Trojans could carry gun pods, rocket pods, napalm canisters, or bombs on their six hardpoints which made them an ideal attack aircraft for counterinsurgency.

Having acclimated to the heat and humidity when he had arrived by plane a few days earlier, Lieutenant Scott Dickson joined the others to ensure that the helicopters were not damaged during the unloading process. Scott was happy to finally be deployed and

DAVID LEE CORLEY

anxious to get back to flying. The H-21s were still new to the young lieutenant and the other pilots that were part of the 8th and 57th Transportation Companies. Everyone knew that they would soon be flying into combat and their skill behind the controls could very well determine the life or death of the aircrew and passengers. The more time behind the controls the better.

Their destination and home for the foreseeable future would be Tan Son Nhut Air Base a few miles outside of Saigon. Although Vietnam was wider at the southern end, Saigon's central location gave the helicopters and their aircrews a broad area of operation. In addition to the aircrew, each Shawnee helicopter could carry twenty troops and their gear into battle in a matter of minutes. Like most warriors, the Americans were restless to prove themselves. They would soon get their chance.

December 16, 1961 – Pearl Harbor, Hawaii, USA

McNamara stood in front of a room full of senior US generals and admirals as he concluded his comments. As usual, he had a plethora of charts and graphs to aid the discussion of expanded military aid to South Vietnam. "The president is with us, and we are on the same page with what needs to be done. Money is no object. We will find the necessary resources to achieve victory," said McNamara. "The only restriction is that no US combat troops will be allowed in Vietnam. We can expand our US advisor program and airlift capacity using American pilots and equipment if required but they cannot engage in combat unless it is a training mission. The job of the US military is to win the conflict now unfolding in South Vietnam. If we are not winning, you gentlemen need to come up with the necessary solutions and tell me what we need to win."

January 12, 1962 – Saigon, South Vietnam

Like most in the American aircrews, Scott could not sleep the night before his first mission. The Americans had been training with the South Vietnamese battalion that was to be transported by helicopter to the battlefield ten miles west of Saigon. The objective was to capture a communications station used by the Viet Cong to coordinate with undercover enemy units inside Saigon and the surrounding area. The training exercises consisted of loading a skid of troops, taking off, landing in a nearby field, unloading the troops, then taking off again to transport another load of troops.

Everyone wanted this mission to go off without a hitch. The helicopters were weaponless. This technicality meant that the American aircrews were only transporting South Vietnamese troops and not actually participating in the battle. In addition, the helicopter aircrew included a South Vietnamese soldier that was being trained to fly the aircraft. In reality, the recruit that sat in the backseat of the cockpit knew nothing about helicopters and would have preferred to stay on the ground.

Limited by their load capacity of twenty passengers, the helicopters would make two trips to transport the 1,000 ARVN troops and their equipment. Scott was a co-pilot in the first wave. The pilot was the company commander. Once the first group of soldiers was loaded up, thirty-three H-21s took off from Tan Son Nhut Air Base and headed west. They flew low, discouraging anti-aircraft fire as they were only insight of anyone on the ground for just a few seconds. The Viet Cong were not experienced shooting at helicopters which traveled slower than the planes and jets they were accustomed to. They would lead their shots more than necessary firing the bullets in front of the helicopter. In time, they would learn, but not on this day.

The journey to their target only took a few minutes and was uneventful. Scott seemed disappointed. But as they landed in a field, Scott saw the side window next to his head spider-web from a bullet hit. Somebody was trying to kill him. He froze for a moment unsure of what to do. In fact, there was nothing he could do. He could feel his hands shaking and hid them from view so his commander would not see that he was a coward. His commander said something, but Scott didn't hear him through his headset. His mind was racing and hyper-focused. How to survive? He looked at the floor-to-ceiling window around the cockpit. He had never felt so exposed in his entire life. He didn't know when the next bullet would come and if it would hit him. He tried to feel the pain of a bullet entering his body so he wouldn't be surprised. But he had no frame of reference beyond the stories he had been told by a WWII veteran that fought in the Battle of the Bulge.

And then it was over. The ARVN troops had exited the helicopter and the pilot was lifting off. It was a miracle. He had survived. He wasn't going to die that day. He was flushed with excitement and grinning. "Nothing like it," said his commander over his headset. His fear gone, Scott turned him and said, "No. Nothing like it."

Then two more bullets shattered the front windows at Scott's feet and the fear was back. He checked his flight suit for wet blood spots where he might have been hit. He found only one in his crotch, and it was urine, not blood. "Why are they only shooting at me?" said Scott wide-eyed.

His commander laughed in response as he banked the Shawnee and headed back to the airbase. There were no more cracked windows on the return flight.

Just as they had practiced a dozen times, the ARVN troops had jumped out of the helicopter and formed a defensive perimeter around the field. The artillery platoon set up their 81mm mortars capable of reaching the village where the Viet Cong were located. Should that ARVN troops meet heavy resistance as they advanced, the heavy mortars could help pin the enemy and allow the ARVN time to dig in or escape. Each platoon carried a 61mm mortar and a light machine gun that would be set up once they made contact with the enemy.

Once the helicopters took off, the ARVN didn't wait for the rest of the battalion. Their American advisors knew that every minute they waited gave the enemy a chance to escape or worse, prepare an ambush. They advised the company commanders to advance their forces toward the reported location of the enemy. They did so.

Having heard the strange whooping sound from the choppers' blades, the Viet Cong moved to investigate and ran straight into the ARVN troops. A fierce firefight broke out with both sides diving for cover. The Viet Cong numbered only fifty against 660 ARVN with more soldiers on their way. The ARVN units were carrying the latest American weapons while the

Viet Cong were using Chinese and Soviet remnants from WWII and their ammunition was limited. Taken by surprise, the Viet Cong were disorganized while the ARVN had practiced their unit maneuvers until everyone knew them by heart. Using their superior numbers, the South Vietnamese troops maneuvered to surround the Viet Cong positions. But the Viet Cong were fierce fighters unwilling to give up ground until forced. The American-supplied light machine guns pinned the enemy down, while the ARVN mortar squads used anti-personnel rounds to pound the Viet Cong positions.

By the time the helicopters returned with the second load of troops, the battle was over. It was a clear victory with no South Vietnamese or American losses. The Viet Cong had been shocked by the speed of the attack. After six of their troops had been killed and a dozen more wounded, the Viet Cong broke, fled the battlefield, and dissolved into a nearby forest. Not wishing to tempt fate, the ARVN let them go. On their first mission using helicopters, a clear win was more important than prisoners. The ARVN troops located the radio transmitter and brought it back with them as a trophy, evidence of their domination of the enemy.

The Americans continued to ferry the ARVN troops to the battlefield until the entire battalion was on the ground and sharing in the victory. It was a very good day for the South Vietnamese. It was also an important day for the Americans as they had begun to prove the effectiveness of their air mobility strategy against the Viet Cong.

When they returned to base, the Americans celebrated with a barbeque and a couple of dozen cases of beer. Large blocks of ice were brought in, and the aircrews rolled their warm cans on the ice until the beer was cold. The beer and the barbeque never tasted so good. They had won… and more importantly, they had survived.

Washington DC, USA

As President Kennedy and the First Lady were heading off to a weekend ski vacation, a gaggle of reporters shouted out questions hoping for a comment. "Mr. President, there are reports out of Saigon that American helicopter aircrews have participated in a combat operation against Viet Cong forces outside of the capital. Are these reports accurate? Have American troops now entered the war against insurgents in South Vietnam?" said a reporter.

Annoyed at being asked an important question on the fly, JFK stopped and turned to the reporters. "I am sure you are aware it is not the policy of our government to comment on US military operations wherever they occur. We do not want to assist the enemy in any way, shape, or form," said Kennedy. "That being stated, I can say that the US military has been helping the South Vietnamese military in the training and transportation of their troops which includes the use of helicopters. It is common sense that our advisors cannot train South Vietnamese pilots and aircrews without flying with them."

Hanoi, North Vietnam

Sipping tea on the patio of the Politburo headquarters, Le Duan sat with General Giap. Giap has fallen out of favor with many of the Politburo members when Ho Chi Minh stepped aside to allow Le Duan to ascend to Party Chairman. But Le Duan did not get to his current position as the most powerful leader in North Vietnam without using his head. He knew Giap was a great military strategist, and he took advantage of that resource whenever he thought necessary no matter what the other members thought. "General, the Americans have started using helicopters to assist the South Vietnamese military against the Viet Cong," said Le Duan.

"Yes, I read the report," said Giap.

"Should we be concerned?"

"Yes, but not overly. Like the French, the Americans will bring their superior air power to bear against our forces. Helicopters are a dangerous extension of those forces. But like all weapons given time we can develop strategies to defeat them."

"It's the speed at which they can now bring their troops and reinforcements to battle that concerns me most."

"As it should. But their mobility will not make up for their lack of esprit de corps. In whatever manner they are carried into battle, the ARVN troops are poorly led, and they know it. It is demoralizing. The helicopters will be seen as a great advantage and temporarily boost their morale. We should bide our time and look for an opportunity to soundly defeat their helicopters in battle. When that happens, it will crush the spirit of the South Vietnamese troops and their leaders. The novelty of their helicopters will fade like a voice in the wind, and they will once again be faced with the reality of the situation – the revolution will not stop until our country and all Vietnamese are reunited under the communist flag. That is the unstoppable force, not their helicopters."

January 10, 1962 –Vung Tau Port, South Vietnam

After months of aerial spray tests in the Central Highlands which had been judged a success, the US military was ready to fully deploy the use of defoliants throughout South Vietnam. JFK was still cautious but could not come up with a reason not to implement the program. He signed off on the generals' plans and Operation Ranch Hand went forward.

Agent Orange was most effective against the South Vietnamese stubborn vegetation. The defoliant was sprayed by USAF aircraft for several miles along Highway 15 leading from the port of Vung Tau to Bien Hoa Air Base northeast of Saigon.

Kennedy had hoped to keep the use of American defoliants in South Vietnam a secret. But Diem's press secretary announced that US herbicides were being used to reduce vegetation along highways through the country. The cat was out of the bag and there would be no putting it back in as tons of the chemical were shipped to South Vietnam in 55-gallon containers marked with an orange band.

FARM GATE

January 13, 1962 - Bien Hoa Air Base, South Vietnam

It was the dry season in South Vietnam with plenty of sunshine and blue skies. The maintenance crew of the 4400th Combat Crew Training Squadron (CCTS) was busy reassembling their aircraft that had been airlifted by C-124 Globemasters from their airbase at Hurlburt Field in Florida to Bien Hoa Air Base in South Vietnam.

Through NSAM 104, President Kennedy had ordered McNamara to introduce American aircraft and aircrews into South Vietnam for purpose of training the South Vietnamese Air Force in close air support missions.

The package that consisted of eight T-28 Trojan fighters and four SC-47 transports was code-named Operation Farm Gate. One hundred fifty-five American volunteers supported the aircraft. Although their official mission was to train South Vietnamese aircrews, it wouldn't take long before the American pilots were flying combat missions to support ARVN ground forces against the Viet Cong. There was always a South Vietnamese air cadet around that could be grabbed at a moment's notice and forced to sit in the backseat as a trainee. Farm Gate was far more extensive and critical than a simple training operation.

Originally designed as a training aircraft, the single-engine T-28s had a long, spacious cockpit that seated two. With a 1,200 lb. load capacity, the Trojans also had six hardpoints under the wings that allowed the aircrews to switch up the aircraft's armament depending on the mission requirements. Although they were far slower than a jet, the fixed-wing aircraft were versatile and easy to fly. They were ideal for close air support missions.

Later in the year, the 4400th would receive B-26 bombers that were being rebuilt in Taiwan for deployment in South Vietnam. Considering the threat the Viet Cong posed, 4400th CCTS wasn't an overwhelming fighting force, but it was the first American Air Force squadron to be deployed in South

Vietnam. Like a camel slowly edging its way into a tent, America was entering the war.

The American airmen of Farm Gate were not impressed with the Bien Hoa facilities. Originally built by the French during the Indochina War, the old colonial airfield was in bad shape. There was only one runway covered with steel plates that needed constant repair, especially during the wet season. The maintenance buildings were dilapidated and leaked constantly during the frequent thundershowers. The airfield was off-limits to the press. The American aircrews had been instructed to keep a low profile and not answer any questions posed by foreign journalists when off-base.

In the beginning, the air commandos as they were called technically belonged to the Air Force section of the Military Assistance Advisory Group (MAAG.) But as the American presence expanded, the air commandos eventually became the USAF in Vietnam. With the additional American aircraft, the airbase at Bien Hoa grew dramatically in size adding more runways, maintenance hangars, and administrative buildings.

As they worked assembling their planes, the Farm Gate aircrews saw some of the South Vietnamese soldiers wearing bush hats like those worn by the Australian soldiers. With a wider brim, the hats protected the face, neck, and ears from the sun and rain when needed. The bush hats were superior to the baseball-style hats that were issued by the US Air Force. Many of the commandos purchased and wore their own bush hats ignoring the uniform regulations. The longer a soldier was in-country, the more likely they were to disregard other uniform regulations and work without shirts or even pants.

Born in Boulder, Colorado, First Lieutenant Dean Adams was among the first group of Farm Gate pilots to arrive in South Vietnam. Few had seen combat including Adams. He, like the others, was anxious to test his skill against the enemy. He was also frightened although he wouldn't admit it, especially to his commander. He didn't want anything to prevent him from flying his first combat mission. He figured his nerves would eventually settle down once he got a few missions under his belt.

His hands would shake with tremors when he held them out straight. He kept them in his pockets whenever possible. Alcohol seemed to help. It took his mind off the danger. Of course, he couldn't fly if he drank, so he kept a pint of whiskey in a flask that he hid in his locker. It was against regulations, but he didn't care. His commander never performed inspections of the flight officers. They were considered gentlemen and supposed to be responsible for themselves. When he returned from training missions and his tremors were at their worst, he would sneak a slug and they would go away. He saw the occasional drink as self-medicating and harmless.

While at Hurlburt Field in Florida, the 4400th CCTS had trained extensively on night navigation and close air support. This made them the ideal unit for South Vietnam where the Viet Cong preferred to attack their targets under the cloak of darkness. The VC relied on stealth and surprise.

The American aircrews were tasked with protecting the South Vietnam hamlets and ARVN outposts. The outposts were set up between the imaginary border that divided the Viet Cong bases and the South

Vietnamese hamlets. This forced the Viet Cong to attack and destroy the outposts before they could assault the hamlets. If the VC bypassed an outpost and were forced to retreat if things didn't go well, they risked being cut off by the ARVN troops within the outpost. It was similar to the medieval technique of building small castles in strategic locations.

For Vietnam, the 4400th had been experimenting with night flares. Even though American forces had used flares extensively during night fighting in Korea, the techniques had not been documented well and the Americans were forced to start from scratch. The SC-47s were assigned the role of flare ship, while the T-28 were to be used for nocturnal air-to-ground assaults. Between sunset and sunrise, one SC-47 and two T-28s were loaded for bear and always on call year-round.

Outside Tay Ninh, South Vietnam

A South Vietnamese outpost was stationed on a hill eight miles northeast of Tay Ninh. It was a hodge-podge of leftover blockhouses built by the French during the Indochina War and connected by thousands of double and triple layer sandbags that formed the perimeter. Thirty feet in front of the sandbags were several layers of barbed wire with tin can noise-makers attached. Beyond the barbed wire were several layers of anti-personnel mines. There were nine light machine guns placed around the perimeter trenches and three .50 Cal heavy machine guns positioned on top of the blockhouses allowing a wide field of fire. Artillery was seven 60mm mortars, three 81mm mortars, and a smattering of 57mm recoilless rifles mounted on tripods. The ARVN battalion station there also had two rusty World War II flamethrowers that nobody was brave enough to operate. Most of the battalion was outfitted with M1 Garand rifles with their eight-round internal bloc clips. It was an accurate and reliable weapon if well maintained. In addition, many of the sergeants were armed with Thompson machine guns. Everyone had three or four grenades and knew how to use them correctly. Like most battalions, they were well led by their non-commissioned officers but that was as far as it went. Most of the officers were politically motivated, seemingly overconfident, and did not have strong leadership skills. They mostly sat back and watched the battle unfold from afar, never putting themselves in danger. They were too important to the units they commanded to engage with the enemy.

The ARVN troops were far from home and the hillside was dangerous, especially at night which was fast approaching. Everyone wanted to fight for their country, but few wanted to fight for the current government. Diem and his family had a bad reputation of interfering with the military and giving promotions only to those they felt were loyal to Diem over the country. That did not sit well with the men in the trenches and blockhouses.

The Viet Cong had surrounded the outpost and were taking potshots from the far-off tree line to keep the ARVN pinned down and to prevent any from escaping. Their weapons were even more eclectic and obsolete than the ARVN forces. Many of the rifles were captured from the French toward the end of the Indochina War, while others were captured from the ARVN and South Vietnamese militia. Still, others came from the Soviets and the Chinese. Many of the rifles had been captured by Mao's communist forces from the national forces of Chiang Kai-Shek and were turned over to the VC as part of an overall military aid package. The VC's weapons were also portable and could be easily carried to and from the battle without slowing down the troops. Knee mortars were supplied to every unit as portable artillery. More like grenade launchers, the knee mortars lacked the punch of a regular mortar but could be very effective when the VC grabbed the enemy "by the belt." Little of the ammunition they carried was interchangeable. Which meant that when their ammunition was gone, their weapon became a club or a spear if they were lucky enough to have had a bayonet.

As the sun set, everyone inside the outpost knew the VC would be coming soon. There was no way to know how many or what they had in the way of armament. The VC followed Mao's doctrine of only attacking when they knew they could win and that the assaulting force needed to be two to three times the size of the outpost defenders. The tension in the ARVN was visible in their twisted expressions and sullen mode. Nobody wanted to talk. It was going to be a bloody battle and many on both sides would not survive the night.

Bien Hoa Air Base, South Vietnam

When the call came of a South Vietnamese outpost being under attack by Viet Cong forces, Adams was pumped. It would be his first combat mission. The fact that the battle would be at night didn't affect him. His training took over as he jumped into his aircraft and prepared for takeoff. His co-pilot, a South Vietnamese cadet, climbed in after Adams and did as he was instructed… nothing. Once strapped in, he was ordered not to touch anything. Just sit back and enjoy the flight.

Adams was the wingman of Captain Tillman, a veteran pilot, and the flight commander. Tillman also had a cadet as a co-pilot and had given him the same instructions… touch nothing. Neither of the cadets spoke understandable English and were therefore useless during battle.

As they prepared for takeoff, the aircrew of the SC-47 made a quick check of their cargo – sixty MK-6 magnesium flares. The MK-6 was housed in a three-foot aluminum cylinder filled on one end with twenty-five pounds. of magnesium and a parachute inside the other end. A steel cable lanyard was used to activate a five to thirty-second delay fuse right before the flare was thrown out the cargo door by the loadmaster or another crew member. It was a simple system. Once the flare canister had dropped a few hundred feet, the parachute would deploy slowing the device's descent and the fuse would ignite the magnesium producing a star-shaped brilliance above the intended target. The flares were used in pairs and dropped seven seconds apart. This eliminated the harsh shadows that could be confusing to the attack aircraft pilots.

The flares only lasted two to three minutes before burning out or landing on the ground. This meant that the follow-on attack aircraft had to identify their targets and fire their ordinance within a very limited time window. Coordination between the aircrews on the flareship and the fighter pilots was essential. The ground forces also played a big role in identifying where the enemy was positioned. The obvious problem with all of this was that the ground forces were Vietnamese, and the aircrews and pilots were

American. Neither spoke the other's language very well making communication all but impossible. Some of the cadets that were often abducted by the aircrews and pilots were helpful in this regard if they had English skills. But the cadets soon learned that admitting or demonstrating one's language skills was almost always a guaranteed method of being coerced into volunteering for the night assault missions. Most concealed their language skills from the Americans and their commanding officers. Although some South Vietnamese cadets felt it was their duty to their country to help the Americans in defeating the enemy. Unfortunately, they often did not last long.

The other problem with air-ground coordination was the radios themselves. The radios carried by the South Vietnamese units were usually World War II or Korean War hand-me-downs. The American aircraft were outfitted with more up-to-date radios that operated on high-frequency FM and had coding capabilities. This meant that any mission that involved radio communication with the South Vietnamese ground forces required a trip to the airbase quartermaster who always kept a few of the obsolete radio handsets in stock. The problem was that there were never enough to go around, and the quartermaster was stingy on issuing them to the aircrews. The standard procedure was to only issue one handset to the flareship aircrew who would then need to relay communications from the South Vietnamese units on the ground to the attack aircraft. To make matters worse, once in the American's hands, there was little chance the obsolete radios would be returned. Instead, the Americans insisted that the handsets fell out of their aircraft while dispensing flares. As time went on, FM handsets became rarer than a virgin Go-Go dancer.

Tay Ninh Outpost, South Vietnam

As darkness descended, the VC stepped up their attack. The first assaults were non-committal, designed to test the ARVN defenses and look for possible points of entry. The VC would charge up the hill, but when the fire became too heavy, they would hit the dirt and slink back the way they came. The night was long, and they had plenty of time to overrun the outpost.

Next came a charge in force from two directions. One charge was meant to break through while the other was meant to distract their enemy and divert some of its troops to the opposite side of the outpost. The diversion charge would hit the dirt and dig in once the fire from the outpost became overwhelming.

Before the assaults began, the VC sent in their Bo Doi Dac Cong - special force soldiers known as "sappers" to the Americans. The sappers were trained to penetrate the South Vietnamese defenses and create a path for the follow-on troops. They often stripped down to only a loincloth to reduce the amount of clothing that could get snagged in the barbed wire and trigger the noisemaker tin cans. Crude wire cutters were their weapon of choice and could be used to cut the barbed wire. The wire cutters could also be used to cut any electrical wires leading to explosive devices outside the perimeter. Few carried any other weapon beyond a knife. Their job was to penetrate defenses, not engage with the enemy. They smeared mud on the skin as camouflage. They used natural objects in the landscape for cover and belly crawled for 100 yards or more to reach their objective undetected. They were patient beyond reason and would take hours to inch forward with slight moves as they neared the perimeter.

At times, follow-on sappers would bring RPGs, grenades, or demolition explosives with them to use right before the assault to eliminate key enemy positions. Designed to penetrate the perimeter, then bring in a small group of heavily armed sappers to attack the interior of the position, it was known as the "blooming lotus" tactic. The sappers were the bravest and most dedicated soldiers in their unit. They were VC elite and the ARVN feared them.

When the assaults began, the ARVN would use their mortars to launch parachute flares beyond the perimeter. The floating flares were a double-edged sword that blinded both sides with their bright illumination and gave the battlefield an eerie feel with long shadows that at times... moved. Muzzle flashes from rifles and machine guns also illuminated the area just in front of a firing position. Shadows performed a macabre dance between the bursts of light. As a flare burned out, the shadows would often flip to the opposite side like some kind of evil magic that allowed the enemy to shift position instantaneously.

Even from a distance, the pilots in the approaching aircraft could see the battle raging with tracer rounds and explosions. The SC-47 was the first to go in. It made a pass over the outpost to identify the positions of friendly forces and those of the enemy. It wasn't easy, but the placement of the flares was critical. When placed correctly, the shadows created from the flares would cancel each other allowing the pilots in the fighters to see the battlefield more clearly. The flares were transported in aluminum canisters that were shed just before deployment to reduce the chance of a rouge flare being accidentally ignited inside the aircraft. Standing in an open cargo doorway with a safety strap wrapped around his waist, the loadmaster removed the flare from its transport canister, pulled the steel lanyard, and tossed the tube out the doorway. Each pair of flares were dropped at 1,200 feet giving them a three-minute burn before hitting the ground. It wasn't much time. Once it dropped its first set of flares, the SC-47 would fly in a racetrack-shaped oval, dropping more flares with each pass over the battlefield.

Following his flight commander, Adams was not surprised by the bright light of the flares. He had been trained to look away from the brilliance to keep his eyes somewhat dilated. Tillman radioed informing him that he would make the first assault and that Adams would follow. It was standard procedure, but when flying at night with a strong possibility of collision it was always better to take extra precautions. What did surprise Adams were the tracer rounds rising from the battlefield as the fighters approached their target. He watched Tillman's aircraft as it was surrounded by pulses of orange light. Even though it was mostly from small weapons, the anti-aircraft fire seemed inescapable. Tillman dropped his two 250 lbs. bombs on the enemy positions then pulled up and turned his aircraft around for another pass. They exploded below with two bright flashes.

It was Adams's turn. As Tillman's aircraft moved away, the anti-aircraft fire shifted to Adams's plane as it approached the enemy lines. Adams was mesmerized by the tracer rounds until two punched a couple of holes in his right-wing tip. Adams couldn't believe it — someone was trying to kill him. He froze. His hands started shaking. He felt like he was falling and there was nothing he could do about it.

The cadet in the backseat shouted angrily in Vietnamese. Adams snapped out of it, pulled his eyes away from the bullet holes, and shouted back to the cadet in English, "Shut the fuck up."

His aircraft was already halfway over the battlefield. His hands were still shaking when he pickled his bombs, then pulled up and turned to follow Tillman. The bombs dropped and exploded in the surrounding forest. A complete miss. Adams cursed as he watched over his shoulder. The cadet cursed and lectured him in Vietnamese. Adams was embarrassed as he considered what Tillman would think. He was a failure.

Tillman came around for his second pass as the flareship dropped another round of flares. This time he released two canisters of napalm. Both hit their target sending a long tongue of fire through the enemy lines.

Adams followed with his pass. He was even more nervous than the first run and his hands continued to shake. He tried to ignore it as he aimed at the enemy lines below. Tillman's napalm was still burning and illuminated the entire battlefield. Adams could see where the enemy was advancing toward the outpost. He pickled his armament and the napalm canisters dropped. He too had a direct hit as both canisters spread their sticky fire across the enemy. He howled with joy as he pulled up his aircraft and turned to follow Tillman. The cadet reached around the front seat and patted Adams on the back of his helmet.

Stunned by so many of their comrades burning to death, the Viet Cong broke off their attack and retreated into the tree line.

The South Vietnamese in the outpost shouted praise to the heavens as they watched the enemy retreat.

Tillman and Adams made a final run using their machine guns to strafe the fleeing enemy. Adams's hands had stopped shaking making his gunfire more accurate. With their armament empty, the pilots banked their planes and headed for home... victorious.

On the ground, the ARVN troops inside the outpost were drained emotionally. They were relieved to live another day and hopefully see their families again. Many soldiers broke down and cried. Nobody thought less of them. Any battle won was reason to celebrate but for the moment a grateful prayer was all they could muster. There was still work to be done. They needed to repair the damage done to the perimeter defenses by the sappers and tend to the wounded of which there were many. When finished, they would eat then sleep as their guards watched over the tree line waiting for the next attack.

After several more night assaults were broken by the American aircraft, the Viet Cong began to flee the battlefield on the first sign of flares dropped by aircraft. Even without the accompaniment of fighters, an SC-47 could put the fear into the enemy and break off night assaults. The Americans and the South Vietnamese were learning how to defeat the Viet Cong.

But the Viet Cong had a tactic that not even the Americans could defeat – self-criticism. After every battle, the Viet Cong would gather, and each soldier would confess how they could have performed better.

This self-criticism was taken seriously, and the commanders were required to write reports on what happened and how to improve. The Viet Cong leaders would examine the reports and suggestions to come up with new ways to defeat the enemy. It was an effective way of defeating even the deadliest enemy tactics and weapons. Self-criticism was the backbone of the Viet Cong's rapid tactical advances on the battlefield. The VC were very good at learning from their mistakes.

Saigon, South Vietnam

The more he thought about it, the more Coyle felt like a complete ass at the way he had treated Janet when he was back in the states. After all, it takes two to tango and she hadn't forced him to dance. He hated the idea that she didn't trust him enough to confide in him about her situation. But then he remembered who he was in the days before the war. He was reckless and self-absorbed, not the kind of qualities women looked for in potential fathers.

He thought about writing a letter of apology but knew she would see that as a coward's way out. He needed to call her and straighten things out. It wasn't something he looked forward to, but it would be good to hear her voice. He could tell what she was feeling in the way she spoke and if she truly forgave him. Saigon was eleven hours ahead of Washington D.C. He thought it best to reach her in the early evening, so he called at 6 AM his time. Her phone rang four times before she picked up. "Janet, it's Coyle. Please don't hang up," said Coyle over the phone.

"I'm not gonna hang up, Tom. I know the news of you having children was an unwelcomed surprise and you were upset," said Janet.

"It wasn't unwelcomed, but it was a surprise."

"Tom, let's be honest with one another."

"Alright. It was unwelcomed at that moment. But I have had time to think about it and…"

"And what?"

"I keep thinking about the fact that I have a son."

"…and a daughter."

"Yes, of course… and a daughter. You never told me their names."

"Scott and Karen."

"Do they look anything like me?"

"They do. I can send you their pictures if you like."

"I'd like that. You know this is gonna take some getting used to."

"Yes, for all of us."

"So, you haven't told them… about me?"

"Not yet. It's gonna be a shock."

"I'll say."

"You're not helping."

"No, I suppose I ain't. Janet, I'm sorry about the way I spoke with you the last time we talked. But I wasn't wrong. I don't think I should be the one to talk to him about deploying to Vietnam."

"Why not? You're his father."

"Well, for starters… I think he's doing the honorable thing in serving his country."

"I do too, but he doesn't have to do it in Vietnam."

"Yeah, but it's like you said… they need helicopter pilots. And when you're in the military, you go where you're needed the most."

"Don't tell me about the military, Tom Coyle. I sacrificed a father and a husband to the military. I've paid my dues. They have no right to take my son."

"I understand how you feel, but I'm not going to talk him out of it."

"It's too late anyway. He's already been deployed."

"He's in Vietnam?"

"Yes."

"Alright. I will watch out for him the best I can while he's over here."

The phone was silent for a long moment, then Janet said, "It's not what I had hoped for, but I suppose that's something. You'll keep him safe?"

"Janet, it's a war and he's a soldier, but I'll do my best."

Bien Hoa Air Base, South Vietnam

Having received his monthly ration allotment, Adams shopped in the base PX with several other members of his squadron. Standing with his back to the other officers, he held up his hand and saw that it was trembling. He didn't smoke, so he traded his cigarette chits for heavy alcohol chits and purchased three bottles of Johnny Walker Red. "Are we having a party or are you gonna drink all of that yourself?" said one of Adams's roommates.

"Ain't none of your damned business what I do with it," said Adams, annoyed and a little embarrassed.

"Relax, Lieutenant. I was just kidding. You can drink yourself to death for all I care."

Outside the PX, Adams purchased a block of ice from a Vietnamese vendor. With the ice block under one arm and the bag of liquor under the other, Adams headed back to his living quarters.

The engineers had assembled several rows of Quonset huts on one side of the airbase for the aircrews. Originally designed in World War I, the Quonset huts were made from corrugated metal with plywood walls and doors on the ends. They were cheap and quick to build, allowing the engineers to assemble the required number of barracks within weeks.

Adams would have preferred a tent with flaps for better ventilation, but like most things in the military, he wasn't given a choice. The Quonset huts provided little privacy but at least the officers were given more space between their bunks than the enlisted men.

In his quarters, Adams used a KA-BAR to break off chunks of ice and slipped them into a heavy-based glass he had purchased in Saigon a few days earlier. He opened one of the bottles and poured himself three fingers. After taking a long pull of the scotch, he looked down at his hand and saw the trembling dissipate. He felt better. More relaxed. Less anxious. He slowed to sipping the cool, caramel-colored liquid as he sat on the edge of his bunk.

Each carrying a case of beer, his roommates returned from the PX. "Are you okay?" said a roommate.

"Oh hell, yeah. Just a little on edge," said Adams.

"I hear, ya. Been a chaotic couple of weeks."

"Yep. Chaotic. Nothing a Johnny Walker Red can't handle. Do you want some ice for your beer? I bought a block."

"We don't wanna hog your ice."

"It ain't gonna last long in this heat anyway. Best make use of it before it melts."

"Alright."

The officers moved to his bunk and placed their beer cans on the ice to cool them down. They joked and talked freely with one another. Alcohol did that… took the edge off.

Lam Dong Province, South Vietnam

The aircrew of a C-47 dropped thousands of PsyOps leaflets over the highland villages near the district capital of Bao Loc. The leaflets were cartoons showing the communist forces burning villages and poisoning rice crops. The leaflets were not a convincing argument, but they did sow doubt among the villagers.

After dumping several boxes out the cargo door, the crewman looked down and saw the flashes from a dual-mounted .50-cal machine gun firing from below. As he turned back to his fellow crewmen, the large bullets ripped through the cargo deck, hitting him in the crotch, and almost split him in half. He fell dead on the deck. More bullets ripped through the aircraft cockpit killing the pilot, co-pilot, and flight engineer. Both engines were hit and caught fire. The aircraft tilted to one side and headed for the ground.

Bien Hoa Air Base, South Vietnam

Adams was asleep when Captain Tillman, his flight commander, entered the Quonset hut and kicked the base of his bunk. "What the hell are you doing still sleeping, Lieutenant?" said Tillman.

"What?" said Adams groggy and hungover.

"Have you been drinking, Lieutenant?"

"No, sir. I must have overslept."

"Well, get your ass up and get your gear. We're flying escort for a rescue mission. Grab yourself a cadet and meet me on the flight line."

As the captain left, Adams jumped out of bed. His head was spinning, and he had to sit back down for a moment. As the adrenaline kicked in, he gathered his wits and the spinning stopped. He was going into battle. He rose again, put on his flight suit, grabbed his gear, and headed out the door.

Tan Son Nhut Air Base, South Vietnam

Coyle had no idea what Scott looked like when he drove into Tan Son Nhut airbase. He could see the helicopters stationed in the distance and drove toward them. He parked and asked a passing corporal where he could find Lieutenant Dickson. The corporal pointed to one of the helicopters and moved off. Coyle could see the helicopter's aircrew prepping the helicopter. He was about to meet his son and felt weak in the knees. He had played this moment repeatedly in his mind throughout the previous night in a fit of sleeplessness. He thought the rehearsal would make things easier. It didn't. He walked toward the helicopter.

He saw a young man in a flight suit that looked familiar. It was like looking in a mirror. The closer he got, the more the resemblance took hold. It was his son. He was sure of it. "Scott Dickson?" said Coyle.

"Yeah. Who are you?" said Scott turning around to see Coyle.

"I'm Tom Coyle. I knew your mother. I mean... I know your mother."

"That's nice, but I'm kinda busy right now."

"I can see that. Are you heading out?"

"What are you doing here, Mr. Coyle?"

"I work here. I'm a pilot."

"Where's your uniform?"

"I don't wear a uniform."

"You're a civilian?"

"Not exactly."

"Look, I don't have time for guessing games. I have a lot of work to do before takeoff."

"I understand. Maybe we could sit down for a drink when you return."

"I'm not much of a drinker."

"Well, then… maybe dinner… or just sit down and talk."

"Sure. But I don't know how long I'll be."

"I can wait."

"It might be a long wait."

"I know. I'll wait."

"Suit yourself. Now, if you will excuse me?"

"Sure. Good luck."

"Thanks."

Coyle started to move off, when a captain approached and said to the aircrew, "Alright. Let's wrap it up. Our escort is inbound, and we got an aircrew to rescue."

Coyle stopped and watched as two Trojan T-28s, nicknamed "Tangos" approached the airbase. He was surprised when one of the fighters broke from formation and swooped low aligning itself with the runway. "Why is he landing?" said Coyle to the captain as he passed him.

"Who's landing?" said the captain looking around and spotting the aircraft as it lowered its landing gear. "What the hell is he doing?"

The fighter landed, taxied over to the helicopter, and stopped. Adams opened his cockpit canopy and vomited on the side of the aircraft. "Well, that can't be good," said Coyle.

The second Tango landed and parked next to the first. Tillman climbed down from the cockpit and marched over to Adams who was holding his stomach. "What in God's name do you think you're doing, Lieutenant?" said Tillman.

"Sorry, Commander. It must have been something I ate," said Adams. "It's those damned food carts outside the main gate."

"Bullshit. I can smell the alcohol."

"No, sir. It's food poisoning."

"Food poisoning takes hold two hours after you eat. If you weren't feeling up to it, you should have told me before we took off, Lieutenant. Now, you've jeopardized the mission."

"I'm sorry, sir. I thought I could handle it."

"You thought wrong, Lieutenant."

Adams vomited again splattering on Tillman's boots.

"Don't matter what he thought, does it, Captain?" said Coyle moving up beside Tillman. "He can't fly like that."

"No, he can't. Get your ass to the base hospital, Lieutenant."

"Yes, sir," said Adams moving off.

Coyle turned to Tillman and said, "You're in a bit of pickle, ain't you?"

"Yeah, I am. It'll take too much time to get another pilot here. I guess we'll just go it alone."

"Probably not the best idea."

"You got a better one?"

"I'm afraid I do. I'll take his place and fly the mission."

"Like hell, you will. You ain't in my air force."

"No. Not anymore. But we're on the same side and right now you got a downed aircrew that needs help. Those are our men out there. Do you really want to stand on formality?"

"Have you ever flown in combat before?"

"Yeah. I have. Pacific War and Indochina."

"What about this aircraft?"

Coyle lied, "Yeah. I'm checked out on it."

"Where?"

"Subic Bay."

"Subic Bay don't have any T-28s."

"Yeah, they do," said Coyle, bluffing.

Tillman was unsure. "Look, Captain. You need me. I can do this," said Coyle.

"If you crash, it's my ass."

"If I crash there won't be any inquiry. The US government will deny I even exist. The whole mission will get buried."

"Are you one of Lansdale's spooks?"

"If I was, I couldn't admit it publicly. Now, could I?"

"I suppose not."

"Look, if you get your ass shot down, that helicopter and the aircrew they rescue are gonna be defenseless. So, how about letting me be your wingman... just in case?"

Tillman considered for a long moment, "What about your co-pilot?"

"Leave 'em here. He ain't any use anyway."

"Regulations say you've got to have a South Vietnamese in the aircraft at all times."

"Well, we ain't exactly going by regulations now, are we?"

"No, we ain't."

"Daylight's burning."

"Right. You stay close and do as I say."

"You're the flight commander."

"Damned right I am."

Coyle and Tillman moved toward their aircraft. Coyle motioned for the South Vietnamese cadet to stay behind and took his parachute. He glanced over at the armament under the wings and memorized the weapon on each pilon position. Closest in were the machine guns, then the two bombs, and finally two rocket pods. Nearby the helicopter spun up its rotors.

Coyle climbed into the cockpit and strapped in. It had been years since he had been in the cockpit of a fighter. He had sworn he would never fight again. But that was before he had a son that was in danger. He took a moment to familiarize himself with the instruments. He had never flown a T-28, but it was designed to be a trainer and the controls were simple. The armament selector was different than what he was used to, but he was sure he could figure it out before they were on station.

The two T-28's cranked up their engines and pulled onto the runway. A few moments later, they took off. The helicopter followed. All three aircraft headed north toward Bao Loc.

It didn't take long to reach the crash site. Black smoke rose from the forest canopy revealing the downed aircraft in the distance. Tillman radioed Coyle, "I figure the anti-aircraft emplacement should be between the crash site and Bao Loc where they were dropping the leaflets. I'm going to take a look. You stay with the rescue team. Over."

"Roger that," said Coyle.

Tillman's aircraft peeled off and headed northeast over the forest-covered hills. Coyle's plane stayed with the helicopter. As they came closer to the black column of smoke, Coyle sped ahead of the helicopter to draw any potential enemy fire from the ground. There was none that he could detect. He passed the crash site and looked down at the wreckage. It was a bad crash with a large debris field. The smoke was too thick to spot any survivors, but Coyle was not hopeful. He radioed back to the approaching helicopter and began scouting for a landing site close to the crash site. He spotted a clearing less than a quarter of a mile from the crash and radioed back the location.

Several miles to the northeast, Tillman was passing over a sparsely tree-covered area of the highlands. There had been no signs of enemy anti-aircraft. It was one thing for the Viet Cong to take potshots at a weaponless transport plane and quite another to shoot at a well-armed fighter. His main concern was preventing the Viet Cong from firing on the helicopter once they had rescued the downed aircrew. Then he saw it – a stream of orange spotter rounds rising in front of him. He banked the plane hard to avoid the bullets but caught two in his left wing. He was fortunate. The bullets punched through the end of the wing without hitting any hydraulics or rupturing the wing fuel tank. He followed the trail of bullets down to a group of trees. Somewhere down there below the canopy was a gun crew manning a twin-mount machine gun.

He swung his aircraft around as he descended. Hugging the tops of the trees, he increased his speed and aligned the aircraft with what he thought was the location of the anti-aircraft gun. He punched up his rockets on the armament selector. With rockets, he could kill at a safe distance. He wasn't going to give them a second shot at his aircraft. There was nothing fair about it and he was okay with that. Pilots hated anti-aircraft gunners and loaders. As he approached the grove of trees, he unleashed his rockets. When the rockets made contact, they exploded in a hail of shrapnel and fire.

Although there was no way to know for sure the anti-aircraft emplacement had been destroyed without visually inspecting the site on the ground, Tillman felt confident that the Viet Cong had been killed. He passed over the burning grove of trees without seeing any tracer rounds rising. Tillman wasn't a vengeful person but felt it was important that the Viet Cong were punished for shooting down a South Vietnamese aircraft. Having silenced the threat, he banked his aircraft, gained altitude, and headed back in the direction of the crash site.

As the helicopter landed in the clearing near the crash site, Coyle flew in a wide arc using the crash site as the center of the circle. He glanced down at the forest below looking for the enemy moving toward the helicopter or downed C-47. He would be the early warning indicator of any potential attack during the rescue.

A nine-man air commando team with two medics exited the helicopter as the wheels touched down in the long grass. The commandos formed a defensive perimeter. Once they were sure the helicopter was not under any immediate threat, six commandos and the two medics disappeared into the trees leaving three commandos to protect the chopper.

Sitting in the cockpit, staring out at the wall of trees that surrounded them, Scott reached down to the machine gun by his seat just to make sure it was available if needed. Strapped into his seat, he felt exposed with nothing but the windshield to protect him and the flight commander sitting next to him.

The rescue team moved quickly but cautiously through the forest. It had been over an hour since the mayday message broadcast by the C-47 had been received. There was little doubt the Viet Cong would close in on the crash site hoping to capture the survivors. It was a race to see who got there first.

Fifteen minutes later, the rescue team reached the crash site. If there was a Viet Cong ambush waiting for them, it was most likely staged in the woods around the crash site. The ground and debris were charred with some pieces of the aircraft still burning and others smoldering. The haze obscured much of wreckage and surrounding vegetation. It was a catastrophic crash with the plane's fuselage torn into large chunks that had toppled through the forest until they were stopped by a tree or boulder. There was no movement that the air commandos and medics could detect. That wasn't a good sign. The air commandos formed a defensive perimeter while the medics searched for survivors.

They found four of the aircrew still strapped to their seats in what remained of the cockpit. Their bodies blackened and smoldered. Two more of the aircrew, two South Vietnamese soldiers, and a cadet were scattered across the debris field. All were dead.

There were no survivors. The medics showed little remorse. It was their job and they needed to keep their wits about them, especially with a potential enemy closing in. They checked the bodies for wounds caused by small-arms fire that would indicate the presence of a Viet Cong ground force. There were none. They had beaten the enemy to the site. The medics quickly loaded the corpses into body bags. They would not leave the fallen to be desecrated by the enemy. They expected the same treatment by their fellow air commandos if they ever died in the field themselves.

The job of carrying the bodies back through the forest would be arduous and time-consuming. The terrain was rough with lots of undergrowth to tangle the feet and twist ankles. Time was still a very real factor. Four of the air commandos stayed in place at the crash site, while two escorted the two medics carrying a body back to the helicopter. The air commandos could not help the medics since their hands needed to be free in case of any attack.

When the medics reached the helicopter, they informed the others that there were no survivors. It was a disappointment, to say the least. Rescuers always hoped for the best and planned for the worst. "Commander, if it's okay, I'd like to help carry the bodies back," said Scott unbuckling his harness.

"Good idea. Take as many of the crew that want to volunteer. The less time we are on the ground, the better," said the pilot.

Scott was joined by all the other aircrew volunteers as they made their way back to the crash site. Even with the extra help, it would still take several trips to bring back all the dead.

Coyle was joined by Tillman. They flew in formation patrolling the forest surrounding the crash site. They both could see the last of the body bags on the ground below. The recovery was almost done. Their luck had held out… almost. It was Tillman that spotted the Viet Cong company moving beneath the forest canopy. He radioed Coyle and the ground recovery team that a company-sized element was moving toward the crash site from the east. Tillman knew that the air commandos would not leave the dead even if it meant risking their lives. "We've got to buy them some time," said Tillman over the radio to Coyle. "I'm out of rockets. You make the first pass north to south. I'll follow with bombs. Over."

"Roger that," said Coyle.

Coyle banked his fighter then straightened out as he descended to make his rocket run. He fired everything he had in the rocket pod at the Viet Cong below. The forest exploded with balls of fire and smoke. The enemy slowed but didn't stop.

Next Tillman dropped his two 250 lbs. anti-personnel bombs. The earth shook from the explosions. Again, the Viet Cong slowed but continued toward the crash site.

The two aircraft turned for a second run. This time it was Coyle's turn to drop his bombs. The Viet Cong fired their weapons skyward as Coyle zoomed past releasing his bombs. One of his bombs landed near a grouping of Viet Cong blowing their bodies through the air. Tillman followed with a strafing pass. His under-the-wing machine guns only carried 100 rounds each and were emptied on his final run. He was weaponless. "I'm out," he said over the radio.

Coyle could see the air commandos, aircrew, and medics picking up the last of the body bags and moving away from the crash site. The air commandos were firing their weapons. They were in contact with the enemy.

Coyle lined up his aircraft and descended as close as he dared, his wings clipping the tops of several trees. The more horizontal the angle of fire, the more effective his machine guns would be against the enemy. Closing in, he fired his remaining ammunition. At 750 rounds per minute, it was less than ten seconds before his guns were empty.

Fortunately for the retreating recovery team, Coyle's aim was deadly accurate killing three Viet Cong and causing the enemy to recoil seeking cover. As if to scare away a rampaging beast, they fired wildly into the air as the fighter passed over them. It would only delay them for a few moments, but in a firefight, a few moments were an eternity.

The recovery team made good use of the time, falling back, and taking up new defensive positions. Then firing and falling back again. Each time driving the pursuing enemy to the ground.

The team was exhausted when they broke through the tree line and stumbled toward the helicopter, tripping, dropping the body bags, then picking them up, and continuing their escape. The air commandos fired the last of their ammunition at the enemy once again driving them to cover, buying time. Having listened to the firefight over the radio, the pilot already had the rotors at speed and was ready to lift off. Scott dropped the last body bag on the deck and climbed into the co-pilot's seat. On hearing that the last man was on board, the pilot lifted off the clearing, banked hard, and headed back to the airbase. "Bet that got your blood pumping," said the pilot.

Out of breath, Scott responded with a halfhearted nod. He looked out his side window as the two T-28's formed up next to the helicopter. It was the first time he realized that one of the pilots was the mysterious man named Coyle that he met at the airbase earlier that day. His curiosity was piqued.

Sitting in the cockpit of his fighter, Coyle looked down at his hand and saw that it was trembling. In all his years of combat and flying, that had never happened before. He wondered if he was losing his edge.

When the helicopter landed, the two T-28s turned to head back to their airbase. Coyle looked down and saw no sign of Scott. *It's probably better this way*, thought Coyle. He didn't want to appear weak when Scott found out who he was and why he hadn't made contact with him sooner. It was not going to be an easy conversion no matter when it happened. But Coyle was grateful it was not today.

Sitting in the helicopter cockpit, Scott watched the T-28s heading for the horizon. The stranger had probably saved his life, but why.

BETRAYAL BEGINS WITH TRUST

Saigon, South Vietnam

Cu's father was released after only a month in prison. As Pham had predicted, Luc revealed the name of another member of the political organization. He had been careful whom he chose. Not only did the person need to be an enemy of the people, but he also had to be believable as an enemy of the government.

Almost a year before being arrested Luc had been in a local restaurant having lunch with friends when he saw a tax collector extorting a bribe from the restaurant owner. Luc inquired as to the government official's name and knew that one day it might come in handy. He chose the man because he believed that there were probably others from which the tax collector had extorted bribes and that somebody had probably reported him to the police. Being reported to the police didn't mean that the man would be arrested. The police were just as corrupt as other government officials and would have accepted an appropriate bribe to keep the tax collector out of jail. But it did mean there were others out there that might collaborate Luc's submission. It worked and Luc was freed. Freedom after being arrested almost always came with strings attached. Luc was required to periodically report other members of the political party which he was happy to do whenever he discovered another enemy of the people.

As his father's troubles continued, Cu too started to be persecuted. As a family member of a dissident and an officer in the military, Cu was seen as a threat to the regime. It was standard procedure and well known that Diem and his family rewarded loyalty and punished infidelity, especially in the armed services. This extended to family members. Officers were often guilty by association. Diem and his family took no chances. Only those with the cleanest of records and family histories were promoted.

When Cu received a letter from his commanding officer denying his expected promotion to first lieutenant, he was dejected and fell into a depression. When word got out, Cu became a plague among fellow officers. Nobody wanted to be caught befriending a marked man for fear that the same fate would await them. He was an outcast. Most officers would resign, but Cu had no other career to fall back on and stayed in the military. As time went on, he became more resentful against Diem and his family.

Cu spoke with his father. Luc felt terrible that his political actions had hurt his son. That was not his intent. But he also knew that there was little future for his family or his country if Diem stayed in power. Cu revealed that he too felt the country was doomed unless something was done soon to change the government. "Do you have any idea on what to do?" said Luc.

"No. If I did I would do it," said Cu.

"What about a coup? Surely there must be others in the air force that feel the same way."

"Everyone is too afraid to speak their mind. Nhu has spies everywhere. Besides, a coup could take a year to plan and execute. I don't think our country can wait that long."

"Perhaps it doesn't need to."

"What do you mean?"

"We only need to remove Diem from the presidency."

"What about his family? They're worse than him."

"That is true. But maybe we could eliminate all of them in one swift strike."

"Are you talking about an aerial assault?"

"More like an aerial assassination of Diem and his entire family."

How would I do that?"

"Bomb the palace in the middle of the night while they are sleeping. Is it possible?"

"I don't know. It's never been tried before. In theory, it could work."

"Are there others that would join you?"

"It would be dangerous to ask. Even hinting at it could land me in prison."

"Perhaps someone close... that you trust?"

"Perhaps."

"Then you will consider it?"

"Of course. I'm not a coward, Father."

"I know that son."

"I need to think about it."

"If something is to be done, you must hurry. Our country grows weaker by the day. Ho Chi Minh is no fool. He will strike if he sees an opportunity. And if he does, all may be lost."

Bien Hoa Air Base, South Vietnam

When Cu returned to his airbase, he studied each of the men in his squadron and listened in on their conversations. The more he listened, the more he understood how untrustworthy they were. Cu didn't dare approach them about participating in his plan. There was one person he trusted above the other men in his squadron – his commander Quoc. Cu didn't know how Quoc felt about Diem and his family. Quoc was smart and kept his own counsel, never revealing his political views. Cu decided to wait until the right moment.

The right moment came a few weeks later as Cu was on his way to the mess hall. Quoc was on a payphone outside the mess hall. As Cu was passing through the doorway, he heard Quoc yelling at someone on the phone. Cu kept going inside but then moved to an open window near the payphones. He listened. Quoc was accusing the person he was talking to of sabotaging his military career. After a few moments, he slammed down the phone and walked into the mess hall. Cu waited a moment then fell in chow line behind Quoc. "Have you heard anything about our next mission?" said Cu.

"What?" said Quoc, angry.

"Our next mission... do you know where it might be?"

"Even if I did, I wouldn't tell you. You'll know when you need to just like all the others."

"Sorry. You're right. I just—"

"Just what?"

"I was passed over for a promotion. I want to get back out there and prove myself to command. Like you did."

"That has nothing to do with getting a promotion. You know that."

"I suppose I do. But I have to do something."

"Save your money for bribes and stay out of trouble."

"Is that what you did?"

"None of your damned business," said Quoc as he threw his tray on the floor and stormed out of the mess hall.

Cu knew Quoc well enough that it was only a matter of time before he would approach Cu with a quasi-apology. Being Cu's commander, Quoc could not apologize blatantly, but he would make sure that

Cu knew that he bore no ill will from their argument. Cu also knew that would be the best time to cautiously approach Quoc.

Several days later after flying another mission, Quoc asked to speak to Cu as they walked back to the officer's quarters. "The other day, when I lost my temper, I didn't mean anything by it. It was just a bad day. I probably would have barked at anyone that tried to talk to me. It was just bad timing," said Quoc.

"I understand," said Cu. "This has not been a great week for me either."

"What's wrong?"

"Politics."

"Your father?"

"Yes. He's been branded a troublemaker."

"And you are guilty by association?"

"Something like that. I think that may be why I didn't get my promotion."

"I know the feeling. I have a cousin that wants to join an opposition party against Diem. I fear it will end my career."

"A cousin?"

"It doesn't take much these days. Diem is more paranoid than ever and Nhu is feeding his fear."

"So, what are we supposed to do?"

"Nothing. Stay out of harm's way if possible. Avoid contact with troublemakers."

"That's not going to be easy. He's my father."

"Look, just keep your meetings out of the public eye where Nhu's spies can see you. Maybe go to the country for a family picnic or something. Spies are lazy when it comes to going outside of Saigon."

"All right. That is good advice. What are you going to do?"

"I'll do my best to talk my cousin out of it. But I don't think he is going to listen. He wants Diem and his family gone."

"And how do you feel about that?"

Quoc looked over at Cu as if wondering and said, "Are you a spy, Lieutenant?"

"No. Of course not. It's just that… your cousin is not wrong."

"What do you mean?"

"Are you a spy, commander?"

"No."

"I mean… Diem and his family are difficult at times."

"Now there is an understatement."

Cu decided to stop there and not push any further. "I need to write a letter to my grandmother… if that's okay."

"Of course."

Cu saluted his commander and moved off.

A week later, Cu conveniently ran into Quoc when he was walking across the base. "Did you see the article in the American magazine *Newsweek*?" said Cu showing Quoc the article.

"Have you been carrying that thing around?" said Quoc.

"No. I was just reading it. I use it to practice my English."

"That's a big waste of time. What does it say?"

"The Americans are questioning Diem's commitment to the war. They are especially critical of his brother Nhu and Madame Nhu."

"That's not surprising."

"Really?"

"Look everyone knows that Diem and his family are more interested in power than persecuting the war."

"I agree. But the fact that the Americans just come out and say it. I mean… don't you find that strange?"

"It's not the Americans saying it. It's a magazine and magazines say lots of things. That doesn't mean they are right."

"But in this case, they are."

Quoc considered for a moment, then yanked the magazine out of Cu's hand and started reading. "You speak English?" said Cu.

"No. I read English. All the flight and maintenance manuals are in English. Now, shut up and let me read the damned article."

"Yes, Commander."

Cu once again moved off leaving Quoc to consider. "Hey, don't you want your magazine?" said Quoc.

"I can read it later, Commander," said Cu.

Cu continued feeding Quoc bits of information and questioning him cautiously about his beliefs. It was a very dangerous game. Cu knew that at any time, Quoc could turn him in to the authorities, and it would most likely end his career and maybe his life. Cu knew that he would never be 100% sure of Quoc's loyalties. There would always be a risk in including him in the operation. But Cu knew that the potential success of the mission would be vastly increased with Quoc's participation. Even though he was young, Quoc's experience in mission planning was vast. He had planned more than one hundred air assaults against the Viet Cong. Cu felt he needed someone with Quoc's experience.

After several more weeks, Cu decided it was time. He waited until Quoc was alone before approaching him as he performed his weekly inspection of the aircraft in his unit. Cu did his best to ensure that nobody else was listening when he said, "I think our country will not survive much longer with Diem and his family in charge. The Viet Cong are taking control of more and more territory in the South. Soon, only the big cities will remain. Then it is just a matter of time before all our defenses crumble."

"What is your point?" said Quoc slightly annoyed.

"I think... I think we should assassinate the president and his family."

Quoc stopped what he was doing, turned to Cu, and said, "Are you insane?"

"No. I mean... no. I am a patriot that desperately wants to save his country."

"By overthrowing the government?"

"No. By killing those who would bring about its downfall if left unchecked."

"You will solve nothing except your death."

"I think we could succeed."

"There is no 'we' in your plan."

"Commander, you know the danger our country faces. How can you just let it fall without at least putting up a fight? It's not like you."

"That's because I value my life."

"At least consider it."

"I will consider nothing. You are a traitor, and you will hang."

Quoc stormed off leaving Cu distraught. Cu knew that Quoc was right – if revealed as a traitor, he would surely hang.

Cu went back to his quarters and waited. There was nowhere to run. He considered taking one of the aircraft and making a run for the Cambodian border, but he knew Quoc and the rest of his unit would most likely hunt him down before he reached his sanctuary. There was nothing he could do but wait to meet his fate.

The night passed without incident. With no sleep and high stress, Cu was a wreck. He wondered if Quoc had told anyone yet. If not, there might be an opportunity to stop him by simply killing him. It would have to look like an accident. Perhaps pushing him into an aircraft's spinning prop or igniting a nearby fuel truck. Whatever it was, he knew he would only get one shot at it. Thinking about it, even more, Cu decided to just stab Quoc with a knife. People often survived bullet wounds, but few survived the severing of an artery with a sharp knife. A knife would make little noise, and if nobody witnessed the murder, Cu was likely to get away with it. After all, Cu and Quoc seemed to be friends in the eyes of his comrades.

It was early morning, and the kitchen staff was busy preparing the morning meal. Cu went into the mess hall. He slipped into the kitchen and stole a carving knife when no one was looking. He wrapped the knife in a dish towel and tucked it into his waistband between his shirt and t-shirt.

Cu went back to his room. He stripped down and wrapped a towel around his waist as he did every morning. He pulled out a clean uniform and underwear, then hid the carving knife between them. Finally, he grabbed his shower kit and headed toward the officer's showers. He knew Quoc would be one of the first to shower. He was a creature of habit. It was a point of pride that the commander of the unit was the first to rise and get ready in the morning. Cu entered one of the stalls, pulled the curtain closed, removed his towel, and began to shower. He waited, keeping watch for Quoc.

A few minutes later, Quoc entered the showers. Cu turned away, so Quoc would not recognize him. Cu readied himself. Killing a man with a knife was not like shooting him. It took real commitment on the part of the assassin. He had killed men from afar in his aircraft but never up-close... and never with a knife. There would be blood... lots of blood. Cu became dizzy and nauseated. The knife in his hand began to shake. He thought about dropping it so he didn't hurt himself if he fainted, but others might see it. Suddenly the shower curtain to his stall opened. Quoc was behind him and said, "There you are. I looked in your room. You were already gone."

"I didn't sleep well. I thought a shower might help wake me up," said Cu stilling holding the knife and turning away from Quoc.

"I have given your plan more thought. You're right. It's the only way to save the country. I'm in. Let's talk after breakfast."

"Yes. Of course. Thank you, Commander."

"Don't thank me. We are probably going to be caught and executed. But at least you won't hang alone."

Quoc closed the curtain and moved off. Cu was shaking but relieved. He opened the drain in the floor of the shower, shoved the knife down inside, and replaced the drain cap. He was pleased he didn't need to kill Quoc.

Quoc and Cu met multiple times over the weeks that followed. Quoc was a stickler for detail and demanded that everything within the plan be thoroughly researched to the best of their ability. He wanted nothing left to chance.

Cu did everything Quoc requested. He was relieved that Quoc had taken command of the mission to assassinate Diem and his family. Cu felt more confident that the operation would be a success and was able to sleep better at night. He knew there was still a good chance that they would be hunted down after the assassination, but he didn't want his life to go to waste. If he and Quoc killed Diem and his family that would be enough. That would be a life well-lived no matter what happened after.

Saigon, South Vietnam

Coyle stood outside the presidential palace watching a quad machine gun being lifted on the bed of a truck by a tall crane. Coyle had arranged to secure one of the anti-aircraft weapons just as he had suggested he might to Nhu. Plus, he was hot on the tail of a second weapon located at an airbase in Guam. Nhu was not a man that Coyle wanted to disappoint.

Coyle had climbed up on the roof with an engineer and found a location with support beams capable of handling the weight and recoil of the weapon.

Coyle was hoping Bian might look out the window and see him at work. The machine guns were mean-looking pieces of machinery and he thought it might impress them.

As the crane lifted the weapon, Nhu appeared and walked over to Coyle. "You've done well, Mr. Coyle," said Nhu.

"Just Coyle," said Coyle not taking his eyes off the weapon hanging above them.

"Very well, Coyle. How long will it take before we can test fire it?"

"I'm not sure. We need to make sure the mount is secure before we put it under a lot of stress. A meat chopper has an incredible kick. I won't want to damage your roof."

"Yes. That would not be wise."

Coyle and Nhu heard a loud pop and saw one of the canvas straps holding the weapon snap under the weight. "Oh, shit! Bring it back down. Now!" said Coyle to the crane operator.

The crane operator lowered the weapon toward the ground. The second strap snapped, and the weapon fell three feet landing on the pavement with a loud thump. "Dammit," said Coyle inspecting the damage. "It's not like these things are growing on trees."

"Is it damaged?" said Nhu.

"I don't know. I think we had better take it back to the base and have a weapon's specialist take a closer look."

"No," said Nhu. "Have your mechanic come here. I will make sure he has everything he needs."

"Why?"

"It's an impressive weapon. Now that we have it, I don't want it misplaced."

"You mean stolen?"

"Yes. Our enemies would prize such a weapon and use it against us."

"I suppose that's true. All right. I'll leave it here, but it may take a few days before the specialist is available."

"That's okay. It will be well guarded."

"I don't doubt that. We should cover it with a tarp, so no dirt or lawn clippings get in the mechanisms."

"I will see that it is done."

It was Sunday. A day of rest for Catholics. Diem did not work on Sundays. He and his family used the day to reflect and attend mass at Saigon's cathedral. In the afternoon, there was usually a family dinner and a movie afterward. Diem was partial to light comedies and historical adventures. He avoided romantic movies, and anything considered provocative. Most of the movies were American that had been dubbed in French. The palace had its own movie theatre, a commercial projector, and a popcorn machine with real butter. Snow cones with different flavors were passed out to guests during the movies. The cushioned seats were the same used in commercial movie theaters and there were even red velvet curtains that covered the screen in between showings, then drawn open as the movie started. Diem also liked to watch newsreels before each movie, especially if the news was about Vietnam or him. Everyone in the theater was expected to clap and cheer if he or any of his family appeared onscreen.

With her translations services not required, unless a foreign dignitary was invited by Diem to attend mass or some other family function, Bian had most Sundays off. Coyle cleared his flying schedule a week in advance to make sure he was available whenever Bian had time available for him. Bian did most of the planning for their dates since she knew the area well and always knew the best places to eat. She enjoyed showing Coyle the hidden sites of Saigon and watching him eat unusual food dishes prepared by street vendors. Coyle was a good sport and always acted like he enjoyed whatever he was fed. Bian knew Coyle's tastes were far from exotic but enjoyed watching his expressions as he swallowed some ungodly cuisine like raw eel or roasted chicken embryos.

Bian and Coyle strolled along a tree-lined cobblestone path deep within the Saigon Zoo and Botanical Gardens. There were potted orchids with brilliant colors sitting on carved stone columns along the route.

The commander of French forces in Indochina commissioned the building of the zoo and gardens in 1864. Like much of the architecture in Saigon, the buildings had a French feel to them and were painted in soft green and yellow. Once inside the park, visitors felt transported to the streets of Paris or Lyon. Dozens of gardeners kept the lawn and hedges neatly trimmed in-between tending to the thousands of flowers and trees from around the world. A tiger roared in the distance. "Must be lunchtime," said Coyle.

Bian liked Coyle's wry sense of humor and laughed at his jokes, even when she didn't understand them. "So, you were born in Hanoi?" said Coyle.

"Yes," said Bian. "My father was a manager of a textile mill before he joined the French military."

"Which unit?"

"Sixth Colonel Parachute Battalion."

"Bigeard's battalion?"

"You know of it?"

"Yeah. Bigeard and I were... friends at one time."

"Not anymore?"

"It's complicated. Your father fought at Dien Bien Phu?"

"Fought and died when the fortress fell."

"I'm sorry to hear that. It's possible we may have met."

"You were there? …at Dien Bien Phu?"

"I was there. I was flying for the French."

"My father was a captain. Logistics. But in the end, he was fighting in the trenches. A huge landmine blew up the hillside on which he was stationed. Everyone was buried beneath the dirt and rock."

"Elaine 2. I was there with Bigeard when the landmine blew. It almost killed us."

"You were lucky. My father was not."

"What was your father's name?"

"Captain Chien Hoang. Did you know him?"

"I don't remember the name, but it's possible we met, especially if he was around Bruno a lot."

"Bruno is Lieutenant Colonel Bigeard?"

"Yeah. That was his nickname… Bruno."

"You knew him well… Bruno?"

"Yeah. I knew him well."

"But you are not friends now?"

"I don't know what we are now. We had a falling out. It was never the same after that."

"A woman?" said Bian sheepishly.

Coyle laughed and said, "Yeah. A woman."

"I am sorry to hear that."

"Don't be too sorry," said Coyle taking her hand for the first time. He was happy she didn't pull it away as they continued their walk.

After a stroll through the gardens, Coyle took Bian to see some of the animal exhibits. They fed bananas to the elephants and nuts to the macaws. Coyle wondered if Bian thought it was childlike to feed the animals.

She did but in a good way. Men were so serious. She knew Coyle was trying to impress her but liked when he relaxed, and she got to see the real Coyle. As they sat on a bench to eat ice cream that Coyle had purchased from a vendor with a refrigerated cart, Bian moved closer to his side hoping he would put his arm around her. He did. "Are you married?" said Bian.

"What?! No. Of course not," said Coyle.

"One never knows with a foreigner... who waits for them when they return home."

"Well, I'm not married, and I don't have a girlfriend waiting for me in the states. What about you? Do you have an old boyfriend hiding in the bushes?"

"Me? No one."

"I find that hard to believe."

"You think I am not honest?"

"No. I think you are very honest. It's just... you're so composed... and beautiful. I just don't see how it is possible someone hasn't snatched you up."

"And you are ngọt ngào-noi chuyen."

"What's that mean?"

"Sweet-talker," said Bian with a smile and kissed him on the cheek.

Coyle and Bian rode in a trishaw on their way back from the zoo. It was often quicker to use a trishaw than a taxi in the afternoon when the traffic in Saigon increased in density. While less agile than a motor scooter, a trishaw with a skilled driver could easily navigate its way through the log jam of cars and trucks that clogged the boulevards. "Bian, we are close to my office, and I need to pick up a map for a flight tomorrow morning. Would you mind if we stopped for just a minute?" said Coyle.

"Of course, it is fine. But I thought your office was at this airbase," said Bian.

"It is. This is a different office," said Coyle as he began giving new directions to the driver.

A few minutes later, the trishaw pulled up in front of Lansdale's headquarters and Coyle hopped out leaving Bian to wait in the trishaw.

As he entered the large house used as a headquarters, Coyle passed Granier on his way out the front door. "Are we all set for tomorrow morning?" said Granier.

"Yeah. I'm just picking up the map. I'll see you at seven," said Coyle.

Satisfied that everything was on track for his mission, Granier exited through the doorway and turned down the sidewalk. As he did, he glimpsed at an attractive woman sitting alone in a trishaw. She looked familiar, but Granier couldn't place where he had seen her. He kept walking and noticed her taking a discreet glance at him as he passed then turn away… just as she had done in the alley outside of Zhou Youyong's office. With his curiosity piqued but resolved not to show any reaction, Granier continued down the sidewalk then crossed the street and entered a small restaurant. He sat by the window and peered out at the lady in the trishaw.

A few moments later, Coyle appeared with the map in his hand. He walked to the trishaw and hopped in next to the attractive woman. The trishaw sped off.

Granier exited the restaurant and hailed a trishaw. It was best to travel in the same type of vehicle, so he didn't lose them in traffic. He pointed to the trishaw speeding down the street. The driver nodded that he understood and followed the other trishaw.

Twenty minutes later, Granier signaled for his driver to pull up across the street from Bian's apartment. He watched as Coyle and Bian stepped from their trishaw.

"Would you like to come up for some tea?" said Bian.

"Sure. I usually get a drink before dinner, but tea is fine."

"Maybe we have dinner later."

"Why do you want to wait… Oh, I see. Of course, later is definitely better."

Coyle paid the driver and followed Bian inside her apartment building.

Granier waited almost an hour watching the building. Bian appeared in a window and drew the drapes shut. A few moments later, a light illuminated the drape-covered window. "Coyle, you dog," said Granier to himself. "What have you gotten yourself into?"

Convinced that he was probably facing a very long wait before Coyle appeared again, Granier made a mental note of the street and address, then signaled the driver to take him back to where they came. The trishaw sped off.

On his way back to headquarters, Granier mulled over the situation and the problems it created. While he didn't exactly consider Coyle a close friend, he didn't want to hurt him either. Coyle was a good pilot and good pilots were hard to come by in South Vietnam. But he couldn't just let it slide. Lives were at stake. If Coyle's woman was involved with Youyong, she could be an informant or even a spy working for the North Vietnamese or Viet Cong. She could get Coyle in a lot of trouble if the information passed was traced back to him. Granier decided to follow the woman and see where she led. If he was going to

251

accuse her of anything, he wanted to know beyond a reasonable doubt.

The next day, Coyle flew Granier to Ben Tre in a Cessna O-1 Bird Dog. Ben Tre was the capital of the province eighty-five miles south of Saigon. There had been reports of Viet Cong sniper activity near a fishing village at the mouth of a Mekong tributary. Granier had been sent by Lansdale to check it out.

It only took two hours before Granier determined it was probably an inner village dispute between two fishermen that used to be partners in a boat. There was no sniper. Just an angry fisherman taking a potshot at another fisherman with an antique musket.

When they landed back at the airbase, Granier offered to buy Coyle a beer at a nearby bar. Coyle was immediately suspect. Granier was not the friendly type. "Why?" said Coyle.

"Because I want a beer and I don't want to drink alone," said Granier.

"Bullshit."

"Alright. Fine. I need to talk with you about something."

"Why don't you just say what's on your mind?"

"The woman you're seeing…"

"Bian? What about her?"

"I've seen her before."

Coyle's expression darkened. "Where did you meet her?"

"It's not like that. I didn't meet her. I don't even know her."

"Okay. So, what in the hell are you talking about?"

"I was on a reconnaissance operation for Lansdale in downtown Saigon. He wanted surveillance photos of a suspected North Vietnamese intelligence officer. I passed your girl in a dead-end alley where the suspect had an office – a gem trading company."

"And?"

"There is no "And?" I saw her near a suspected enemy operative that's all."

"Did you take a photo of her?"

"No. It was before I was set up. I just passed her in the alley."

"And you think she is a spy?"

"No. I mean… I don't know. It's kinda weird, right?"

"You tailing my new girlfriend? Yeah, that's kinda weird."

"I told you, I wasn't tailing her. I was there for someone else."

"And she just happened to be there?"

"Exactly. Look, it could mean something, or it could mean nothing. Either way, I thought you should know."

"Are you gonna tell Lansdale?"

"No. Should I?"

"No. He could tell Nhu or Diem and she could lose her job. Maybe even be brought in for interrogation."

"It was probably just a weird coincidence. I'll leave it up to you whom to tell or not tell."

"All right. Thanks."

"But you are going to check her out?"

"Of course. But there is not much of a need. Her father was a war hero that fought against the Viet Minh in the Indochina War. She would never help the North Vietnamese."

"That's good to know. But still…"

"Still what?"

"You haven't known her very long."

"I've known her long enough."

"Coyle, think about it... you're CIA. You're a prime target for North Vietnamese counterintelligence."

"Granier, you're making an imaginary mountain out of a molehill. She's not a spy. She works as a translator for Diem and his family. You don't think they checked her out?"

"Yeah. You're probably right. I'm just being cautious."

"Good. Thanks for telling me."

The next day, Granier woke early and told Lansdale he needed a couple of days off. Granier was technically a civilian, not a soldier. He had a ton of vacation time saved up, so Lansdale had no choice even though they were in a war zone. Granier borrowed another camera and loaded it with film.

It was 8 AM when Granier spotted Bian emerging from her apartment building and hailing a trishaw. Granier snapped a photo to document his trailing her, then followed her in his own trishaw.

As usual, Bian went straight to the palace and entered through the guarded gate. Granier was forced to wait outside. He set himself up at a teahouse near the palace that allowed him a good view of the main gate.

Bien Hoa Air Base, South Vietnam

Coyle was a wreck. He hadn't been able to sleep since Granier had told him about Bian. He kept replaying the timeline of their relationship over and over in his mind. He had approached her in the teahouse, not the other way around. He never bothered to consider why she was at that particular teahouse. It wasn't close to her home or the palace where she worked. He remembered seeing her at the palace. Again, that was his doing, not hers. He had pursued her, not the other way around. At least not in the beginning. He couldn't help thinking that she might have set it all up. That she wanted to meet him. She was attractive but not overly, and smart. The kind of girl he liked to date, not just sleep with. The perfect honeypot. He had been trained to watch out for such things. How could he miss it? Did he miss it or was all this some strange coincidence? He knew if he accused her, he would lose her forever. One doesn't recover from an accusation like that. It doesn't happen.

As he replayed everything in his mind, he finally realized there might be an easy way to check at least part of her story – Bruno. She said her father was under Bruno's command at Dien Bien Phu. Bruno would know him… or not.

He was nervous about calling Bruno. They hadn't talked in years, and they hadn't left things on the best of terms. And then there was Bridget. The wound of their betrayal took time to heal. He didn't want to open it back up. It was too painful. He looked at his watch. It was almost midnight in Saigon and that meant it was 7 am in Paris. If he was going to call, he would need to do it before Bruno left for the day. He picked up the phone and dialed…

Paris, France

Sipping her second cup of coffee, munching on a croissant, and reading the morning newspaper, Bridget sat on the balcony of the apartment she shared with

Bruno. The phone rang. She answered it and was surprised to hear Coyle's voice, "Bridget?"

"My God. Tom is that really you?" said Bridget.

"Yeah, Brig, it's me."

"It's so good to hear your voice. Where are you?"

"Saigon."

"We miss you, Tom. When are you coming back to Paris?"

"I'm not. That's not what this is about."

"Oh, I'm sorry to hear that."

"Brig, I need to speak to Bruno."

"Oh," said Bridget realizing that Coyle was not calling to speak with her.

"Is he there?"

"Not at the moment. He went out for his morning run. He should be back shortly."

"Can I give you a number and have him call me as soon as he gets in?"

"You don't want to talk with me?"

There was a long silence and then, "I want to but…"

"It still hurts?"

"Yeah. Something like that."

"I'm sorry, Tom."

"I know. We're all sorry. The good news is that I've met someone."

"Really? That's great," said Bridget half-heartedly. "I'm happy for you. Is she American?"

"No. She's Vietnamese. Her name is Bian."

"Pretty name. Are you… in love?"

"I don't know. Maybe. She's special that's for sure."

"When can we meet her?"

"I don't know. Things are a bit up in the air right now. That's the reason I need to speak to Bruno."

"Really? She says she knows Bruno?"

"No. That's not it. I think he knows her father."

The front door to the apartment opened and Marcel Bigeard, his workout clothes drenched in sweat, walked in. He pulled off his shirt to reveal a chiseled body. He knew Brigette liked to see his stomach and chest muscles and he didn't mind showing them off whenever he was given the chance.

"Speak of the devil. Bruno just walked in. I'll get him. It was good hearing from you, Tom. I wish you luck with your new girl."

"Thanks, Brig. I think I'm gonna need it."

"Bruno, it's Tom. He's in Saigon."

"Really?" said Bruno grabbing the phone. "Coyle?"

"Hi, Bruno. Did you have a nice jog?"

"Jogging is for pussies. I run."

"Of course, you do."

"You should try it yourself and work off some of that fat."

"Right. Look, I'm calling for a reason. Do you know a Captain Chien Hoang?"

"Yes, very well. He was a good officer and a good fighter. We were at Dien Bien Phu together. I'm sure you met him."

"I might have. I don't remember. I'm not good with Vietnamese names. But that's good that you remember him."

"I could not forget him. He saved our lives when Elaine blew up."

"He saved our lives?"

"Yes, he fought off the Viet Minh while we hunted for Bridget under the dirt and rocks."

"And then he was killed?"

"No. He wasn't killed. Not then."

"What do you mean?"

"I mean, he survived Elaine. I remember seeing him once again after the fortress fell... before the death march. He was a prisoner of war like all the survivors."

"Bian said he died on Elaine."

"Bian?"

"My girlfriend."

"You have a girlfriend?"

"Yes. Is it that hard to believe?"

"No. It's just... You're so fat."

"I'm not fat, Bruno."

"I think that is a matter of opinion."

"You're such an asshole."

"That's what Brigette keeps telling me. I think she is wrong."

"She's not, Bruno. You should listen to her."

"What is the point? I don't want to change."

"Of course, you don't."

"Besides, how does one improve on perfection?"

"So, Captain Hoang was Bian's father. She said he died on Elaine."

"No, Coyle. She is mistaken. He was alive when the fortress fell and was taken prisoner."

"Do you know what happened to him after that?"

"No. The Vietnamese were separated from the French. I never saw him again and we received no word about the whereabouts or condition of the Vietnamese prisoners. It was a tragedy, but there was little we could do at that point. We were fighting for our own survival."

"I understand."

"Why do you need to know?"

"It's not important."

"So, your girlfriend. Is she sexy?'

"Fuck off, Bruno," said Coyle.

"I'm kidding. I'm kidding. Can't anyone take a joke anymore? Why so serious all the time?"

"Thanks for your help, Bruno. I gotta go."

Coyle hung up. Bridget slugged Bruno's arm and said, "Is she sexy?"

Bruno shrugged it off like it was nothing and said, "Where's my breakfast onion?"

Bien Hoa Air Base, South Vietnam

Returning from a mission, Quoc and Cu flew over the palace grounds. Holding a 35mm camera, Quoc took several aerial photos of the palace and its surrounding compound.

When they returned to the air, Cu went to the base photography lab and asked if he could use the lab once they were finished for the day. When asked why Cu explained he had taken some private photos of his girlfriend that he did not wish a civilian lab to see. The lab commander understood and agreed he could use the lab one hour in private, but a guard would be posted outside.

When the time came, Cu developed the role of film then used the enlarger to make several photos of each shot, zooming in on points of interest. There was one blown-up image that caught his eye and caused him to panic – a photo of a quad .50-cal anti-aircraft gun being inspected in front of the palace. He waited until the photos were dry, then rushed off to find Quoc.

Cu found Quoc in a conference with the sergeant in charge of aircraft maintenance. Cu did not want to raise any suspicions, so he waited until they were done. When the sergeant left, Cu entered Quoc's office and closed the door. Quoc could see the panicked look on

Cu's face and said, "What's wrong? You look like you swallowed a bad egg."

"We have a big problem," said Cu as he opened the manila envelope holding the photographs and spread them across Quoc's desk. Quoc looked down at the photographs as Cu shuffled through them until he found the ones he had just developed showing the Quad-50s.

"Where in the hell did that come from?" said Quoc.

"I don't know. It's the first time I've seen it. Maybe it was recently delivered."

"I think that's our weapon specialist working on it," said Quoc examining the photographs closer. "He must be checking it over before it becomes operational."

"Oh, great," said Cu looking a little green. "What are we gonna do?"

"Nothing. We go as planned."

"Now, who is insane? That thing is gonna rip us to shreds."

"Maybe. But it's not installed yet. If we go before it's operational, our odds of success are greater."

"And our odds of survival."

"You still think we are going to make it out of this alive, don't you?"

"Well, yeah. I figure the people and maybe even the army will rise up once Diem and Nhu have been eliminated."

"What do you think Nhu's secret police are going to do once they find out we killed the president and their commander?"

"I don't know, but I sure as hell know what a meat chopper can do to an aircraft."

"This isn't the first time we have gone up against anti-aircraft guns."

"Right, but never this low. We're flying on the deck."

"At the speed, we will be flying we will only be within its range for a couple of seconds. The gunner would have to be pretty lucky to hit either of us and that's assuming the weapon is functional when we attack."

"Then I say the sooner we go, the better."

"I agree."

February 26, 1962 - Saigon, South Vietnam

Bian didn't reemerge from the palace until after 5 PM. She hailed a trishaw. Waiting in a nearby trishaw, Granier followed her home. There was no sign of Coyle that evening. Granier waited outside until he saw her turn off the light inside her apartment. Believing that she was in for the night, Granier left. He felt foolish but something was still bothering him. It was the way she had casually looked away in the alley and on the trishaw. It seemed well-rehearsed... like she had been trained to act that way when under surveillance. It seemed professional.

The next morning, Granier again rose early. He had decided to change tactics. He did not follow Bian. Instead, he followed Youyong.

He positioned himself at a milk bar across from the alley where Youyong had his trading company office and where he had first seen Bian. Granier placed the camera on the table hidden under a magazine. He lined up the lens, so it pointed at the mouth of the ally.

Granier sat for four hours discreetly watching the entrance to the alley. The owner of the milk bar kept hovering over him until he ordered another pastry. After the first two, he just ordered the pastries and let them stack up on the table without eating them. When there were too many, he asked that they be taken away so as not to cause suspicion.

When Youyong finally appeared, Granier casually leaned over and pressed the shutter button under the magazine. He paid his tab while he watched Youyong hail a trishaw and head off toward the main boulevard. He hailed a trishaw and followed Youyong.

Youyong made several stops downtown before making a final stop in front of Saigon's post office where he paid the trishaw driver. Granier followed Youyong inside the French colonial-style building and watched him purchase some stamps. Nothing was unusual. Granier was beginning to wonder if Coyle had been right, and he was wasting his time.

When Youyong exited the post office, he didn't hail another trishaw. Instead, he walked across the street to Notre Dame Cathedral with its 19th-century architecture. He didn't go inside. He walked past the entrance to the end of the corner. He trotted across a busy street and entered a heavily forested park. Granier followed giving Youyong a good lead.

It appeared to Granier that this was a common stroll for Youyong. He wasn't in a hurry and even stopped to sit on a park bench. He fed some pigeons from a bag of breadcrumbs he kept in his pants pocket. Granier watched patiently. After a few minutes, Youyong tucked the empty bag in the ironwork of the bench, then rose, and continued his walk. Reaching the other side of the park, Youyong hailed a trishaw. But before climbing in, he dropped a coin. When he bent down to pick it up, he used a small piece of chalk to mark a small "O" on the base of a lamppost. It was almost imperceptible.

Granier did not follow Youyong. He suspected he was going back to his office, but it didn't matter. Instead, he walked over to the lamppost and studied the chalk mark. He could see that there was a previous chalk mark of an "X" that had been erased. Granier thought for a moment, then walked back to the park bench and sat down. He looked around to ensure nobody was watching before retrieving the discarded paper bag. There was nothing inside the bag and no writing on the inside or outside. He thought for another moment and decided it didn't contain the message. It was a visual marker for the park bench. He felt underneath the edge of the bench seat and encountered a dry piece of old gum that fell off. He picked it up and studied it. He determined it was a dry piece of old gum and pitched it into the grass beside the bench. He continued to feel under the bench seat and didn't encounter anything more. He moved his hand to the back of the bench seat and checked underneath. Once again, he came up with nothing. When he moved to the side of the bench seat, he felt a slip of paper wedged between the iron brace and the wood slats. He pulled it out, checked to make sure nobody was watching, and opened the slip of paper. There was writing in Chinese characters. Granier didn't read Chinese and thought it was probably coded anyway. He folded the slip of paper back the way he found it and placed it back in its original place underneath the side of the bench. He rose and walked off leaving the dead drop undisturbed.

Granier repositioned himself on the opposite side of a hedge fifty feet from the park bench. He broke off several small branches within the hedge allowing him a good view without being seen. With only a few leaves in front of his face, he could easily poke the camera lens through and snap some photos without causing attention. It was what Granier did best... not being seen.

He waited five hours and watched several people sit on the bench. But nobody reached for the message underneath. His elbows were aching, and his forearms were sore from holding the camera in position. If the time came, he wanted to be ready.

When Bian appeared on the park path through the forest, Granier was sad. He had hoped he was wrong, and it was someone else he had seen in that alley. That he had made a mistake. But his memory was solid. He snapped several photos as she sat down, opened a book, and began to read. Granier didn't need to see her do anything more. He was sure she was one of Youyong's operatives. A spy for the Chinese, North Vietnamese, Viet Cong, or even all three. But still, he watched. Others would need proof. Coyle would need proof.

She read for twenty minutes and checked to make sure nobody was watching before reaching down the side of the bench and retrieving the message. Granier snapped several more photos. She placed the slip of paper in her book like it was a bookmarker. She read for another five minutes then rose and walked off. Granier didn't try to stop her. He knew where she was going.

When Bian returned to her apartment, she carried a paper bag filled with vegetables she had purchased on her way home. She flipped on the light switch and turned to find Granier sitting in a chair staring at her.

In his hand was a pistol with a silencer on the barrel. His face was familiar, but she didn't know him. She froze. "Put your groceries on the table and sit," said Granier.

Bian obeyed. She went to the far end of the table, set the bag down, and sat placing her hands in her lap. "Why Coyle?" said Granier.

Bian thought for a moment wondering how much this man really knew. "He is a handsome man and I like his jokes," she said as she discreetly reached under the table and felt around for the pistol she had hidden.

"Are you looking for this?" said Granier holding up her pistol with his other hand.

She said nothing. "You should put your hands on the table where I can see them. You don't want me to react to any sudden movements."

Bian obeyed and said, "What do you want?"

"That's a tough question. I am not sure. I don't want to hurt Coyle, but I don't see how I can avoid it at this point."

"You could let me go."

"No. That's not an option."

"I see. You are CIA?"

"…like Coyle?"

Bian said nothing. Granier aimed the barrel of his pistol at her right knee and said, "You best answer. I am a very good shot, and we don't want things to get ugly. You are going to answer my questions one way or another."

"Yes. Like Coyle," she said.

"You were sent to recruit him?"

"Not in the beginning."

"Diem was your target?"

"Coyle was an additional assignment."

"You didn't answer my question."

"Yes. Diem was my original assignment."

"That's a pretty big assignment."

"Yes. It wasn't easy… arranging things so I could be recruited as his translator."

"But it worked."

"Yes. It worked."

"So, why Coyle then?"

"My handler wanted to infiltrate Lansdale's operation. Coyle seemed like the best choice. Are you going to kill me?"

"I haven't decided yet."

"It would be better than turning me into Brother Nhu."

"For you perhaps."

"He will torture me."

"Probably."

"He will seek revenge on Coyle."

"Also, a possibility."

"You like Coyle?"

"I don't dislike him."

"Then kill me. It is better for me and better for him."

"If you wanted to die, you would have made a move against me. You haven't."

"Yet."

Granier smiled and said, "Sassy. I can see why Coyle likes you."

"He's a good man."

"I understand your father was a patriot and a hero. Why are you working for the North Vietnamese?"

"It's complicated."

"I've got time."

"I'd like to hear why too," said Coyle standing in the doorway with a pistol in his hand.

Bian and Granier were both surprised. Coyle pointed the pistol at Granier and said, "Put your gun down on the floor and kick it over to me, Granier."

"What are you doing, Coyle?"

"Do as I say."

"Don't make me kill you."

"Don't make me kill you."

"Alright. Relax," said Granier lowering his pistol to the floor. "How long have you been listening?"

"Long enough. Now, kick it over here."

"Kicking a gun is a bad idea. It could go off."

"That's the least of my worries at the moment. I'll take the risk."

Granier kicked the gun toward Coyle. Coyle knelt while keeping his gun on Granier and picked up the silenced pistol. Bian rose from the chair. "Sit, Bian," said Coyle with a stern tone.

Bian obeyed and sat back down. "Answer the question? Why did you betray your country and your father's memory?"

"I didn't betray my father. I saved him," said Bian.

"Because he is still alive?"

"Yes. A prisoner in Hanoi. They tortured him."

"And they offered you a deal?"

"Yes. My life for his."

"How do you know he is still alive?"

"He is allowed to write me a letter once a year. And I him. There are things mentioned that only he and I share. So, we know that the letters are authentic."

"And your handler delivers the letters?"

"Yes. It is what I live for."

"And you give him information in return?"

"I do his bidding, yes."

"None of this matters, Coyle. She's an enemy operative," said Granier.

"I may not matter to you, but it matters to me."

"You can't let her go."

"I don't know, Granier. I am the guy holding the gun. Seems like I can do whatever I want."

Granier reached down and slipped his fingers around Bian's pistol. "He has my gun," said Bian.

Coyle took aim at Granier. "Don't move, Granier. We don't want any misunderstanding. At this range, I won't miss."

"I don't know. I can move pretty quick," said Granier.

"We don't need to do this."

"Have you got a better idea?"

"We can come up with one. We just need to think about it."

"Always the optimist."

"Pick up the gun by the barrel with your fingers and set it on the floor."

"That hardly seems fair."

"Please, Granier. Don't make me kill you."

"It's you I'm worried about, Coyle. Even if I die, she will have no choice but to kill you."

"She won't."

"Have you been listening to our conversation? Of course, she's gonna kill you. It's the only way she can save her father."

"She won't."

"You're an idiot."

"I ain't gonna argue the point considering the circumstances. But I still need you to put her gun on the floor."

Granier considered for a moment, then picked up the gun's barrel with his fingers and placed it on the floor. "I hope you know what you're doing," said Granier.

"I admit… I'm kinda winging it," said Coyle.

"I can see that."

"He's right, Tom. You should shoot me. If I die while loyal to the North Vietnamese, they may let my father live."

"I'm not going to shoot you, Bian. We are going to find a way out of this."

"And we are just going to sit here until we do?" said Granier.

"Exactly."

At 2 AM, Coyle was sitting in a chair with the pistol still in his hand but not pointed at anyone in particular. Bian's and Granier's pistols sat on an end table beside him. Bian had served a light supper and was pouring tea to keep everyone awake. Granier looked annoyed and bored. "I'm not hearing any ideas from the peanut gallery," said Coyle.

"This is your show, Coyle. I'm just along for the ride… or until you fall asleep, and I can blow your brains out."

"Don't be a smart ass, Granier. I need your help."

"You have a gun pointed at me, Coyle. That's not a very good sign of gratitude."

"I just don't want you getting any crazy ideas."

"This whole thing is a crazy idea. As long as her father is a captive of the North Vietnamese, she's gonna spy for them. I can't allow that, and neither can you."

"If I don't show up for work tomorrow morning, Nhu will send someone to check up on me," said Bian.

"We'll jump off that bridge when we get to it. We still have time. Let's use it," said Coyle.

"The solution seems obvious…" said Granier.

"How's that?" said Coyle.

"We've got to break her father out of prison and smuggle him back across the border."

"Is that possible?" said Bian.

"Anything's possible. We just have to come up with a feasible plan and execute it."

"And you'll help?" said Coyle.

"Not if you keep pointing that gun at me."

Coyle studied Granier, then laid his pistol on the table next to the others. "Happy?" said Coyle.

"Let's just say I'm slightly less anxious," said Granier.

"So, how do we do this?"

"I have no idea. I came up with the required solution, the actual plan is gonna take some time."

"But you think it's possible?"

"I'm covert paramilitary. We live for this stuff. The biggest problem is not breaking him out or even getting him across the border. It's when Nhu finds out Bian has been spying on Diem."

"He'll kill her for sure," said Coyle.

"I imagine he'll torture her to find out the secrets she revealed, then kill her."

"You say that like it's a joke."

"I'm stating the truth of the situation. I'm not trying to be funny, just realistic."

Bian listened and realized Granier was right. Even if they freed her father, Nhu would never let her live. She let the teapot slip from her hand. It smashed on the floor breaking into a dozen pieces. "I'm sorry," said Bian. "It slipped."

"It's okay. Just get a towel from the toilet and clean it up," said Coyle.

Bian retrieved a towel and sopped up the tea, then picked up the pieces of shattered porcelain. She stepped into the kitchen and opened the trash bin.

Before dumping the remains of the teapot, she took a long shard from the pile and used its razor-sharp edge to cut a long gash down her forearm. Blood flowed. The broken shards crashed into the trash bin. She placed the towel in her hand to allow the blood to be soaked up. She walked out of the kitchen and sat down keeping her slashed forearm out of sight of Coyle and Granier. She sat quietly and listened. Her eyes became heavy as her blood pressure dropped. She was sad to leave this life. A tear welled up in her eyes and rolled down her cheek.

Coyle caught a glimpse of Bian's head sagging from across the room. "Bian, are you okay?"

She said nothing. Coyle rose and moved toward her, "Bian?"

He saw the crimson on her forearm and panicked, "BIAN?"

He grabbed the wound with his hands and tried to stop the bleeding, "What have you done?"

"She found the solution," said Granier.

"Fuck you, Granier."

"Let her go, Coyle. It's what she needs."

Coyle looked into Bian's eyes. They filled with tears, pleading, "He's right, Tom."

After a moment, Coyle loosened his grip and the blood flowed freely once again. Bian smiled weakly. Coyle tried to smile back but couldn't. He tightened his grip on her forearm once again restricting the wound. "No. We can get you out of this, Bian. You need to believe me," said Coyle.

"Goddammit, Coyle," said Granier. "You're being very selfish."

"Make yourself useful and find me a sewing kit, Granier. Maybe the bedroom."

Granier sighed, then walked into the bedroom and shuffled through the drawers in the dresser until he found a sewing basket and brought it to Coyle. "I'll hold the wound closed while you sew the artery that was cut," said Coyle.

"I ain't no doctor, Coyle."

"You don't have to be. We just gotta stop the blood long enough to get her to a hospital. It'll work. I know it will."

"Sure. Why not?" said Granier threading a needle. "Bian, I imagine this is gonna hurt a bit. Blame your boyfriend. I liked your idea better," said Granier as he went to work on the wound.

HEROIC TRAITORS

February 27, 1962 – Bien Hoa Air Base, South Vietnam

Quoc and Cu arose early on reports that the Viet Cong attacked an ARVN company thirty-seven miles south of the capital in the Mekong Delta. Their planes were being loaded with bombs, napalm canisters, and rockets. The four autocannons on each aircraft were already loaded with 800 rounds of 20 mm shells. It was a heavy load. "It's not going to get any better than this," said Quoc watching the ground crews load up the aircraft.

"I agree," said Cu.

"Then we go. Say your prayers and prepare yourself."

"You too, Commander."

"We take off as soon as the ground crew is done loading the munitions."

Ten minutes later, the two Skyraiders lifted off the runway and headed south toward the Mekong Delta. After flying out of sight from the airfield, Quoc used hand signals to Cu and the aircraft changed course back to downtown Saigon. They flew low over the city. It was seven in the morning and people were just waking up when the two aircraft flying overhead shook their houses and apartments as they zoomed past.

Saigon, South Vietnam

It was early morning. Coyle and Granier sat in Bian's hospital room. With an IV drip attached to her uninjured arm, Bian slept. Her forearm was covered in bandages after being sutured by Granier, then resutured by a surgeon at the hospital. Coyle had been right. Granier's sutures had kept her from bleeding out on the way to the hospital and saved her life. "I'm in love with her, Granier," said Coyle looking down at her.

"I know, Coyle. You're also an idiot," said Granier.

"But you'll help me, right?"

"Yeah, if I think it's possible."

"It's possible. It's got to be."

"Spoken like a true idiot. We've got a lot of details that still have to be worked out. The question is what do we do with her in the meantime?"

"We leave her in place. Like nothing has happened."

"I'm not sure that is the wisest thing. After all, she is the enemy."

"She's not the enemy. Not really. Look, you'd do the same thing if you were in her position, wouldn't you?"

"Probably not. I didn't like my father very much."

"But you get my point."

"Sure. But Diem is still our ally."

"I know but maybe we could use this to our advantage."

"How's that?"

"Youyong has been giving her messages for things that he wants her to find out. We could get our hands on those messages. We'd know what the North Vietnamese are trying to find out. That's gotta be worth something."

"If Nhu finds out, he is still gonna torture and kill her."

"So, we make sure he doesn't find out."

"How are you gonna do that?"

"We'll tell Lansdale what we are up to. We'll bring him in on it."

"That's a really bad idea. Lansdale is loyal to Diem. If you tell him that Bian is a spy, he's probably going to go straight to Diem."

"So, we don't tell him the spy is Bian. We just forward the information."

"Oh, Coyle. You are walking a dangerous line."

"Yeah, well... all options are risky."

"Lansdale's not stupid. What would you tell him when he asks where you got the information?"

"I don't know. Maybe we make up an informant."

"He's gonna want to meet your informant. Made-up or not."

"So, we stall him."

"What's this 'we' crap? This is your operation."

"I know. I know. I'll stall him."

They heard the engines of two planes passing over the hospital. The building shook. "What the hell is that?" said Granier.

"Fighters by the sound of it. Why are they flying so low this early in the morning?" said Coyle.

"Let's go have a look."

"What about Bian?"

"Doctor said he drugged her up pretty good. She'll be sleeping for hours."

"You're not worried about her escaping?"

"Nah. She's got nowhere to go. Besides, I think she likes you."

"Yeah?"

They left the room and headed toward the main doors.

Presidential Palace, Saigon, South Vietnam

President Diem had awoken early that morning. As a celibate, he slept alone, emulating the pope and cardinals he revered. He had been dreaming of the great generals of the past that had led his country to victory over those that would oppress his people. Diem felt he had been chosen by God to lead his country at this critical moment in time when so many foreign invaders had descended upon it. Diem saw the United States as a foreign invader, but also a necessary evil required to battle the communists. Refreshed from a good night's sleep, he propped himself up in bed and continued to read a book about George Washington that he had begun the night before. He often read in the morning while it was quiet, and his advisors and diplomats were not vying for his attention. He enjoyed his alone time.

Madame Nhu was still asleep in her bedroom. She did not sleep with her husband who was prone to getting phone calls in the middle of the night and waking her needlessly. Her husband was fine with the arrangement as it allowed him to have other companions in his bed-chamber without disturbing his wife. He wasn't trying to hide anything. Madame Nhu often arranged for other women to satisfy her husband's desire for variety. She saw it as the best way to keep her husband from straying, especially when she controlled whom he slept with and when. Several times a month, she would share her husband's bed just to remind him that only she understood his deepest fantasies and needs.

Brother Nhu was already up. He had just finished dressing and was getting ready to go down to breakfast on the veranda. He disliked eating in his bedroom because he felt it attracted bugs. He was the first to hear and feel the approaching aircraft. The building shook slightly as the aircraft drew closer and the drone of their engines grew louder. Aircraft passing over the palace was commonplace, but never this early and never this low. Nhu moved to a window and looked out.

Two royal deer that Diem kept as pets stood on the lawn munching on the grass. Both looked up for a moment, then ran off frightened by the approaching aircraft engines. The two Skyraiders appeared hugging the city's skyline. Nhu didn't like it and told himself that he would personally see to the punishment of the two arrogant fighter pilots flying the warplanes so close to the palace.

Quoc and Cu had decided to make one pass over the palace to do a quick reconnaissance and hopefully spot the quad-50 anti-aircraft gun still on the ground and not operational. They were both relieved to see the weapon on the ground, covered with a tarp, and unmanned. There were few signs of life on the palace grounds beyond the guards and two frightened deer run wildly around the palace gardens. The two pilots did see a man on the second floor staring out at them through a window as they roared overhead. They had no idea who he might be. They were flying too fast to see clearly.

Nhu felt the building shake and listened as the two aircraft passed overhead and headed north. He relaxed as the thrum of the aircraft engines faded but tensed again as he heard the sound level off then grow once more. "They are turning," he said to himself.

Nhu burst into Madame Nhu's bedroom and yelled, "Get on the floor!"

Madame Nhu was startled by his outburst and said, "Why? What's going on?"

"Get on the damned floor, woman," he said pulling her from the bed, pushing her to the floor, and laying down next to her.

As usual, Quoc was the first to attack while Cu waited his turn circling above. Swooping low, Quoc dropped a 500 lb. bomb on the residence chambers on the far side of the palace. The bomb smashed through a window and exploded. A maid was thrown against a wall and pierced with large pieces of shrapnel shredding her body. She died instantly. The palace shook forcefully as several rooms were blown to smithereens sending flames and broken masonry into the air.

The explosion was next to Madame Nhu's bed chamber and shook the room violently. A French armoire holding her dresses tipped over and came crashing down landing on her arm. She screamed in pain. Nhu lifted it off her, freeing her broken arm. He pulled a pillowcase off one of the bed's pillows and fashioned a sling for his wife's crushed arm. He lifted her in his arms and carried her out of the room.

Startled by the explosion and still in bed, Diem was unsure what to do. He climbed out of bed and put on his robe and slippers. He considered his situation for a long moment, then sat on the edge of his bed, and waited for someone to come to get him.

Outside the hospital, Granier and Coyle watched the aerial assault from a distance. "Those are Skyraiders. What the hell is going on?" said Coyle. "Why are they bombing the palace? Has there been a coup we didn't know about?" said Coyle.

"I don't think so. There would be fighting in the streets and a lot more gunfire," said Granier. "We should take a closer look."

"Why?"

"Aren't you curious?"

"At this point... no. I think Diem and his family deserve whatever happens to them."

Coyle considered Coyle's comment and said, "A well-placed bomb could solve a lot of your problems, ya know?"

"Exactly."

"I still want to see what's happening. Are you coming?"

"I suppose."

Granier and Coyle jogged toward the palace as a plume of black smoke rose into the morning sky. Except for the explosions at the palace, everything seemed normal. There was even an old man pushing a cart filled with vegetables down the street and a woman sweeping the sidewalk in front of her coffee shop. It was surreal.

As Quoc pulled out of his bombing dive and ascended back into the sky above the palace, Cu dove his aircraft making his run. He aimed to the left of where Quoc's bomb had landed. He pickled the bomb release dropping a 500 lb. bomb from his aircraft's hardpoint. The bomb dropped.

Diem heard something heavy smash through the roof and looked up to see the huge bomb break through his ceiling and crash into the floor. And there it stopped; its fins sticking out of the hole it had created. Pelted by pieces of the broken ceiling, Diem looked down at the unexploded bomb. He wondered how long it would take the device to explode and end his life. He just stared at it, unmoving. It was a very big bomb and he was sure he would not survive the explosion when it came.

In the hallway, Nhu handed his wife off to Diem's butler and said, "Take her to the basement and get her a doctor. I'll go after my brother."

The butler obeyed. Nhu ran towards Diem's room. He opened the double doors and saw Diem looking down at the unexploded bomb. "What are doing?" said Nhu incredulously.

"Waiting. It didn't go off," said Diem without taking his eyes off the bomb.

"Brother, look at me."

Diem tore his eyes away from the bomb to see his brother standing in the doorway. "Walk toward me slowly," said Nhu motioning.

Diem nodded and rose from the side of the bed. He walked toward the doorway skirting around the bomb in the floor. Nhu reached out and grabbed Diem's arm pulling him through the doorway. "Are you hurt?" said Nhu.

"No. Jesus protected me," said Diem.

Nhu put his arm around Diem and moved toward the stairway. Nhu could see a dozen palace staff lying on the floor below while others tended to their wounds. "You. Help me," said Nhu to a servant standing at the bottom of the stairs. The servant obeyed and ascended the stairway. A napalm canister crashed through a window, broke through a banister at the top of the stairway, and slammed into the wall on the second floor. The napalm ignited. Nhu could feel the heat and knew immediately what was about to happen. He pulled Diem tight and rolled over the stairway railing dropping twelve feet. Nhu landed first with Diem landing on top of him. A sofa had broken their fall. Its front legs snapped off from the impact and tipped over on top of them. A huge ball of flame rolled down the stairway engulfing the servant coming up the stairs. The intense heat incinerated the man's body in an instant. Everything caught fire, including the couch that had rolled on top of Diem and Nhu saving their lives. The clothes of several staff members caught on fire. They rolled on the ground attempting to extinguish their burning clothes.

Nhu pushed the burning sofa off him and his brother. He could see the flames were consuming most of the oxygen and the room was filling with smoke. "We've got to make it to the basement stairs," said Nhu belly crawling on the floor. "Follow me."

Diem crawled after his brother. They passed several seriously wounded staff members, some with burning clothes. They didn't stop to help but continued toward a staircase leading down to the basement across the room. Another napalm canister exploded on the floor above and more flames burst down the stairway. The entire residence wing was burning out of control. Diem became faint from lack of oxygen and smoke inhalation. Nhu pulled this brother toward the basement stairs just a few feet away. Servants that had survived crawled through the smoke and fire to the exits. When the outside doors opened, smoke poured out and the air was sucked into the palace feeding the oxygen-starved fire. The inferno flared as Nhu and Diem reached the stairway to the basement. They slid and tumbled down the stairs until they could once again breathe. They were safe for the moment. A doctor was tending to Madame Nhu's arm. "Help my brother," said Nhu.

The doctor left Madame Nhu and rushed to help the president. Multiple HAV rockets exploded in the rooms above again shaking the palace but not as severely as the bombs. Nhu could hear the screams of the staff workers. "Whoever did this must pay," said Madame Nhu in tears.

"They will, my dear," said Nhu. "They will."

Quoc and Cu continued their attack on the palace for almost thirty minutes using their remaining rockets and 20mm autocannons to strafe the building. Believing that they had killed the president and his family, they did not use all the bombs they carried. Before the attack, they both agreed that their objective was to kill Diem and his family and not the people that served them. They did not want to cause the needless death of civilians or the destruction of the palace. Instead, the two pilots elected to use rockets and autocannons which they could target much better than bombs. They wanted to keep rescue crews away from the residence as long as possible to ensure that Diem and his family could not be saved.

With a view of the palace, Coyle and Granier stood in an alley, occasionally peeking around the corner to watch the air assault unfold. The royal guards were stationed around the palace's perimeter ready to fight off any ground forces that might attack. The two Americans were not anxious to get caught in the crossfire and decided to keep their distance. "I wonder if they're still alive... Diem and his family?" said Coyle.

"You'd better hope not," said Granier.

"I don't want them to be harmed."

"Bullshit."

"Alright. The world would be a better place without Nhu and his wife. But Diem's not a bad guy. He's just caught between a rock and hard place."

"And how do you think he got there? Diem never would have survived all these years if it wasn't for his brother Nhu. The man is truly merciless."

"...and evil."

"Evil is a relative term."

"You sound like you admire him."

"No. I have limits. But this is war, and we should be wary of passing judgment. The side that usually wins is the side that is most committed."

"What's that?" said Coyle hearing the approach of vehicles.

Granier moved to the opposite corner and peeked out to see – a column of tanks, armored cars, and troop trucks rolling up the street toward the palace. "I'm not sure if they're good guys or bad guys," said Granier. "But there's a lot of them. I think it's time to skedaddle."

"Let me see," said Coyle moving up beside Granier and peeking around the corner. "I'll follow you," said Coyle wide-eyed.

Granier and Coyle moved back down the alley as the first tank rolled past. The convoy took up positions around the palace perimeter with their cannons and machine guns pointed outward. The forces were loyal to Diem and there to protect the palace. A few minutes later, government aircraft flew overhead in search of the assassins.

It was the appearance of ground troops and government aircraft that caused Quoc and Cu to break off their attack. The ground units were armed with 50-cal machine guns and mobile anti-aircraft vehicles with 20mm cannons. The two Skyraiders were running low on ammunition, so Quoc and Cu flew up into the clouds overhead and disappeared. But before leaving the field of battle, Quoc and Cu made one more strafing run emptying their rockets and autocannons on what remained of the residence wing. They had done all that they could short of leveling the entire palace with their remaining bombs.

As planned, Cu and Quoc split up causing the government aircraft to divide their forces in pursuit of the two rogue pilots. Quoc headed for the river. A minesweeper in the river opened fire with their twin 50-cal machine guns and hit Quoc's Skyraider. With the engine pouring out smoke and his aircraft losing altitude, Quoc bailed out and his parachute opened. As he descended local police followed him from the ground and captured him once he landed. He was taken directly to the palace.

Cu headed West. He was low on fuel and had no hope of reaching the relative safety of Cambodia. He flew as far as he could. When his engine began to sputter from lack of fuel, he attempted to land on a dirt road at the base of a mountain. The road was poorly maintained and had dozens of ruts and potholes. He only traveled a few dozen feet before his right tire hit a rut and tore the landing strut from the plane's wing. The plane spun around, and the second strut folded under the left wing when it hit a pothole. It probably saved Cu's life because the plane did not flip. It spun like a frisbee across the road and into a nearby field until the aircraft came to a stop.

Unharmed, Cu climbed out. He could smell the fuel from a ruptured wing tank. He pulled out his pistol from his flight jacket and shot the plane's wing until the fuel caught fire and engulfed the downed aircraft. He wasn't exactly sure why he wanted to destroy the plane. He just didn't want it captured. He walked toward the mountains. A few minutes later, the remaining bombs ignited and blew the plane to smithereens. He was alive and on the run. But he was satisfied with himself. He had done what he set out to do. President Diem and his family were dead. He was sure of it.

Except for Madame Nhu's broken arm, the president and his family survived the air assault with only small cuts and bruises. Madame Nhu was in pain as the doctor prepared to inject her with opium. A lieutenant entered with a message for Nhu. Nhu read the note and said, "Our navy has captured one of the treasonous pilots. They are bringing him to the palace."

"I will kill him myself," said Madame Nhu.

"Not yet. We need to find out who was behind this."

"Obviously, it's another military coup."

"I don't think so. There were no ground troops involved. If it was a coup, the coup leaders would want to occupy the palace, not destroy it."

"So, who was behind it?" said Diem.

"I'm not sure. But the American pilot, Coyle, delayed the installation of the anti-aircraft weapons that could have protected you."

"But they were his idea."

"I know. That is what is troubling. Someone must have given him an order to delay."

"You think the American's are behind this?" said Madame Nhu.

"It's possible. I think we need to be very careful how we portray what has happened."

"How do you mean?" said Diem.

"If the Americans are behind it, we need to show them that you were never in danger of being assassinated or overthrown."

"I wasn't. God was protecting me."

"Divine providence… that's good," said Madame Nhu. "The people will believe that."

"Yes. But it's the Americans that concern me most."

"Kick them out, I say," said Madame Nhu. "They constantly stick their noses where they do not belong. We will be better on our own."

"I don't think we would survive long without their help. We need their weapons and their money to pay our military," said Nhu.

"But if they want us dead, is there any hope?" said Diem.

"There is always hope… if we can find who is behind it. It could just be the CIA or the Ambassador acting on his own."

"I always thought he was two-faced," said Madame Nhu.

"Whoever it is, we must unmask them quickly. In the meantime, we should reassure our military and the public that you remain in control, brother."

Within the hour, Diem was broadcasting over the radio to all of South Vietnam. He assured the listeners that the assassination attempt had failed and was an isolated incident carried out by two rogue pilots. "It is by God's grace that I and my family survived this vile attack. Now, more than ever, I know that God has chosen me to lead you, my people and that he will protect us against the many challenges that will come our way," said Diem into the microphone.

Once he finished the radio announcement, Diem went immediately to Bien Hoa Air Base and addressed the troops. He reassured them that he and his family did not blame them or their leaders for what had happened. He knew their loyalty to his government and its war against the communists. There would be no punishment beyond the two rogue pilots, one of which was already in custody.

Madame Nhu appeared before women's organizations proudly displaying the cast on her broken arm and telling the audience it was a small sacrifice for her beloved Vietnam. She proclaimed that those responsible for the attack would hang in the royal park until their corpses rotted away.

It didn't take long to figure out that Cu was the second assassin even if Quoc was uncooperative. Brother Nhu used all his resources to hunt down Cu. He suspected that the young pilot was trying to escape to Cambodia or possibly Laos. Hundreds of patrols combed the mountains between the countries.

In the meantime, Nhu interrogated Quoc. Quoc insisted that he and Cu acted alone, and his only regret was that Diem and his family were still alive. Nhu wanted him dead but realized that Quoc could easily become a martyr and stir up even more trouble for the government. It was better to keep Quoc alive and imprisoned under harsh conditions. Death was too easy for the assassin.

Cu traveled at night and slept during the day when Army patrols scoured the countryside looking for him. It took several weeks before he entered Cambodia. He surrendered himself to the Cambodian Army and was brought to the capital. Cu was proclaimed a people's hero by the prime minister and permitted to stay in Cambodia as long as he wished. He had lost his home but found another.

White House, Washington DC, USA

JFK, Robert Kennedy, McNamara, and Rusk were gathered in the oval office listening to John McCone who had recently replaced Allen Dulles as the director of the Central Intelligence Agency. McCone informed the group of the aerial assault on the palace and the attempted assassination of President Diem and his family. "Jesus, Diem's own air force is trying to kill him," said JFK.

"I'm not so sure about that, Mr. President. Based on our current intelligence, we believe the two pilots were dissidents acting of their own volition. The air force and other military forces don't seem to be involved," said McCone.

"So, there is no coup?" said Robert Kennedy.

"No. No military force beyond the two aircraft involved in the bombing has attempted to take the palace or any key installations in the capital. In fact, things are rather quiet at the moment."

"Well, that's good news," said Rusk.

"I am still concerned that one of our key allies was almost assassinated and we knew nothing about it," said the president.

"It was a failure of intelligence, Mr. President. No doubt about it. I'm going to look into personally," said McCone.

"See that you do, Jim. At times, I feel like I'm flying blind here. We've got to do better."

"Yes, Mr. President."

"So, the big question is… have we chosen the wrong horse to run with?" said the president.

"I don't think so, Mr. President. While some of the tactics of President Diem and his family leave much to be desired, we've got to admit… he's getting the job done," said McNamara. "Now that we have Operation Farm Gate in full swing and with the guidance of our military advisors, the South Vietnamese forces are more willing to confront the Viet Cong in the countryside. Diem's military is driving them out of the villages. It's not happening as fast as we would like, but it is happening, and we can see real progress. If we allow Diem to continue, he could reduce the Viet Cong forces back to a gang of disorganized bandits."

"When?" said JFK.

"A few years I would imagine."

"And what if the North grows impatient and decides to invade the South?"

"That's a different problem, Mr. President. Any invasion from the North would have to be checked by our own forces. South Vietnam could not withstand such an invasion, at least not in its current state."

"So, when will they be capable of standing on their own?"

"I'm not sure, Mr. President. I am still crunching the numbers on that one. But I think it is fair to say we must be ready to step in with our own forces if any invasion of South Vietnam occurs."

"I don't like it."

"Neither do I, Mr. President. But it is the reality of the situation. The communists are not just going to walk away. Sooner or later, they will attempt to overrun the South and take Saigon. It's just a matter of when and what we do about it."

"We've got to find a way to win this thing."

"Yes, Mr. President. We are working on it. We just don't have a solution yet. There is one more thing I want to make you aware of."

"What's that?"

"We are seeing a lot of back-channel discussions about America's possible involvement in the attempted assassination."

"What?! We weren't involved in any way, were we?"

"No, Mr. President. However, Diem and his family seem to feel that it was the foreign press that encouraged the actions of the dissident pilots. Diem is focusing on American journalists more than others."

"The United States has a free press. This administration cannot be held to account for the stories our newspapers choose to print."

"Yes, Mr. President. But Diem and his family do not see it that way."

"How do they see it?"

"As a disloyal brother as Madam Nhu put it."

"A disloyal brother?! What a crock of shit."

"Yes. But still… I think we should be prepared for some pushback."

"Pushback? We are giving his country damned near a half billion a year in financial and military aid. If that's not a loyal ally, I don't know what is. He should be thanking us."

"And I am sure our diplomats will remind Diem of that. But to keep things stable we might wish to reassure him of our intentions."

"He does understand that if America pulls its support, North Vietnam will attack and South Vietnam will be lost forever, doesn't he?" said Robert Kennedy.

"There are those in his circle of advisors that are feeding him alternative realities of what might happen should America pull its support. Some are saying it would be easier to defend the country and root out the enemy because the 'gloves would be off' so to speak."

"That's delusional," said McNamara.

"Yes, but not an uncommon sentiment in the South Vietnam government and military," said McCone.

"Alright. Enough. Let's not kill the messenger. I want suggestions on how to deal with Diem and his family by tomorrow morning," said JFK.

The meeting ended as everyone rose and exited. Seeing his brother hold his lower back and the anguish on his face, Robert Kennedy hung back and said quietly, "Are you all right, Jack?"

"Yeah. I'm fine. I just need a handful of aspirin and to lie down for a bit. All this sitting and talking… My back is killing me," said the president.

"I'll see that you get the aspirin and that you're not disturbed," said Robert. "Is a half-hour long enough?"

"Better make it fifteen minutes. Back or no back, I still have a full day and a country to run."

Saigon, South Vietnam

Viet Cong attacks continued to increase across the countryside. It seemed that whatever pressure was placed on the communists only made them more resolved like swatting a hornet's nest. The South Vietnam commanders called for more air support for their embattled ground troops. With more and more outposts and hamlets coming under attack, the American advisors realized that the South Vietnamese Air Force in its current form was wildly inadequate for the job at hand. They had no night fighting capability which is when most of the assaults occurred. The South Vietnamese commanders increasingly turned to Farm Gate to provide the assets and aircrews to fly the sorties needed to drive back the Viet Cong.

The American Air Force commanders expanded their reach by creating forward operating air bases at Qui Nhon and Soc Trang. Brigadier General Rollen Anthis, the commander of the 2nd Air Division, asked for additional air force personnel and aircraft to supplement Farm Gates's current squadrons. He wanted more B-26s, T-28s, and SC-47s to be used as flareships. His forces also needed more spare parts, bombs, rockets, ammunition, napalm canisters, and a lot more white phosphorous bombs than were currently being supplied. While napalm was highly effective against troops caught in the open, white phosphorous was proving to be more useful against an enemy that used the forest canopy as protection and stealth. The napalm canisters spread across the top of the canopy while the white phosphorous bombs penetrated the canopy and exploded on the forest floor. However, napalm was cheaper to manufacture, and the supply was almost unlimited. The enemy feared both.

When McNamara received Anthis's request, he was hesitant. The plan was to train, supply, and expand South Vietnamese forces, not American forces. Farm Gate had originally been designed as a training mission and was not approved for combat operations. It was mission creep. McNamara knew there was little chance of stopping it once it started. At the same time, he realized the danger of not helping the South Vietnamese forces in their struggle against the Viet Cong. He approved the request and even threw in a couple of U-10s which were ideal for cargo and transport in the South Vietnam countryside because of their short takeoff and landing ability.

In addition, the 1st Air Commando Squadron exchanged its T-28s for A-1 Skyraiders. The hand-me-down T-28s were built during World War II and were no longer suitable for the number of sorties being required in Vietnam. Several had already crashed because of catastrophic wing failures caused by stress cracks and metal fatigue. The newer A-1s were the world's biggest, most powerful prop-driven, single-seat combat aircraft. With almost twice the horsepower as the T-28s, the A-1s were capable of lifting freakishly heavy weapons loads and had a total of fifteen hardpoints under the wings and fuselage. With a full load of ordnance and fuel, the Skyraider wasn't fast, but it was agile, and in Vietnam, that was more important than speed. It was slower than the T-28s it was replacing, but because it could carry more fuel it had a longer range. The 1st Air Commando Squadron gave it the call sign "Hobo," but everyone nicknamed it the "Spad" after the legendary World War I fighter.

The American air force was growing at an incredible speed and so was America's involvement in Vietnam. There were still less than 5,000 American advisors, Special Forces, CIA officers, and aircrews in South Vietnam, Cambodian, and Laos, but that would soon change as North Vietnam expanded its own commitment. It seemed nobody in power took the time to stop and think about where it was going and what it all meant... and if they did, they seemed powerless to stop it.

Saigon, South Vietnam

Secluded in her apartment, Coyle sat in a chair beside Bian's bed. She was asleep.

Before leaving, Granier had agreed to allow Coyle to convince Lansdale that an imaginary double agent was feeding him information and threatened to stop if his identity went beyond Coyle. It was a lousy plan and Granier knew it, but he wanted to let Coyle at least try. Granier no longer wanted to assassinate Bian, but still thought it might come to that if they could not free her father from the North Vietnam prison. There were far too many loose ends to make Granier comfortable and he had agreed to help only if the plan was solid. They were a long way from that and time was short. In Granier's mind, if anyone found out about Bian and the deception, she would have to die. There were no other feasible options. It was the only way to save Coyle from being accused as a traitor.

Bian was fortunate that Nhu was busy searching for more potential assassins and any sign of a coup. He had accepted Bian's excuse of being injured on her way into work on the day of the attack and needed a few days to recover. But then what? Diem, Nhu, and Madame Nhu were paranoid beyond reason, and everyone that worked in the palace was a suspect in the plot to assassinate the president and his family.

Coyle wondered how long Bian would be able to avoid interrogation and when it happened, he didn't know how she would react. He would do whatever he could to protect her but even he knew that in the end, it may not be possible. It wasn't fair and it wasn't just, but it was his reality… and hers.

LETTER TO READER

Dear Reader,

I hope you enjoyed *Kennedy's War*. I must admit, it was a bit of a labor of love and took longer than expected. I am especially proud of the chapter called "ANNISTON."

I missed writing about Tom Coyle, one of my favorite characters, and I finally got my chance to insert him back into the series in a big way. You'll see him again in *The Uncivil War,* book 11 in the Airmen Series, along with many of the other characters. It's available as eBook and Paperback. Here's the link:

https://www.amazon.com/gp/product/B09HJRP5ND

Sign-up for my never-boring newsletter and you will receive a free book – Prophecies of Chaos (one of my favorites) in addition to new release updates, special offers, and my thoughts on history. Here's the sign-up link:

Newsletter Sign-Up
https://dl.bookfunnel.com/5tl2favuec

Reviews and recommendations to friends and family are always welcome. Every sale helps support my taco addiction.

In gratitude,

David Lee Corley

LIST OF TITLES WITH READING ORDER

The Airmen Series
1. A War Too Far
2. The War Before The War
3. We Stand Alone
4. Café Wars
5. Sèvres Protocol
6. Operation Musketeer
7. Battle of The Casbah
8. Momentum of War
9. The Willful Slaughter of Hope
10. Kennedy's War
11. The Uncivil War
12. Cry Havoc

The Nomad Series
1. Monsoon Rising
2. Prophecies of Chaos
3. Stealing Thunder

Facebook Page: https://www.facebook.com/historicalwarnovels

Shopify Store: https://david-lee-corley.myshopify.com/

Amazon Author's Page: https://www.amazon.com/David-Lee-Corley/e/B073S1ZMWQ

Amazon Airmen Series Page: https://www.amazon.com/dp/B07JVRXRGG

Amazon Nomad Series Page: https://www.amazon.com/dp/B07CKFGQ95

Author's Website: http://davidleecorley.com/

Author's Biography

Born in 1958, David grew up on a horse ranch in Northern California, breeding and training appaloosas. He has had all his toes broken at least once and survived numerous falls and kicks from ornery colts and fillies. David started writing professionally as a copywriter in his early 20's. At 32, he packed up his family and moved to Malibu, California, to live his dream of writing and directing motion pictures. He has four motion picture screenwriting credits and two directing credits. His movies have been viewed by over 50 million movie-goers worldwide and won a multitude of awards, including the Malibu, Palm Springs, and San Jose Film Festivals. In addition to his 23 screenplays, he has written ten novels. He developed his simplistic writing style after rereading his two favorite books, Ernest Hemingway's "The Old Man and The Sea" and Cormac McCarthy's "No Country for Old Men." An avid student of world culture, David lived as an ex-pat in both Thailand and Mexico. At 56, he sold all his possessions and became a nomad for four years. He circumnavigated the globe three times and visited 56 countries. Known for his detailed descriptions, his stories often include actual experiences and characters from his journeys.

Made in the USA
Monee, IL
10 June 2022

97749212R00177